CAKE POPPED OFF!

Cupcake Catering Mystery Series Book 2

KIM DAVIS

Cinnamon & Sugar Press

"A delightful new cozy with a cool California setting and an imminently likable heroine." *Ellen Byron*, Best Humorous Lefty Awards winner and author of the Agatha Award-winning and USA Today Bestselling Cajun Country Mysteries and The Catering Hall Mysteries.

"This very well-written first-in-a-series from Kim Davis is a great read, hard to put down, and filled with intense "come-uppances" and realistic family dynamics." – *Kathleen Costa*, Kings River Life Magazine

"If you love cozy mysteries, murder stories, and a great plot, then Sprinkles of Suspicion is a must-read." – *Trudi LoPreto*, Readers' Favorite

"This book has all the qualities of a top notch cozy mystery." – *Karen Kenyon*, Reviewer

". . . .a fun debut. . . Sprinkles of Suspicion sets up a promising new series. You'll enjoy meeting Emory here and be anxious to find out where cupcakes and murder take her next." *Carstairs Considers*

"This story moves along at a great pace and doesn't lag anywhere. There is always something happening, drama, twists, and yes, cupcakes. So well-plotted, I was totally taken in by the entire story and flabbergasted when the real killer was revealed." *Escape With Dollycas Into A Good Book*

Chapter 1

A low roar filled my ears right before a whoosh of hot blue flames raced toward my face. Blistering heat singed my bangs, but I stood still, rooted in place. I couldn't move. My mind screamed for me to get a fire extinguisher, except I had no idea which cabinet held it. Large hands shoved me aside then slammed the oven door shut. I watched, mesmerized, as the flames flickered out.

"What are you trying to do, burn my grandmother's house down?" The deep voice sounded angry.

I turned to see dark-green eyes that smoldered in a classically handsome face. A scowl created furrow lines in his forehead that his carefully coiffed blond hair didn't quite cover up. He must have been the heir apparent to the Skyler family business and fortune. I had been warned about him… by his own grandmother. Just my luck he had caught me in the middle of a bad cupcake experiment.

"Uh, no. That was definitely an accident." I held out my hand. "I'm Emory Martinez. Thanks for putting out the flambé."

He looked at my offered hand, studied my ample figure, then turned away. Apparently, he didn't want to get his impeccably manicured fingers sticky with the smear of buttercream on my palm. After I washed and dried my hands, I smoothed my frizzy red hair away from my face. I had made an impression, but unfortunately, it wasn't a good one.

"What's all this?" He gestured at the row of liquor bottles lined up on the butcher block island. "My grandmother isn't supposed to consume more than four ounces of red wine with dinner each day. Has my father allowed an alcoholic to care for my grandmother?"

My face burned, and I wished someone had warned me that Theodore Preston Skyler was going to make a surprise visit. I would've scurried back to my pool house after preparing his grandmother's breakfast and hidden until the coast was clear. The man seemed as pretentious as his name.

"No, definitely not. I almost never drink." That might have been true up until almost three months ago. However, since I'd moved there to care for Tillie, the feisty octogenarian had made it her mission to educate me on the finer points of creating then sipping cocktails every evening by the pool. Tillie's favorite, the gimlet, had become one of mine. Of course, her son and grandson's recommendation that she limit herself to four ounces of wine with dinner had been met with outright disdain from the woman herself. When I voiced my concern, Tillie assured me that her doctor saw no reason to limit her consumption to the small quantity because she was in perfect health.

"Well, what is all this alcohol doing in the kitchen? Are you stealing from my grandmother?"

"No! These are my own supplies. Tillie—"

"That would be Mrs. Skyler to you, Ms. Martinez," said the pompous man, who was only a few years older than my twenty-eight. "I'll have a talk with my father. It's obvious you're not the right sort of caretaker for this position."

My stomach clenched, and my mouth went bone-dry. Ever since I'd discovered that my no-good cheating husband was having an affair with my supposed best friend, my life had spiraled out of control. This job had been a second chance for me to get back on my feet, and I truly loved the elderly woman I lived with. Besides, if I got fired, my mother would kill me.

"You'll do no such thing, Teddy." His grandmother marched past her grandson and stood at my side to face him. "This is between your father and me. We both happen to think Emory is perfect for the job."

He blanched. "Grandmother, please call me Theodore. It's absurd that I have to keep reminding you."

"You'll be called Teddy until you remember to call me Grams or at least Tillie. Honestly, 'Grandmother' reminds me of my former mother-in-law, and those memories are best forgotten."

I cringed. Words like "forgotten," "memories," and "remember" were best not brought up. Her son thought she suffered from dementia and wanted me to spy on her so they could move her into a care facility. It appeared her pretentious grandson shared or hoped for the same outcome. I wondered if both men were after her money and property. Despite what they thought, Tillie's mind was as sharp as a tack, and she lived life to the fullest. It would crush her to lose her independence.

I tuned out their bickering as they went back to the living room to wait for David Skyler, Tillie's son, to arrive. He'd scheduled a family meeting and requested that I prepare muffins and tea for his sons and mother. Since it was autumn, I had baked pumpkin-spice muffins and put them in the warming drawer. Tillie had recommended a chai blend from her favorite tea shop, and I would steep the tea when Mr. Skyler arrived.

Mr. Skyler paid my generous salary and allowed me to live in Tillie's luxurious pool house. In exchange, I cooked for his mother and did some accounting and administrative chores for him. The arrangement suited me and left me plenty of time to experiment, bake, and deliver the cupcakes for my fledgling cupcake catering company.

My specialty was creating cupcakes that tasted like cocktails. Fireball Pumpkin-Spice Coffee Cupcakes had been the morning's experiment. Apparently, I had used too much Fireball in the recipe, which had caused it to flambé. I giggled when I realized the whiskey had lived up to its name. Unfortunately, the centers of the little cakes had cratered like giant sinkholes when I removed them from the oven.

I needed to get the recipe right, since I planned to showcase them at Tillie's Halloween party the following evening, two weeks before the actual holiday. I hoped the cupcakes would generate some new orders from the seventy-five guests. My sister would cater the party food while I provided the desserts. Besides the Fireball Cupcakes, I planned to make Poison Apple Cupcakes and Poison Apple Cake Pops. Smashed Pumpkin Cupcakes were already in the refrigerator, ready to be consumed. Tillie had arranged for a live band and a bartender, which was more evidence of her living life to the fullest.

The gong of the doorbell made me jump, and I rushed to fill the teapot with steaming water to steep the chai blend. I placed the warm muffins on a serving tray and covered them with a pumpkin-print cloth napkin before putting the teapot beside it. I jumped again when a deep masculine voice whispered in my ear, "Let me carry that for you."

Tillie's youngest grandson, Brian, was standing right behind me. He could've been the twin of his slightly older brother, but whereas Theodore seemed uptight and pretentious most of the time, Brian was happy-go-lucky and quite thoughtful of others. Well, I might have been a bit biased because Brian was a huge flirt and stroked my ego whenever he visited his grandmother.

"Thanks."

"My father wants you in on this so-called family meeting." He picked up the tray.

"Why? I'm not family."

He shrugged. "I'm only his messenger boy."

I followed Brian into the living room and noticed a woman standing next to Mr. David Skyler. She looked to be in her late twenties, but it was difficult to tell because of the dramatic makeup troweled onto her face. I suspected that regular visits to a salon resulted in her perfectly coiffed shoulder-length golden-blonde hair, while her toned figure was probably the result of hours spent with a trainer. I took in her designer dress and stiletto heels, which pushed her height to about five foot eight, but she was still six inches shorter than Mr. Skyler.

"Thank you for joining us, Emory. Please make yourself comfortable." Mr. Skyler motioned toward the couches. The slim European cut of his trousers made him appear lean, while his eyes appeared darker than their normal light-blue hue because of the sky-blue of his buttoned-down shirt.

I sat next to Tillie on the uncomfortable formal loveseat and stared out the window to watch a sailboat bob past in Newport Bay. Tillie squeezed my hand before she picked up her teacup.

"Let me introduce you to my new wife, Barbara." Mr. Skyler smoothed back his graying hair before putting his arm around the young woman's waist. "While I realize this is sudden, I hope you'll be happy for us."

I finally noticed the quail egg–sized diamond that sat on her ring finger. The teacup clattered against the saucer in Tillie's hand. I reached out to take it from her before the hot chai spilled onto her cream-colored slacks. The color drained from her face, and she placed her shaky hands back on her lap.

Theodore didn't hold back, though. "What the…? Your third wife is barely cold in the ground, and you have another to replace her?"

Theodore was the son from Mr. Skyler's first wife, while Brian was the son from the second. Both marriages had ended in divorce, and Mr. Skyler still paid out a substantial amount of money in alimony each month. I knew because I wrote and mailed the checks to the two women. Brian had told me the third trophy wife had died in a tragic hit-and-run a few weeks before I started working there, and the case hadn't been solved. Trophy Wife Number Four appeared to be at least thirty years his junior… right around my age.

"I realize this is sudden." Mr. Skyler's voice sounded low and angry. "But I expect you to show respect for my decision and for Barbara."

I glanced at Barbara, expecting to see her to seem embarrassed or shy, given Theodore's outburst. Instead, she looked like she was gloating over the family's squabble. Tillie shivered beside me.

"Welcome to the family, Barbara." Brian's face looked as if he had bitten into a sour lemon. "How did you two lovebirds meet?"

With her age and her Barbie-doll looks, I expected her voice to be high and breathy. Instead, it was sultry with a hint of an accent, possibly French. I tried to focus on what she was saying instead of her looks.

"We met at a tea shop in London over Easter, and it was love at first sight." She beamed up at her new husband, who returned her gaze with adoration. "I quit my job and returned to my home in Washington, DC, so we could be together more often."

Tillie gasped. I might have done the same. Mr. Skyler had still been married to Wife Number Three during Easter. The new Mrs. Skyler had just insinuated that they had been carrying on an affair for quite a while. I found it suspicious that Wife Number Three was conveniently out of the way, with no arrests in the hit-and-run.

"And what's your job?" Theodore's question sounded more like an interrogation. "Are you still working in DC?"

"Not that it's any of your business, but I'm a consultant. I've completed the work for my clients and moved here permanently. Being your father's wife is my top priority."

Her description of her background was so vague that I wondered what she consulted on.

Theodore scowled, Brian kept his face bland, and Tillie's hands still shook. I questioned why Mr. Skyler's remarriage bothered them so much, aside from the fact that he was making a fool of himself by marrying someone who was clearly in it for the money. Then it dawned on me. Mrs. Skyler would take money from her new husband that otherwise would have gone to his sons.

Mr. Skyler's voice invaded my thoughts. "Emory, you'll be providing social secretary services for my new wife," he said. "Since your mother has connections to the best clubs and philanthropist societies in Orange County, I want you to facilitate getting her introduced and involved."

I gulped. My cupcake business kept me busy as word of mouth was spreading. I had gotten used to working on Mr. Skyler's accounting on my own time... like late at night or at the crack of dawn. Being a "social secretary" wasn't anything that appealed to me, and I didn't like the sound of my new responsibility. I especially didn't like the way the new Mrs. Skyler looked at me—her new minion.

"Um, sure."

"We'd better go." Mr. Skyler looked at his Rolex. "I've chartered a jet to take my bride to St. Thomas for our honeymoon. Theodore, I told the managers that you're in charge while I'm gone. I don't want to be disturbed unless it's an emergency."

Theodore's eyes grew wide, and his face turned red. "I hope you have a prenup."

Mr. Skyler glared at his eldest son. "That is none of your business. I demand respect for myself and my wife."

"If your new marriage impacts the family business, then it is my concern." Theodore's voice was loud in the quiet room.

"Remind me, is your name on the ownership papers of the Skyler Development Company?" Mr. Skyler turned his back on his son and held out his elbow to his bride. "Now, my dear, let's go start our honeymoon."

Theodore and Brian exchanged looks that would have ignited a feud if their father had seen them. Witnessing the family quarrel was embarrassing, and I tried to quell my unease over the marriage. I didn't want to be that woman's social secretary because I was sure she would go out of her way to make my life miserable.

Chapter 2

We sat in stunned silence after the front door had slammed shut. Tillie looked as if she might pass out. Theodore's face was still molten red, and I prayed he wouldn't have an aneurysm. I had no idea what to say or do and wished that I had stayed hidden in my pool house with my golden Labradoodle mix, Piper, instead of attending this awful family meeting.

Brian broke the silence. "So… we have ourselves a new stepmommy. I wonder what Daddy dearest has in store for us this time."

I didn't like the bitterness in Brian's voice. He was the happy-go-lucky brother. Tillie had once confided in me that Trophy Wife Number Three had convinced Mr. Skyler to cut off his trust fund unless he worked full-time in the family business. Brian had a creative flair and was half owner of a hip Laguna Beach restaurant into which he had poured his heart and soul. While popular, the restaurant wasn't making a livable income yet, and so Brian relied heavily on the monthly income provided by the trust. Since he didn't work full-time for his father—and, as far as I could see, hadn't changed his lifestyle—I assumed Mr. Skyler had relented and reinstated the fund after the accident.

"Did you notice the size of that rock on her finger?" Theodore sputtered. "And a private jet to St. Thomas? She's already digging her fingers into our inheritance. Why can't he see these women are only after our money?"

Tillie spoke up, but her voice held a tremor. "You mean your father's money, don't you, Theodore?"

"Well, yes, but eventually it will be our company and our money." He glared at his grandmother. "Either way, it's bad for all of us."

"Unfortunately, I have to agree with you." Tillie sighed. "The gall of that woman to come right out and say they've been having an affair all this time. It's disgraceful."

I needed to get back to preparing the desserts for the party the next night. I was happy that Mr. Skyler and his "bride" would be out of the country for a while, since I didn't think I could bear having to work for her anytime soon. Not after that parting glance she gave me. Just thinking about the malice in Barbara's eyes before she left the room made me shiver again.

I stood up and placed the teacups and saucers back on the serving tray. "Let me get out of your way so you can talk about this."

"Nonsense, this marriage concerns you too." Tillie snorted. "'Social secretary'! The nerve of him."

"I know. It sounds awful." I wasn't happy about my new responsibilities, but I desperately needed this job and a place to live. I couldn't afford not to do what they asked of me. "Maybe it's not as bad as it seems. But right now I have to get the cupcake recipe figured out for the party tomorrow."

Theodore's scowl deepened. "Party? What party?"

Uh-oh. Me and my big mouth. Brian had been invited, but "Teddy" hadn't.

Even though Tillie was in her early eighties, she never

failed to impress me with her ability to think up lies at the drop of a hat. "Didn't you get the invitation? I mailed them out three weeks ago."

"No, I never received it." Theodore looked annoyed, like he wasn't sure whether he believed his grandmother or not.

"I wondered why you hadn't RSVP'd yet." She pursed her coral-colored lips together and patted down her short platinum hair kept coiffed by frequent salon visits. "I thought you were ignoring me, since costumes are mandatory."

"Costumes?" He scrunched his eyebrows together. "Uh, I just remembered I have a board meeting tomorrow night, so I can't make it."

"Oh, that's too bad, dear. I'll be sure to hand deliver the invitation for the next party."

"Thank you." Theodore studied his grandmother. "We have bigger problems than lost invitations. What are we going to do about Barbara?"

I took that as my cue to leave the room and the emotionally charged conversation behind, so I returned to my refuge: the kitchen.

As I mixed the ingredients for a new batch of Fireball Pumpkin-Spice Coffee Cupcakes, I thought about the reactions to Mr. Skyler's bombshell announcement. Theodore and Brian's concerns about Barbara going after their father's fortune and their inheritance were understandable. But Tillie's reaction had been odd—her pale face, her shaking hands, the tremor in her voice. Then I realized she wasn't angry... she was frightened.

What is she worried about? I wondered.

I placed the cupcake tin into the preheated oven and crossed my fingers I wouldn't see any more blue flambé flames. With the timer set, I went to work on the buttercream frosting. Something magical happened when butter and confectioners' sugar were whipped together until fluffy. The concoction was an empty canvas waiting for whatever flavors I chose, then that first bite would melt in my mouth with a rush of deliciousness. I would even say that a cupcake was a pedestal for the ethereal buttercream frosting.

When the timer chimed, I checked on the cupcakes. So far, no flambé, and they were rising like they should have. I opened the oven and turned the tin around to help them bake and brown evenly. So far, so good. The smell of pumpkin spice filled the kitchen as I whisked the glaze ingredients together and heated the mixture in the microwave to dissolve.

One secret to really moist cupcakes was to give them another layer of flavor using a simple syrup infused with complementary ingredients. So as soon as they came out of the oven, I pierced them several times with a fork, going about halfway down, then brushed the tops with the simple syrup. A few minutes later, I put them on a cooling rack. Once they were completely cooled, I would pipe on the creamy buttercream and garnish them with a candy pumpkin.

After I had put the last sticky dish into the dishwasher, Tillie came into the kitchen. Her face was still pale, and she had chewed off most of her lipstick. This was the first time I'd ever seen her so feeble. My heart ached for her.

I rushed over to give her a hug. "It's going to be okay."

"I'm not so sure, my dear." Her voice quivered.

"Sit down and let me fix you some tea." I led her to the small kitchen table that hosted two chairs. "Did you eat this morning?"

Tillie sank into an offered chair. "I had some cereal and fruit before you arrived. I planned on eating one of your pumpkin muffins once David and the boys came, but with that bombshell…"

"Let me fix you some strong black tea with honey and a splash of brandy and lemon." I touched her shoulder. "I hate seeing you so upset. Do you know Barbara?"

Tillie sighed. "I've never met her, but I've certainly met

her type. She could be the identical twin of Katrina in both looks and greediness."

"Katrina?"

"That's right, you moved here after she was killed. Katrina was his third wife."

Even though I had never seen her give any indication of being religious before, Tillie crossed herself.

"No one deserves to have their life snatched from them," she went on. "But I think karma finally caught up with Katrina."

"Let me get that brandy for you." I skipped the tea and pulled down a snifter glass from the cabinet. I looked at Tillie and pulled out a second glass for myself and generously poured the amber liquid into each. After I handed her a glass, I excused myself and ran out to my little slice of heaven— Tillie's pool house—where I called for Piper. There was something comforting in having a dog to pet and stroke when I was distraught. Piper followed me back to the main house and laid her furry golden head in Tillie's lap. I sat in the empty chair across from her.

Tillie stared absentmindedly at the snifter, and I was startled to see tears well up in her pale-blue eyes. Another first.

"Do you want to talk about it?" There seemed to be a personal family tragedy that had happened, and I wasn't sure I should intrude. Yet my morbid curiosity over why Katrina could turn such a strong, independent woman into this sad person who sat in front of me made me ask. Plus, I was drawn to the unsolved crime of Katrina's death. Maybe it had been a tragic accident… or maybe it was murder.

"Katrina was the force behind convincing David that I had dementia bordering on Alzheimer's. She hired someone to follow me and plant things to make me look like a fool, like putting my wallet in the freezer, an empty gin bottle in the entryway planter. Stuff like that." Tillie took a long sip of the brandy and shuddered. "But what I'll never forgive her for is turning my own son against me. He bought her stories about me hook, line, and sinker."

"Oh, Tillie, I am so sorry that happened." I gave her hand a quick squeeze. "It's heartbreaking."

"We're in for another tough ride, kiddo." She took a small sip of brandy with her free hand while she stroked Piper's furry ears. "Barbara had the exact look Katrina had every time she came to my house."

"What look is that?" The only strange expression I noticed on Mrs. Skyler's face was malice. While it was out of place, it wasn't mercenary.

"Oh yes, you were in the kitchen when they arrived." Tillie closed her eyes like she was replaying the moment in her mind. "The second she stepped into my house, she calculated the value of everything she saw. And once she examined my artwork, she couldn't keep that greedy look off her conniving face any longer. I'm surprised she didn't drool."

"Maybe she was admiring your paintings?"

"There's a huge difference between admiring and appreciating art and coveting it for monetary value. It was written all over her face." Tillie swiped at her eyes. "When she noticed me watching her, she gave me the most evil glare I've ever seen. She scares me even more than Katrina did."

I hoped Tillie was only imagining things, but unfortunately, the new Mrs. Skyler hadn't filled me with warm and fuzzy thoughts either.

"Is there any way you can share your concerns with your son?"

"No. He didn't listen to me with the last wife and, in fact, turned against me when I mentioned it." Tillie's gaze settled on me, her eyes filling with tears. "He should have married your mother. Then none of this would be happening."

"But she's married to Lars, and as far as I know, they're happy together." Lars became my stepdad a couple of years after my real father had abandoned our family. I hadn't been all that accepting of him when I was twelve, but he had slowly won over my heart. It was obvious to anyone who saw them together that Lars adored my mother, and I hoped she wouldn't do anything to hurt him. "I suspected something might have been going on with Mother and Mr. Skyler this past summer, but I hoped it was only my imagination."

Tillie's hand fluttered dismissively. "No, not now. I meant back in school."

"Wait, what? They dated in school?" This was news to me. My mother had never even mentioned David Skyler until I was desperate for a job and a place to live a few months ago. "Was it high school?"

"I shouldn't have said anything." Tillie swirled the brandy left in her snifter. "I blame it on the shock and the alcohol."

"You can't leave me hanging like that."

"It's not my story to tell, so please don't pry. I shouldn't have said anything." She took the last sip, stood up, and put her glass in the sink. After giving Piper a homemade puppy treat and one last pat on the head, she moved toward the doorway. "If your mother wants you to know, she'll tell you. I suspect you have a lot of work to do for tomorrow's party, so I'll get out of your way."

My mouth dropped open as Tillie left the kitchen. How could I concentrate on baking when I needed to know what happened between my mother and Mr. Skyler all those years ago? Yet my friend was right. I had too much to do for the party, so I needed to immerse myself in sugar and spices.

I didn't want Piper underfoot while I was baking, so I returned her to my abode. It was the perfect spot for my pup to spend her days, especially when I was busy in the kitchen. Tillie had thoughtfully added a doggie door to the luxurious two-bedroom pool house and also installed a mesh pool fence to keep Piper safe, so she was free to wander the huge yard dotted with fruit trees, shrubbery, and pet-safe flowers. She loved to romp, chase squirrels and birds, and flop on the grass for a sunbath. It was heaven for both of us.

After returning to Tillie's industrial-sized kitchen, I sampled the cupcakes and buttercream together. *Perfection.* I didn't need to tweak the recipe any more. After whipping up several more batches of cupcake batter and buttercream frosting, I turned my attention to the cake pops. I loved how fun cake pops were, but making them was time consuming.

The trick was to do each step in stages. I had made the frosting two days ago then baked and shredded the Poison Apple Cupcakes yesterday. First thing this morning, I had removed the frosting from the refrigerator and found it was now soft enough to work into the shredded cake. After mixing the gooey mess and forming it into walnut-sized apple shapes, I dipped the ends of lollipop sticks into melted white chocolate and inserted them into the bottoms of the apples. I arranged them on a parchment-lined baking sheet and stored them in Tillie's industrial-sized freezer to firm up.

While the unadorned cake pops were freezing, I finished frosting the cupcakes then poured a cup of red candy melts into a tall glass measuring cup. The secret to working with candy melts was to melt them slowly using gentle heat, stirring frequently and never overheating. A double boiler worked okay, but I liked the ease of the microwave better. I zapped the candy melts in thirty-second intervals on 80 percent power and stirred after each cycle. It took some patience to get them to melt, but I'd found it was the best way to keep from making a gloppy mess that would be too thick to cover cake pops easily.

I removed a few cake pops from the freezer and, one at a time, twirled them into the melted candy. After tapping off the excess, I stuck the lollipop sticks into a Styrofoam base. Before the candy melt mixture hardened, I added a small fondant leaf and a piece of brown Tootsie Roll candy, fashioned into the shape of a stem, to the top of the "poison apple.

Once I finished coating and garnishing all the cake pops, I stepped back to admire my work then snapped photos of them for my Instagram account and Pinterest boards. They were as tempting as Snow White's poison apple—without the deadly side effects.

Chapter 3

Our Halloween party was in full swing, and I loved seeing the variety of creative and exotic costumes. The live band performed next to the pool, and the atmosphere was spirited, helped along by the bartender, Kenneth, who was dressed as a court jester. His girlfriend, Mandy, served drinks while dressed in a skimpy Bavarian barmaid costume that emphasized her curvaceous figure. She did an admirable job of keeping everyone's glasses full, but I noticed she flirted aggressively with several of the men she served.

A few women were annoyed with Mandy's antics, and at one point it seemed as if a fistfight might break out between the Bavarian barmaid and a cone-chested Madonna. Before it could reach that level, though, Elton John grabbed Madonna and pulled her toward Tillie's house. Even over the noise coming from the band, I could hear Madonna curse Mandy and threaten to smash her face in.

Kenneth had created a festive presentation for our signature drink: Poison Apple Cocktails served from a large witch's caldron, which sat inside a short box. He had decorated the outside of the box with sparkly flames, and inside, tucked around the caldron, dry ice smoldered, creating eerie smoke twining its way around the black vessel. While the special drink was tasty, it was time to water the cocktail down with extra juice and pass water bottles around. We didn't need any more fights breaking out between inebriated guests.

My twin sister, Carrie, had outdone herself by creating a buffet that epitomized the holiday. Guacamole spilled out of the mouth of a jack-o'-lantern, and warm queso dip was nestled in the carved pumpkin's top. Pure genius. She had decorated her layered taco dip with baked tortillas in the shapes of tombstones and served it alongside tortilla chips. For the main course, she had chosen Chicken Cordon Boo Casserole, Yummy Mummy Calzones, mini meatloaves baked in skull-shaped pans, and Halloween Baked Potato Skin Pizzas.

She came up beside me and gave me a hug while I surveyed the buffet table, trying to decide between getting seconds of Stuffed Mushroom Eyeballs, Bloodshot Deviled Eggs, or Monster Bread Fingers. I was already too full and wanted to save room for dessert, but there was something fun about eating decorated food.

"Your Poison Apple Cake Pops look amazing." She leaned in close to my ear so I could hear her over the band's enthusiastic version of "The Monster Mash." "I'm tempted to try one. How much alcohol do they have in them?"

I looked at her growing baby bump while trying to do the calculations. "Not much. Less than a teaspoon per cake pop."

"Perfect." She snatched one of the glossy ruby-red apples off the tiered stand and took a bite. "Oh my, these are so yummy. I think this is my new favorite."

I laughed, noticing there weren't many cake pops left. Since she'd gotten over her morning sickness, most foods were Carrie's new favorite. "I'll make you a batch to celebrate my new nephew's birth. Do you want to share one of the Fireball Pumpkin-Spice Coffee Cupcakes with me?"

"Can I have just a bite?"

"Sure. I'd like to see what you think." I knew they were good. It had taken a lot of willpower not to eat more than two while I frosted them. *Okay, maybe three, but who's counting?*

I peeled away the Halloween-themed cupcake liner, sliced off a generous portion, and placed it on Carrie's plate. At home I would have shoved the cupcake into her mouth, but I didn't want to mess up her elaborate makeup. She'd dressed up as one of the KISS band members, her face painted pure white with elaborate black accents. She had covered up her auburn hair with a spiky black wig. Her husband, Thomas, was costumed as another member of the iconic band, although it wouldn't have surprised me if he kept wearing the wig long after the party ended to cover his recently receding hairline.

My best friend, Brad, joined us by the buffet table. "Hey, girls, what's up?" he asked, eying the cupcake sitting on my plate. His wavy honey-blond hair and handsome looks paired perfectly with his Marc Antony costume.

"I'm sampling Emory's new cupcake flavors." Carrie took a bite, closed her eyes, and moaned. "This is my new favorite. I love the kick the Fireball gives the spices in the frosting. You have to try the Poison Apple Cake Pops. They're my favorite too."

Brad grinned and swiped a cake pop off the tiered serving platters. "I really should watch my girlish figure, but these look good enough to die for."

I laughed, since Brad had perfect six-pack abs. "They exceeded my expectations. I'm glad I figured out how to make the apple shape so they wouldn't come out looking like lumpy golf balls."

He mumbled in agreement, since he had stuffed the entire pop into his mouth.

I turned toward Carrie. "What did Mother and Lars have planned for the girls and Piper tonight?"

Our mother and stepdad had agreed to let my five-year-old twin nieces sleep over so that Carrie and Thomas could attend Tillie's party together. Even though Carrie was the caterer, she had hired extra help so she could enjoy the festivities once everything was in place. My nieces had convinced us that Piper needed to spend the night too. I was relieved my mother had agreed, because I didn't want to crate Piper for the party, and I couldn't let her roam free.

"They're taking them to the pumpkin patch carnival in Laguna. The girls are excited to give their costumes a trial run." She gave me a sideways glance. "Did they tell you they were entering Piper in the pet costume competition?"

"Whatever it is, I hope she cooperates with them and leaves the costume on. What did they decide to be this year?" Last year they were both Queen Elsa. They'd had a mini meltdown when they each wanted the other to be Princess Anna, but in the end, they agreed they could both be queen… along with millions of other little girls.

"They're both Moana, and Piper will be Pua, the pet pig. I'm glad the weather is warm enough so I didn't have to fight them to wear sweaters over their costumes." Carrie licked the sticky frosting from her fingers and walked toward the house. "I need to check on the food and make sure the staff knows when to begin the cleanup. Need anything?"

I giggled, trying to imagine Piper dressed up like a pig. I knew my mother would take lots of photos and video for Instagram. "Can you have your staff bring out more cake pops and cupcakes?"

"You bet." She picked up another cake pop, popped it into her mouth, and headed to the house.

I shook my head before taking another bite of cupcake. My taste buds hummed, and I think I moaned a little as I closed my eyes to concentrate on the flavors.

"I'll have some of whatever you're having," a low voice whispered in my ear before its owner blew on my bare neck.

My eyes snapped open. It was Tillie's grandson. "Brian. I,

um, was just trying to see if I could pick out the individual flavors I used in the cupcake."

"Whatever it is, I want it." He lifted the half-eaten cupcake from my hand and took a bite. "This is good but I think I like the Smashed Pumpkin cupcakes better," he said, turning to gaze at me. "Maybe I should try another one of each to make sure."

"Okay, you've convinced me." Brad picked up a cupcake and took a bite. His eyes widened. "You're a dangerous woman, Em. I could eat the frosting by the spoonful. I might have to buy some Fireball."

I elbowed him and scanned the crowd. "So, where's your new guy?"

Brad pouted. "He ended up having to work late. He'll try to drop by later, but he refuses to wear a costume."

"That's okay. I can't wait to meet him." I gazed into Brad's gorgeous gray eyes. "Come on, give me some background. What's his name? What's he do? What's he look like?"

I watched as Brian picked up another Smashed Pumpkin cupcake from the tray and ate half in one bite. It appeared I had lost his attention.

"No way, girlfriend. You need to wait and take in the whole package all at once." Brad laughed. "Where's your guy? I thought he was coming tonight."

"His flight was delayed. I'm hoping he'll make it before the party ends." I stuck out my lower lip.

Randall. Visions of his sapphire-blue eyes and chestnut-brown hair filled my head, but I knew better than to get my hopes up that he'd ever be "my guy." I'd met him right before the police accused me of murdering his supposed cousin. Things had sizzled between us after the killer was caught, but then Randall moved back to Florida, and our romance fizzled. We exchanged texts daily and tried to chat when our schedules allowed, but I felt like we had become good friends and nothing more. Randall was in the process of moving back to Southern California, and my friends had high hopes for me. I, on the other hand, certainly had my doubts.

Brad peered into my face. "Don't worry, Cupcake. He'll be just as smitten with you as he was before he left."

I wrinkled my nose. "He was never smitten with me."

Over the band yelling out the lyrics to the "Ghostbusters" movie theme song, I could hear heated words being exchanged by the door that led to my pool house. I turned and saw my brother-in-law, Thomas, arguing with Mandy. Even with the pure-white paint covering Thomas's face, I could tell he was turning red. He looked enraged, which surprised me because he was one of the calmest men I knew.

Before I realized what was happening, Brian grabbed me by my wide foam cupcake costume and placed me between him and the arguing twosome. I glanced over my shoulder and could see that he was crouched low as if hiding. I looked back at my brother-in-law.

Mandy, who barely came up to Thomas's shoulders, shoved him in the chest, and I could have sworn I saw his pudgy fist ball up like he wanted to strike her. Instead, he bent closer and whispered something in her ear. Whatever he said, it couldn't have been sweet nothings because her eyes grew large and her overly tanned face went pale. He spun on his heels and strode out of the garden and toward Tillie's house while Mandy rushed inside my pool house. I assumed she wanted to use my bathroom to compose herself after that exchange.

Had I just imagined it was Thomas? Or had it been another guest dressed in a similar costume? I searched the dancing couples and other guests milling around with food and drinks in hand. There were two other men with KISS costumes and makeup but nothing as elaborate as the art Carrie had created on her husband's face. I stood there, frozen, while I tried to decide what I should do: run after

Thomas and ask for an explanation or see if the waitress was okay.

Brad's eyes were huge, and he turned his lips down in a grim line before leaning toward me. "What was that all about?"

"Your guess is as good as mine, but it doesn't look good." I frowned. "I wasn't aware Thomas knew the bartender or his girlfriend."

"Is she gone yet?" Brian's voice was quiet—hidden behind my costume.

"All clear." I turned around halfway just in time to see Brian straighten up as if nothing had happened. "What or who were you hiding from?"

"Psycho Mandy. I've been dodging her all evening."

"How do you know her?"

"I made the poor decision to date her a while back." He pulled at the collar of his shirt. "Let's just say it didn't end well."

Before I could respond, Tillie came up to us. "Hiya, Cupcake, Roman guy, and grandson." She gushed over my cupcake costume while wiping a smear of frosting from my cheek with her paper napkin. "Great party, don't you think?"

"It absolutely is." I took her hand and spun her around. "Your costume is fantastic. It looks authentic."

She was dressed in a beaded gold-and-black 1920s flapper dress. The headband wrapped around her head sported a peacock feather, and her hands and arms were wrapped in long black satin gloves. I had no idea how she was managing to dance in her high heels, but she did.

Brian, who was dressed as a 1920s gangster, sidled up beside her and placed an arm over his grandmother's shoulder and kissed her cosmetically rejuvenated cheek. "Hey, doll. Has anyone told you you're the bee's knees?"

"Thanks, sugar." Tillie bumped her grandson with her hip

then turned back to me. "This dress belonged to my aunt, who was quite the Gibson Girl back in those days."

"I'll bet that dress has stories to tell." Brad fingered the beading on the sleeve of her dress. "Where did your aunt live back in those days?"

"She was born and raised in Chicago but moved to LA like loads of other girls hoping to make it big in the movies." Tillie leaned in conspiratorially. "There's even rumors in our family she partied with F. Scott Fitzgerald."

Tillie, Brad, and Brian chatted on about the roaring '20s. Normally, I would have been fascinated. I loved history, especially as it pertained to family stories, but the exchange between Thomas and Mandy worried me. I looked around the party area but still didn't see the buxom waitress. Nor did I see the bartender or Thomas. I wanted to track one of them down to make sure everything was okay but wasn't sure there was anything I could do even if I did find them.

My sister came back, her servers in tow, as they carried trays of desserts and a few more hors d'oeuvres. She fussed over the placement of the food, scanned the pool area, then joined our group.

"Have you seen Thomas?" she asked.

Brad and I exchanged a quick glance. "No, he walked toward Tillie's house about twenty minutes ago."

"That's odd. I didn't see him." She looked around the pool area again. "Maybe he was in the restroom."

I doubted that was the case—perhaps he was hiding from Mandy, like Brian had been doing all evening. I didn't think she had come out of my pool house, unless she went through the door that led to the garage. There was a small door in the garage that led into a narrow side yard where the garbage cans were kept. Perhaps she was so upset she left the party. The bartender was back, flipping bottles and mixing drinks. Before I asked if he knew where she was, I decided to do a quick search inside my abode.

I excused myself from the group and let myself through the French doors that led into the living room. Soft electric candles illuminated the room, which made it appear cozy. I shut the door behind me, relieved to be away from the booming music coming from the band. The guests were enjoying the music, and most of the couples had danced at one time or another, but I wished they didn't have to play so loud.

The bathroom door was closed, but light spilled out from between the cracks at the bottom and top of the door. I knocked. "Mandy? Is everything okay?"

There was nothing but silence. Maybe she'd gone through the garage and left the bathroom door shut. I knocked again. "Hello? Is anyone in there?"

When I didn't get an answer, I gripped the doorknob. The muted strains of "Thriller" came drifting in from outside. It sounded like the band was doing a creepier version than the original. The electric candlelight sent flickers of shadows across the hallway, and a shiver crept down my spine. I chided myself for letting the spookiness of the evening get to me. Nothing was wrong. It was just my imagination running away from me.

I slowly turned the doorknob, pushed the door open, and screamed. Mandy was splayed out in my bathtub. Her curly dark-brown hair draped over her shoulders, and her unseeing violet eyes were wide open. Several of my cake pops were stuffed in her mouth, and sticky red goo dripped off her chin and onto her substantial décolletage.

Chapter 4

The chatter from police radios and emergency personnel had replaced the band noise. The costumed guests were huddled in small groups, whispering to one another. Thomas held Carrie's hand, and I hoped he had a good alibi for the time he disappeared after arguing with Mandy. Without a doubt, Thomas would never have hurt the barmaid. Unfortunately, Brad and I weren't the only ones who had noticed their heated exchange, and it wouldn't take long for the police to consider him a suspect. I would know, having been a murder suspect myself just a few months ago.

Brad inhaled a sharp breath of air and sucked in his stomach, and I turned to see what he was looking at. A *GQ* cover model–worthy man had entered the pool area. Two uniformed police officers, who were both gesturing with their hands toward my pool house, were walking at his side. He was dressed in sharply pressed black slacks and a white button-down shirt that had to have been tailored to show off his broad shoulders and impressive pecs. In the glow of the tiki torches and patio fairy lights, his skin looked golden.

"That's the new detective." Tillie leaned forward to get a better view. "He's like Adonis."

Brad's voice was quiet. "Gabe is so much more than Adonis."

The admiration in Brad's voice and his use of the detective's first name made me turn to look at him. His gaze followed every move the gorgeous man made. "New friend of yours?"

Brad blushed. "I wish you'd had the chance to meet him in a social setting instead of these circumstances."

Whistling, I elbowed his rock-hard side. "Wow, you set your sights high."

"He's so much more than just a pretty face." Brad elbowed me back. "He's intelligent, well-read, and has a great sense of humor."

Just then, Gabe noticed Brad and gave him a short nod before making his way into the pool house.

"Lucky you." I sighed. My love life was nonexistent, and my pending divorce was moving through the courts just as quickly as the law would allow. My soon-to-be ex had moved in with his new girlfriend before the divorce papers had even been filed. The murder of his other girlfriend—yes, he was, or might still be, a philanderer—was what had introduced me to Randall, a former vice cop, in the first place. I had to admit that sparks had flown between us, especially after our sizzling kiss right before he left for Florida. But despite what my friends might have said, I doubted Randall would want to pick up where we'd left off when he returned to Southern California… which I hoped would be within the hour.

Tillie must have noticed my sigh. "You do realize my grandson is interested in you, right? Brian seems to get along with you and have fun when he comes to visit."

I whipped my head around so fast I saw stars. I hadn't seen Brian leave our group and hoped he wasn't anywhere around to hear this awkward conversation. Thankfully, he had wandered off to cozy up to the voluptuous Betty Boop.

"Brian's sweet and funny, but no way am I going to date him and risk losing you as a friend when things go wrong. You're much too important to me to risk that."

She studied my face. "Why in the world would things go wrong?"

"Because they always do." I didn't want to tell Tillie that her grandson was a huge flirt who left behind a string of broken hearts along the Newport Coast on a regular basis. I didn't need to be with a player and go through that again. "Besides, maybe something will work out with Randall."

"I hope it does, sweetie. Just don't write off my grandson too soon."

Several uniformed officers took down the names of guests before they were allowed to leave. After finding Mandy and screaming for someone to call 911, I had Tillie and Brad ask the guests to stay calm and remain at the party until officials gave word that they could leave. Unfortunately, Kenneth had decided to find out what my hysterics were all about and, once he caught sight of his girlfriend, collapsed into a sobbing heap. As far as I knew, the police still had him in there.

Carrie directed her helpers to pack up the remains of the food. They disposed of the perishables that had been sitting out on the tables, and my sister would later drop off the refrigerated leftovers at her church so they could deliver the food to shut-ins and the homeless. She was thoughtful that way.

She signaled for me to join her. "The police said I can start cleanup, but they want your cake pops left as is."

"I hope people don't think my Poison Apples killed her." I groaned and tried not to picture all the cake pops jammed into the young woman's mouth. "Technically, I guess they did, but it wasn't from poison."

Carrie leaned in to whisper in my ear. "The police won't

let Thomas leave until the detective can speak with him. Do you know what is going on?"

I looked around. There was no one close enough to over-hear our conversation. "Brad and I saw Thomas have an intense argument with Mandy. I didn't realize you knew her."

"I've never met her before tonight." Carrie drew her eyebrows together, forming a deep line between her eyebrows. "What were they arguing about?"

I shook my head. "The band was too loud for us to hear anything. I'm sure it's nothing. Thomas wouldn't hurt a fly."

Carrie turned red, and her voice shook as she leaned in to my face. "Are you insinuating that Thomas might have killed that woman? I can't believe you, of all people, would think something like that."

"Whoa, calm down." I gripped her arm, wondering if her pregnancy hormones were making her irrational. "That's not what I said or even implied at all. Thomas is innocent, but the police will learn that he had a big argument right before she disappeared into my house."

"I hope you won't tell them about the argument." She burst into tears.

"What's going on?" I gave her a quick hug before I grabbed some napkins for her to wipe the tears and smeared makeup from her face. "It'll be okay."

"I just have a bad feeling about this," she whimpered. "Did you see how hot she looked in her costume? Thomas stared at her every chance he could. Do you think he's having an affair?"

I shook my head. The argument hadn't seemed passion driven. "No way. Thomas adores you and your daughters."

"Do you think she was an old girlfriend he wants to recon-nect with?" Big tears rolled down my sister's cheeks, leaving trails through her white-and-black face paint. "I'm getting fat and ugly, and I'm sure he's tired of me."

"Carrie, that couldn't be further from the truth. You're the most beautiful pregnant woman I've ever seen." I wasn't lying either. While we were almost identical twins, Carrie's gorgeous red hair leaned more toward auburn, while my shade of red was better suited on a clown. Her hair was always sleek whereas mine was frizzy. Again, kind of like a clown's. Her eyes were deep green, and mine had muddy-brown flecks mixed with green. And most of all, she didn't have a generous sprinkle of freckles dotting her peaches-and-cream skin. I was almost jealous of her.

"Then why is he never home, and why does he say he has to work late almost every night?" Carrie hiccupped. "It's not even tax season."

My brother-in-law was a CPA, so I knew what early spring was like for him. Fall was generally quiet. "Have you asked him? There might be several reasons for the long hours, like a new client or a start-up."

"He won't talk about it, and he keeps making excuses." She turned to face me. "The worst thing is I found a text on his phone that said 'Meet me at the party. You won't be sorry.' I just know it was from Mandy."

Before I had the chance to reassure my sister or ask any more questions, an officer strode up to us.

He pointed at me. "Detective O'Neill would like to speak to you."

I gave Carrie another hug and followed the officer inside the pool house.

The detective sat at my kitchenette table, which was scattered with papers. An iPad sat in front of him. The tech team crowded the hallway leading to my bathroom, scouring the area for any evidence, no matter how tiny.

"Ms. Martinez, please have a seat." Detective O'Neill's voice was a deep baritone that would have done any voice-over narrator proud. "I'll be with you in a moment."

His use of my last name made me cringe, and I vowed to

change it as soon as my divorce decree came through. I didn't need to be reminded of Philip and his betrayals.

Up close, Detective O'Neill was even more handsome than I had realized. Any girl would be covetous of the long, dark eyelashes that framed his amber-colored eyes. His face was lightly tanned, and he had a constellation of freckles across the bridge of his nose and apple-red cheeks. Despite the late hour, he didn't even have a five-o'clock shadow. His golden hair showed a hint of red in the light that shone from the small pendant lamp that hung over the table.

He finally put down the iPad he had been reading. Straight white teeth and a slow, sensual smile made his face even more handsome. "Now, Ms. Martinez—"

"Can you please call me Emory? I'm really unhappy with my last name. I'm going through a divorce and hope to change it soon. Although I can't decide if I should go back to my maiden name or take my stepdad's last name. Or maybe create a whole new last name. I guess I need to think about it more before I decide."

I was babbling, but I couldn't stop myself. It happened anytime I was nervous. My cake pops had killed Mandy, after all, and then I had found the body. Plus, I was about to be grilled by my best friend's new love, and he would think I was an idiot. I couldn't mess this up for Brad.

"All right." The corners of his mouth tried to edge up on his cheeks. "I understand you hosted this party?"

"Yes, that would be me and Tillie Skyler."

He tapped something into his iPad. "I'm sorry I had to miss it and then meet you under these conditions. Brad's told me so much about you."

My mouth fell open. This detective sounded like a human—unlike the last detective I'd had the misfortune of meeting, who had done everything possible to prove I was a murderer. Detective Gabe O'Neill could carry on a conversation that had nothing to do with the investigation, and I was impressed.

"Uh, it's nice to meet you. Brad has been quite mysterious about you, and I've been dying of curiosity." I cringed. It was a bad choice of words, and I was on the verge of babbling again. I snapped my mouth shut.

"Once this case is over, I'm sure we'll have the chance to get to know each other." He sighed and looked back down at his iPad. "In the meantime, I need to get your statement on what happened tonight."

I took him through everything I had observed over the evening, from the flirting to Madonna and Mandy's fight, and I even told him about the heated exchange with Thomas. I felt as if I were betraying him, but it was certain to come out anyway. Detective O'Neill seemed to have an open mind, and I knew he would find the truth no matter what circumstantial evidence surfaced. I didn't mention the text, since it was hearsay. That would be up to my sister and her husband to discuss with the detective.

He asked me a few more pertinent questions, told me they had bagged up the remaining Poison Apple Cake Pops, and handed me his business card. "Call me if you can think of anything else. And most of all, Ms. Martinez, uh, Emory, please don't go playing amateur detective this time. Let me do my job without getting in the way."

I was a little irritated by his remark, since he didn't know me or understand the circumstances in which I'd had to clear my name or else end up in prison. But knowing Brad, Detective O'Neill had probably heard my entire life story several times already. "When can I move back into my home?"

"Give us another twenty-four hours. I'll text you information on a good cleaning crew who handles these types of situations."

I said my thanks, grateful that Mandy had been in the bathtub instead of on one of Tillie's imported wool rugs. One of the police officers opened the door and ushered me back onto the patio. The cool night air soothed me as I watched another officer escort Thomas into the pool house. The fairy lights that twinkled in the trees lining the pool area didn't look quite so magical now. Most of the guests had dispersed, and the band members were dismantling their equipment. Carrie's helpers had done an admirable job of cleaning off the buffet tables. I guessed that they were in Tillie's kitchen, packing up the remains of the food and serving dishes.

"Are you a suspect this time?"

I jumped at the sound of Randall's voice behind me. Thoughts about who could have killed Mandy were consuming me, and I hadn't been paying attention to my surroundings. I was lucky I hadn't stepped right into the pool. "Randall! You made it."

"I'm sorry I wasn't here earlier." He looked around and ran a hand through his close-cropped hair. His short-sleeved shirt strained against the biceps on his raised arm. "The airplane had mechanical issues, and then they canceled the flight. I had to scramble to find another one."

"I'm glad you're here, but I'm sorry you had to walk in on a crime scene." My arms hung awkwardly at my side. Not sure if I should give him a hug, a peck on the cheek, or a mind-blowing kiss like I wanted to, I decided to let him take the lead. "Carrie is packing up the food in Tillie's kitchen. I can fix a plate for you if you're hungry."

"No thanks, I'm fine." Randall started to reach for my hand but then dropped his arm. "I heard there was a murder and you found the body. Are you a suspect?"

I shook my head and cringed. "I don't think so, although it was my Poison Apple Cake Pops that appear to have killed her."

Chapter 5

Randall's blue eyes widened, and even in the dim lighting, I could see their brilliance. "Poison Apple? Really?"

"It's a Halloween party. You know, Snow White and the poison apple story?"

"It could only happen to you, Em." His chuckle sounded musical. "Does the detective have any theories yet?"

"None that he's sharing with me, but I'm worried about my brother-in-law, Thomas." I looked to make sure no one was within listening distance, even though the words were already out of my mouth. I told Randall about the argument just as Brad was joining us.

"That argument looked pretty gnarly." Brad invoked his surfer vernacular, giving Randall a fist bump. "Did you find out what the problem was?"

"No, I didn't think it was any of my business. Detective O'Neill will figure it out with Thomas. It seems like he's a reasonable detective, unlike my last experience."

Brad's eyes lit up. "So..."

"So... what?"

Brad huffed. "You know darn well what I mean."

Laughter bubbled from my lips. It felt good to forget, even for a moment, about the tragedy that had taken place inside my home. "He's hot. Really hot."

Randall's gaze jumped from me to Brad and back again. I thought I saw concern flit across his face.

"And?" Brad shifted his weight from one foot to the other.

It was obvious Brad had fallen hard, so I relented and sang Detective Gabe O'Neill's praises. The funny thing was that I meant all the compliments, too, including how I thought he was honorable and how I could see myself becoming good friends with him.

Brad sighed. "You just made my day. I've been so worried about what you'd think about him, especially meeting him under these circumstances. It doesn't exactly bring out the best in people."

It appeared Randall had finally figured out our conversation, and I saw the tension ease in his shoulders. He stepped closer to me, and I felt the warmth of his arm next to mine. I hoped that meant he had been just a teeny tiny bit jealous about my description of the new detective.

Carrie sidled up to our group as Thomas emerged from the pool house. He looked haggard. I could have sworn he had aged about ten years—but maybe it was the lighting on the white makeup still covering his face. I realized that with all the elaborate costumes hiding people's identities, it would be next to impossible to ascertain who had killed Mandy.

"The leftover food is loaded in my van, and the assistants will finish the cleanup in Tillie's kitchen. They should be done in about thirty minutes," Carrie said, giving me a quick hug. "I'm going to take Thomas home. Call me tomorrow."

Carrie ran to her husband, took his hand in hers, and pulled him toward the gate that led to Tillie's house. I didn't blame her for wanting to get out of there. What was supposed to be a fun, romantic evening with her husband had turned into a nightmare. I was glad her daughters weren't home so they would have privacy to talk about that text and the argument.

Brad yawned beside me. I nudged him with my elbow. "What are you still doing here?"

He turned his head, staring at my door. "What do you think?"

"I think he's going to have a very long night. Send him a text that you're going home." I chuckled. "Don't let him see you looking so desperate."

"I'm worried about you and Tillie being here alone with a killer on the loose." He yawned again.

"I'll sleep in one of Tillie's guest rooms tonight." My favorite was the room with the French doors leading out to a generously sized balcony overlooking Newport Bay. I loved waking up to the sounds of seagulls and water lapping against her dock.

"I don't mind staying here tonight." Randall leaned in closer. "We have a lot of catching up to do."

Whoa. The way he'd said "catching up" made my face burn. I wanted to fan myself. As tempting as it sounded, though, I wasn't quite ready to jump into his arms. We needed to start out slow and build our friendship first. "That's really not necessary. Her house is more secure than Fort Knox."

Brad gave me a sideways look that told me he thought I'd lost my mind. After all, he was the one I had complained to the most about my fizzling romance. But as emotionally and physically exhausted as I was after this evening, I didn't want to do something I would regret later.

Randall tried to study my face in the dim lighting. "It's no trouble at all. I'm happy to sleep on the couch."

"Thanks for the offer, but we'll be fine." I laid my hand on his arm. "We've both had an exhausting day. I'll call you tomorrow."

. . .

AFTER AN UNEVENTFUL NIGHT, I spent the next morning baking cupcakes for my mother's bridge club's Halloween party. She had wanted to forgo cocktail cupcakes, so I made pumpkin-spice cupcakes with cinnamon-y cream cheese frosting for the ladies. I needed to deliver them before lunch. After that I planned to return several crystal serving pieces I had borrowed for the previous night's events to Mr. Skyler's housekeeper, Marge Maloney.

My twin nieces, Sophie and Kaylee, answered the door when I knocked while Piper danced with joy around my feet. I gave her a good belly rub, but as soon as my nieces scampered back to their playroom, Piper followed them, abandoning me. The girls had informed me they wanted to finish watching *Moana* and do a dress rehearsal for their Halloween hijinks. Apparently, Piper didn't mind her pig costume.

"Why hasn't Carrie picked the girls up?" I stowed the cupcake carrier in the butler pantry along with the display stand. I removed two cupcakes, placed them on pretty autumn china plates, and started water for tea.

"Your sister asked if she could pick up the darlings later today." My mother, Addie Whitendale, sniffed. "She knows I'm going to a party this afternoon, and I hate to impose on Lars if I have to leave."

My mother loved her granddaughters and was over the moon about the upcoming newest addition to our family. However, she and her bridge group were sticklers for punctuality, no matter what.

Today she was dressed in stylish cream-colored pants and, as a nod to the season, a nutmeg-colored silk blouse with subtle leaf watermarks. Her signature pearl necklace and earrings completed the ensemble. As usual, her hair and makeup looked perfect, despite the fact that she'd been caring for her five-year-old granddaughters.

"Under the circumstances, I'm surprised she didn't ask you to keep them until Monday."

"What circumstances? Is Carrie feeling okay? Is something wrong with her pregnancy?" She gazed directly into my eyes as if she needed to reassure herself I would tell her the truth.

"Carrie and the baby are fine, Mother. I didn't mean to worry you." I didn't want to tell her about finding another body, but I didn't want her to be concerned about my sister either. "There was an… incident last night at the party, and, well, Thomas was the last person seen arguing with a woman before I, uh, found her. So, um, the police were called."

There was a horrified look on her face. "Don't tell me you're involved in another murder!"

"It wasn't my fault. I didn't mean to find her, and I don't want to get involved, even though she was killed in my bathtub." After filling the teacups with hot water, I added Earl Grey tea bags and handed a cup to my mother. I nudged a cupcake toward her.

"Do you think the police suspect Thomas?" Mother sank down into a cushioned kitchen chair. She picked at her cupcake with a fork but didn't take a bite. "This can't be good for Carrie and the baby."

For once, I agreed with her. "I'm sure there's a very logical explanation, and the police will find the person responsible."

"I'll run the cupcakes over to Betsy's house and cancel my plans to attend the party. Your sister and Thomas need to work this out. I'll keep the girls as long as they need me to."

"Let me know if you need a pair of backup hands." I gestured toward the playroom. "I'd offer to let them sleep over, but I'm not sure when the police will finish with the pool house."

She looked at me, aghast. "You're not sleeping there, are you? Maybe you should move back here until it's resolved."

I gaped at my mother. She had done everything under the sun to keep me from staying there when I'd been a murder suspect a few months back. Now she wanted me to move back home?

"I'm staying in one of Tillie's guest rooms." It relieved me to know I had another option. If I stayed under my mother's roof, we would both regret it within hours. "She has plenty of space, and I would hate to leave her alone."

"You're right. I wasn't thinking about that."

"So, want the latest Skyler gossip?" I knew that would grab her attention. Tillie had confirmed my suspicions that Mother had once been involved with my boss. But so far, I hadn't been able to drag the secret out of her. "Mr. Skyler called a family meeting on Friday and had me attend…"

My mother eyed me, clearly annoyed that I wasn't getting straight to the point. She picked up her teacup and took a sip.

"He introduced us to Trophy Wife Number Four."

I had expected some kind of reaction from Mother. What I didn't expect to see was the teacup fall from her hands. Golden-brown tea spilled over her cream-colored slacks before the delicate china cup shattered on the travertine floor. Her face was ashen.

"Are you okay?" I jumped up to grab paper towels to clean up the mess.

My nieces must have heard the crash because they came running toward the kitchen dressed in grass skirts, coconut shells, and colorful leis. They were barefoot, with Piper close behind on their heels.

"Stay out of the kitchen. I don't want you to cut your feet on the china." I swiped the damp paper towels over the floor to pick up any shards that might have escaped my first cleanup effort. "Quick, grab Piper before she comes in here!"

"What happened, Aunt Emory?"

"Grammie accidentally dropped her teacup."

My mother still hadn't said a word. She just sat there and stared out the window. I had a feeling she wasn't admiring her well-maintained garden or the water trickling over the rocks that divided the pool from the hot tub.

Sophie held on to Piper's collar. "We're hungry," she said. "Can we go to McDonald's for lunch?"

"I'll take you and let Grammie change her clothes and clean up." I eyed my mother, wondering why Mr. Skyler's marriage disturbed her so much. "But you two need to change out of your grass skirts and coconut-shell tops before we go."

As if on cue and in unison, the twins screeched, "*No!* I don't want to change."

It didn't take me long to decide this was a battle I couldn't win. "Okay, calm down. We just need to make sure you don't get your costumes dirty or tear them. Your mom will be mad at me if she has to fix them before Halloween. You need to put your shoes on before we leave."

Not even giving me a second to change my mind about taking them to lunch, the twins scrambled to find their shoes with Piper trotting off behind them. *Traitor.* I was sure I would have to correct some behavior once we got back home.

My mother tore her eyes from the backyard and stood up. She walked over to a kitchen cabinet, opened a drawer, extracted keys, and placed them in my hand. "You'd better take my car. The girls aren't big enough to be out of their car seats."

"Thanks. I forgot about that." I hugged her and lowered my voice. "We need to talk about Mr. Skyler when the girls go home."

"Don't be ridiculous. There's nothing to discuss." She straightened her posture and seemed back to her old self. "I'll call Carrie and arrange for the twins to stay another few days. My granddaughters don't need to be exposed to their parents being questioned by the police or arrested."

With the tragedy of the murder and her reaction to Mr. Skyler's marriage, I wasn't sure how I was going to tell my mother she had to introduce the new Mrs. Skyler to all her friends, committees, and clubs. So I did what I was good at—

avoidance by procrastination—and I went to find my nieces instead.

After extracting promises that they would be careful to keep their costumes clean, I spent several minutes hunting for their shoes and finally buckled Sophie and Kaylee into their car seats. My mother must have gotten over her shock, because she gave me instructions on what to order and how to help her granddaughters eat their food. Piper whined at the car door, wanting to go with us. Mother gave her a treat and called her into the house. I was relieved when Piper obeyed. Apparently, bribes still worked.

I shook my head as I drove my giggling nieces down the street. My sister and I had survived Happy Meals with no one cutting cheeseburgers or chicken nuggets into tiny little bites, so I was sure the twins would too. But while singing silly songs with them, I mulled over the reaction my mother had had to my news.

Chapter 6

After settling my nieces back in with my mother, I assured her that the girls had eaten well and hadn't had any choking episodes. Okay, there *may* have been a small problem when Kaylee inhaled a slice of apple while sliding down the indoor playground slide. Luckily, she coughed it right up, grabbed a french fry, and headed back to the slide. I kept an eagle eye on my nieces, and I was CPR certified, but I still wanted the girls to be treated like kids instead of fragile mementos. Besides, I'd never once seen Carrie cut their food into tiny pieces, so I was following her lead. Of course, I didn't tell my mother any of this.

The two girls begged me to let Piper stay with them, and when my mother granted approval, I relented and gave my pup a long belly rub. I said my goodbyes and promised to have a Halloween cookie–decorating party with them after kindergarten the next day. While I waited for the guard gates to open, I called my sister and told her I was headed to her house —I needed to find out what had happened and make sure Thomas was not a suspect. When she tried to protest, I gave her a quick "see ya" and hung up.

I parallel parked in front of their craftsman-style home in

Costa Mesa, almost scraping the rims of my wheels. The house was painted charcoal gray with white trim, and even pregnant, Carrie had somehow found time to keep the flower beds weeded. She had a few late blooms on her many rose-bushes, and autumn-colored chrysanthemums dotted the flower bed borders. A variety of pumpkins and gourds had been arranged on the steps leading up to her front door, and a scarecrow graced the porch. I felt a tad jealous.

Carrie answered the door. She looked exhausted, and her face was blotchy with red welts. She led me to the kitchen without a word. A plate of warm lemon crinkle cookies sat on the table, and a fresh pot of decaf coffee was brewing.

I touched her arm. "Are you okay?"

"I've had better days, but I'm not as bad as it looks. I had an allergic reaction to the face paint I used last night."

I gulped. "Can you talk about what's going on with Thomas?" I didn't want to ask, but I had to. "We know he's innocent, but do the police consider him a suspect?"

Carrie's face turned pale, which made the welts stand out even more. "They came and escorted him to the station for further questioning this morning. I wanted to go with him, but he wouldn't let me."

"Please tell me you called an attorney to be with him."

She gave me the big sister look—even though she was only ten minutes older than me—that told me I was an idiot. "I called Mel Shearwood, and he's with Thomas now."

I gave a sigh of relief. Mel was my attorney when I had been accused of murder. While I had heard he was a genius in the courtroom, I hadn't wanted to wait to see if he could get the jury to believe me, so I started my own little investigation. Maybe I needed to help my sister and brother-in-law out and see if I could find the real killer instead of relying on the court system to exonerate Thomas. I didn't think they could afford the massive attorney bills or the loss of income if Thomas lost his clients. Mother and Lars would help financially, but I knew

Carrie and Thomas were proud people and would hate to accept it.

"Did Thomas tell you what the argument was about?" I hoped he'd done nothing stupid that would break my sister's heart—otherwise another murder charge might be leveled against me.

This time it was my sister who sighed. "Yes. She was blackmailing him."

"What?"

"Mandy worked for Thomas doing odd jobs and filing during this past tax season. He gets swamped with all the paperwork, so he'd needed a temp for a couple of months." She rubbed her growing belly. "He gave her a key so she could work around her school schedule and another part-time job. You know how trusting he is of everyone."

Carrie closed her eyes and leaned back in her chair. I let the silence linger. It was her story to tell, and I let her take the time she needed.

"Right around the time Mandy quit, Thomas started receiving phone calls from clients complaining that their identities had been compromised, money disappeared from their bank accounts, or their credit cards showed unauthorized charges. No one accused him, they were just complaining to a friend. If it was ever found out there was a pattern with so many clients, Thomas would have been investigated."

"That's horrible." I reached out and held her hand. "I'm assuming he suspected Mandy?"

"He didn't want to, but when he found ten thousand dollars missing from the company's checking account, he decided he'd better ask her some questions before going to the police." Carrie paused and took a sip of her decaf. "He tried tracking her down, but all the information she had given him on the job application was false. Mandy Graber never worked for any of the employers she had listed, nor did she live at the address she provided."

"So when he recognized her at the party, he confronted her?"

"Oh, it gets even worse." Carrie moaned. "I can't believe he tried to cover it up."

"How could it be worse than that?" I was impatient to hear the entire story, but I reminded myself to let my sister take her time.

"Not long after Mandy 'disappeared,'" she said, making air quotes with her fingers, "he got a phone call from her, demanding money. She said she had enough documentation to prove that it was Thomas stealing his clients' identities and money, and she would go to the police if he didn't pay her."

"That's despicable."

"He wasn't sure she could prove it, but if even a whiff of scandal touched his company, he would have lost everything." Her hands were shaking, so she placed her mug back on the table. "Mandy was a greedy little bi… um, witch, and Thomas kept paying her week after week."

This really wouldn't look good for my brother-in-law when the police found out.

"Em, she's shoved us to the brink of bankruptcy. We have next to nothing left, and I'm afraid we're going to lose our home." Carrie's lips quivered, and then she couldn't stop the flow of tears. "And if Thomas goes to jail, I'll have three children and no one to take care of us."

I jumped up and wrapped my arms around her heaving shoulders. "Shh, I won't let that happen. You have me, you have Mother and Lars, and Thomas isn't going to jail. I'll find out who killed her, and then you'll be safe."

"But you almost lost your life last time. Mother would kill me if anything happened to you."

"Carrie, listen, I can't stand by and let your innocent husband take the blame for this crime," I said, sounding braver than I felt.

I stayed a while longer and tried to console my sister.

When Thomas came home, I left them to comfort each other. He looked ghastly, and my sister looked like death warmed over. I vowed to do whatever it took to make their world right again.

Once I returned to my car, I checked my cell phone. I had turned it off so I could focus while talking with my sister. A text from Randall was waiting for me.

I thought u would call me this am. Is everything ok?

I gave myself a mental head slap. Last night, Randall had made the first overture toward starting our friendship—or was it a romance?—back up. Since I had rebuffed him, it should have been me contacting him. But here he was, trying to make sure I was safe. I was afraid that since I hadn't answered his text right away and had ignored him most of the day that I had given him the signal I wasn't interested. I wondered why I couldn't let myself believe he was a better guy than my ex—or that such a hot guy could be interested in chubby little ol' me. I thumbed a reply.

Family issues. Thomas taken in for questioning. On way home. Do u want to come by?

A quick reply chimed on my phone.

Sure. See u in 1 hr

I had planned on returning the crystal serving pieces, but now it looked like I wouldn't have enough time. I sent Marge a quick text telling her I would try again tomorrow. She replied not to worry about it and that she would plan to pick the pieces up from Tillie.

It was already late afternoon by the time I returned to Tillie's house. I wanted to check on her before I freshened up for Randall's visit. She sat on the patio overlooking the bay, a soft breeze ruffling her white hair. I watched while she used a pen to fill in the spaces of the *Los Angeles Times* crossword puzzle. I shook my head in amazement. I couldn't solve crossword puzzles even when the answers were provided for me.

How was I ever going to solve the puzzle of who killed Mandy?

Tillie glanced up from her paper. "Hey, kiddo. What's wrong? You look worried."

"I am." I ran my fingers through my frizzy red hair that had wrapped around my face from the breeze blowing off the bay. "Thomas could be in serious trouble. Mandy was blackmailing him, and they're almost at the point of bankruptcy now."

She motioned for me to sit. "What are we going to do about it? Who are we going to interrogate first?"

I looked at her pointedly. "*We* are not going to do anything. I'll start by asking a few people some questions, like the bartender. He was Mandy's boyfriend, right?"

Tillie stuck her lower lip out in a pout. "You never let me have any fun."

I groaned. "You realize your son and grandson— Theodore, in particular—would fire me then throw me in jail and then probably put a hit on me if something happened to you."

"You're exaggerating."

"What about Mrs. Skyler? Don't you think she'd look for a reason to take away your freedom if you got involved in a murder investigation?" I didn't want to be mean, but I hadn't been kidding when I said my life would be in danger if Tillie got hurt on my watch.

Tillie's face turned pale, and her eyes became misty.

"I'm sorry, Tillie, I didn't mean…" The words died on my lips as she waved her hands in a dismissive manner.

"You have nothing to be sorry about. It's my son who should apologize for inflicting another gold digger on our family."

I decided now was the perfect time to dig for some information about my mother and her son's relationship. "You should have seen the mess my mother made when she found out Mr. Skyler remarried. She'll be finding shards of the teacup she dropped for days."

Tillie raised her eyebrows and looked at me, but she didn't say a word.

"Why would she be so upset? She seems happy with Lars, and he worships the ground she walks on." I hoped she would give me a hint of what was going on in my mother's head.

"You'll need to ask Addie." Silence filled the air for a moment. "It's not my story to tell."

I was frustrated, but I knew better than to press. "Fine. So, what are we going to do about Mrs. Skyler? She seems to have swooped in a little too fast, if you know what I mean."

Her cheeks turned pink, and her eyes regained their sparkle. "I think we need to investigate her. I'll hunt for her on the internet, and when you start as her social secretary, you'll have the chance to snoop through her things."

I shuddered. The phrase "social secretary" chilled my soul. "When are they coming back?"

"I think David said it would be Wednesday."

Great. Only three days of freedom left.

"Can't you hire a private investigator? That seems like a much easier way to find out her background."

Tillie chuckled. "I'm sure that's the first thing Teddy did after leaving here on Friday."

"Well, maybe we should leave it up to him. He'll tell you what he finds out, won't he?"

She shook her head. "Teddy won't form an alliance. He trusts no one and won't risk having his father find out he had the new wife investigated."

"But if he finds something about Mrs. Skyler that's, uh, not good, won't Mr. Skyler realize it then?"

"My grandson would probably make a good spy. I'm sure his father will be told of any indiscretions his new wife may have, but he won't realize where the information came from." Tillie's face soured. "Of course, there's the risk Teddy will let his father think it was *my* doing. Kill two birds with one stone, so to speak. Trophy Wife Number Four isn't the only one after my money and independence."

It was unbearably sad that this intelligent, vibrant woman would have to worry about her own family. I also worried that if her family found out how concerned she was, they would claim that dementia was making her paranoid.

"Let me know what you find online about Mrs. Skyler, and I'll do some snooping when I work with her." I shuddered. "In the meantime, I'll try to talk to the bartender about Mandy tomorrow."

Tillie looked at her watch. "Why don't we swing by my club and see if Kenneth is working? We can have a drink in the bar."

"You mean right now?"

"Sure. It's five o'clock somewhere."

I glanced at my watch and felt my cheeks warm. "Randall is coming over. He should be here in about twenty minutes."

"Perfect. Bring him along." A sly grin appeared on Tillie's face. "Unless you had planned a private reunion with him?"

"Uh, no. I don't think I'm ready for that. Cocktails at your club sounds great."

She gently poked me in the ribs. "Don't leave that fine young man dangling too long. You don't want some other gal to swoop in and steal him."

My face was flaming now. I needed to divert her attention, and the murder was just the thing. "I doubt Kenneth will work tonight. His girlfriend was just murdered, so he's probably mourning."

"Even if he's not there, we can ask a few servers what they thought about Mandy and her relationship with Kenneth." She poked my ribs again. "Come on, there's no time like the present. Gotta strike while the iron is hot. Don't let grass grow under your feet. Never put off—"

"Okay, okay. I get it." I scowled at Tillie but had a hard

time keeping the corners of my mouth from curling up. "Enough of the cheesy quotes."

My phone chimed with a text from Randall. He was at the pool house gate and wondering where I was. I jumped up and tried to smooth down my hair.

"Relax, dear. Send him a text and tell him to come to my house."

I did as Tillie instructed while she pulled a tube of lipstick from the pocket of her slacks.

"Dab a little on your lips, and you'll be fine."

I smiled at her as I slid the creamy lipstick over my lips then pinched my cheeks for color. Tillie shooed me toward the door, and I made my way to greet the man I was infatuated with.

Chapter 7

Randall stood at the security gate, his back ramrod straight—almost as if he was standing at attention. I wondered if he had spent any time in the military. There was so much about him I didn't know. He was dressed in pressed black trousers and a short-sleeved light-blue buttoned-down shirt. I buzzed the gate, and he pushed it open and walked toward me. My heart felt like rabbits were jumping around in my rib cage.

"Hey, Emory." He paused as if he didn't know what to say. "I hope this isn't an inconvenient time."

"No. Not at all." I gestured toward Tillie's house, feeling a little awkward. *Should I give him a hug or a kiss on the cheek?* "Tillie is worried about the murder and my family, so I was chatting with her. She's invited us to have cocktails at her club. Do you mind if we go with her?"

"I don't want to intrude. We can get together another time." He turned back toward the gate.

"No. Please don't go. You're not intruding at all." My voice sounded desperate. "Tillie is looking forward to spending some time with you."

He looked at me and raised an eyebrow.

"And I've been looking forward to seeing you too." Now it sounded like I was begging him to stay. *Could this get any worse?* I wondered.

Tillie came to the front doorway, saving me. "You kids ready to go investigate? My driver will be here in a minute."

Randall shook his head and chuckled. "Mrs. Skyler, how can I pass up that invitation?"

She walked past me, trotted down the steps, and threaded her arm through Randall's. "You need to call me Tillie, young man. Mrs. Skyler was my dreadful mother-in-law."

It made me happy to see the spring back in Tillie's step as we headed to the car that arrived as promised. While I didn't want her to get involved and risk getting hurt by a deranged killer, letting her help was a good way to get her mind off her new daughter-in-law. Plus, Tillie's idea to talk to the bartender and servers was a good one, and I needed her to gain access to the private country club.

Newport Cove Country Club's imposing wood, stone, and glass edifice always made me think it would be better suited for a forest in the mountains. Inside, the richly detailed wood and sumptuous brocades reflected the feel of a colder climate. I supposed there were plenty of other clubs in the area that carried a seaside or nautical theme, and this one had wanted to be different.

I followed Tillie, who clung to Randall's arm, up carpeted stairs and into the main bar. Small tables with cozy leather club chairs dotted the room. Quiet chatter and the clinking of glasses and ice filled the air as patrons relaxed after a round of golf. I caught the mouthwatering smell of something garlicky, and I could see several patrons had plates of pasta on their table. My stomach growled. An entire wall made of glass over-looked the course, and outside the white sand traps glittered against the green grass as they captured the last rays of the setting sun.

Kenneth wasn't the one mixing up cocktails behind the

bar, so I tried to casually look around the room to see if there was anyone else I recognized.

"Good evening, Vince." Tillie slid onto a high barstool and leaned her elbows on the polished wood bar. Randall and I hung back, uncertain what to do.

"Hiya, Mrs. Skyler." Vince expertly poured generous shots of an amber liquid into a highball glass half-filled with ice. "Can I get you your usual?"

"You bet." Tillie turned toward us and patted the barstool next to her. "What's your poison?"

I grimaced at her use of "poison." The image of my Poison Apple Cake Pops stuffed into Mandy's mouth would forever haunt me. "Merlot is fine."

Randall sat on the stool next to Tillie. "I'll have a bourbon, neat," he said.

Vince nodded to us both, his wavy dark-brown bangs almost flopping over his dark-brown eyes. I was mesmerized as his slender hands poured my glass of wine while almost simultaneously concocting a gimlet for Tillie. He was an artist in top form.

I sat on the barstool on the opposite side of Tillie. This was her party, so I thought we should make her the center. I didn't want to cozy up to Randall and exclude my friend.

After we had been served, Tillie clinked her cocktail glass to my wineglass and Randall's highball then leaned toward the bartender. "So, did you hear about the murder last night?"

His baritone laugh filled the air. "That's the only thing people are gossiping about. Half of them are relieved they weren't invited to your party while the other half are miffed about being excluded."

When preparing the Halloween party-guest list, Tillie had been afraid she would hurt a few people's feelings by not inviting them. Since her space couldn't accommodate everyone, we'd had to exclude quite a few. We had tried to keep the party under the radar and had asked the guests not to talk about it, but it was apparent everyone had heard about it by now.

"What can you tell us about Mandy?" she asked Vince.

He paused his pour of tequila then winked at me. "Are you being a busybody, Mrs. S?"

"You betcha," she answered. "Okay, spill anything and everything you have on her."

He added fresh lime juice to a silver cocktail shaker. "It's not much. She worked here a few months earlier this year but then quit. She didn't give her two-week notice, which was a pain in my… well, ya know."

Tillie swirled her cocktail. "Rumor has it she'd been dating Kenneth."

"I don't get along with him, so who can tell." He shrugged. "It's not like he confides in me."

Tillie opened her handbag and slid a fifty-dollar bill she had folded in half onto the bar. "Let me know if you learn anything juicy about Mandy."

The money disappeared into the bartender's hand so fast that I wondered if he was a magician.

"Thanks, Mrs. S." He gestured toward the outside patio overlooking the golf course. "Talk to Samantha. She might give you an earful about Mandy."

We grabbed our drinks and followed Tillie to the patio. I had become a bump on a log, letting Tillie take over like that, but then again, she knew everyone, and I was a stranger. Plus, most people had a way of opening up to adorable elderly women. Even Randall seemed to be in awe of Tillie. I couldn't help but admire the dimple that appeared in his cheek whenever he grinned at my elderly friend.

We settled ourselves into club chairs that sat beneath an overhead patio heater. It didn't take long for Samantha to amble over to our table to see if we wanted another cocktail.

"Can we have menus, dear?"

"I'll be right back with them, Mrs. Skyler." The young bleach-blonde woman seemed to be talking exclusively to Randall, since her eyes never left him.

I watched her tall figure, dressed in the servers' standard uniform of black slacks and a long-sleeved white button-up blouse, as she walked back into the clubhouse. She looked young, but since she was serving alcohol, I assumed she was at least twenty-one.

I turned my attention to Tillie. "I'll admit I'm disappointed the bartender didn't give us any information."

"Don't let him fool you. He's a cautious one, our Vince." My friend almost cackled. "He won't let members suspect he's gossiping, since that would ruin his reputation. But don't worry. He'll be dropping by tomorrow morning for coffee and breakfast. He'll spill the beans then."

"What?" Randall shook his head. "How did you manage that?"

Tillie's smile was smug. "Admit it. You need someone like me to help in the investigation."

"I'll be the first to admit it." I patted her almost-blemish-free hand. This was Newport Beach, after all—land of excellent cosmetic medical groups and laser treatments. "But I can't risk your son and grandsons finding out. We'll both be in more trouble than it's worth. But back to Randall's question: How can you be certain Vince will visit you tomorrow morning?"

She tittered. "Oh, I have my charms. But if you must know, I included a note with his tip offering additional rewards if he joined us. Now, observe and learn while I grill Samantha."

I looked up and saw the young server approaching our table, three leather-bound menus in hand.

"Here you go, ladies and gentleman." She handed us the heavy tomes, her gaze never leaving Randall's face. "Baked ziti with garlic bread is the chef's blue plate special tonight. I'll let you browse through the menu a few minutes, and I'll check back with you."

"I think I'm ready to order." Tillie handed her menu to the waitress. "But while they look, can you tell me if you've heard about that murder last night? Her name was Mandy?"

"Oh gosh, yes!" Samantha clapped her hand over her lips for a moment. "That's what everyone is talking about today."

"So young. So tragic," Tillie murmured in a soothing tone. "Did you know her well, dear?"

I pretended to browse through the menu—even though I'd already decided on the special—so I could watch Samantha without her realizing it. The slight narrowing of her brown eyes and the minor turndown of her lips made me suspect she hadn't been a fan of the victim.

"No. I didn't really know her." She furrowed her brows. "We worked together a few times earlier this year, but then she quit. I haven't seen her since."

"Did she have any special friends while she worked here?"

Samantha glanced over her shoulder at the clubhouse. I couldn't tell whether she wanted to make sure no one was listening in or if she wanted to get away from the questions.

"Um, if I remember right, she dated Kenneth. He's the other bartender here." She smoothed her long blonde hair back behind her ear and looked to see if Randall had noticed her. "Last I heard she broke up with him a couple weeks ago. He's been heartbroken."

That was a surprise to both Tillie and me. Mandy and Kenneth seemed to have gotten along at the Halloween party and, in fact, had acted like they were a couple. It was time to talk to the grieving bartender and get his side of the story.

I barged into the conversation. "When does Kenneth work? Or do you have his phone number? We'd like to express our condolences."

The cute, fresh-faced waitress turned to me. "I'm not sure

I can give that out. You know… with privacy issues and all. Are you ready to order yet?"

Tillie rolled her eyes at me, then ordered the pasta special along with a glass of red wine. I ordered the same, as did Randall.

Once Samantha left the patio, Tillie let out a long sigh. "I was questioning her just fine. You scared her away."

Randall laughed. "You are an expert interrogator, Tillie. There are several law enforcement agencies who would be thrilled to put you on their payroll."

I glared at him. Tillie didn't need encouragement. "I might have scared her away, but aside from not liking Mandy, she doesn't know anything."

Tillie turned to me. "You're mistaken. She knows more than she's saying."

"Maybe, but she won't tell us." I lifted two fingers and made air quotes. "'Privacy issues' and all that."

"Patience is a virtue." Tillie paused and looked around to make sure no one could overhear us. "Our Samantha has a thing for Kenneth and will eventually want to badmouth Mandy."

"Why do you think that's the case? She never even hinted at that." The way Samantha had gazed at Randall made me suspect she would try to make him her next conquest. Kenneth would be long forgotten.

Tillie chuckled. "It's called experience. When she mentioned Kenneth's name, a slight blush colored her neck, and when she talked about Mandy, her eyes turned dark."

"I caught that she wasn't a fan of Mandy, but Kenneth? He just doesn't seem Samantha's type." Personally, I couldn't see why women were flocking around the bartender.

Randall's dimple deepened. "I have to agree with Tillie. Give it some time, and she'll be ready to spill her secrets."

I felt like there was a lead balloon sitting in my stomach. I had so much to learn, and the responsibility of exonerating Thomas was heavy on my shoulders. What if I couldn't help him? What would my sister do?

Tillie must have sensed my mood, because she reached over and cradled my hand between her own. "Don't worry. We'll find the answers and save Thomas."

"I feel like I'm bungling around, and I'm afraid I won't be able to help Thomas and Carrie." I gave her hand a quick squeeze. "Plus, I would never forgive myself if something happened to you because I got involved in this murder."

"Before you came along, I had no purpose except to stay out of the clutches of my son's wife. These investigations are nothing more than asking a few questions, yet they give me a chance to exercise my brain and relish my freedom."

Randall cleared his throat and briefly touched my arm. "I realize I'm an interloper here, and I acknowledge you're both intelligent women… but please consider the danger you could put yourself in if you accidentally question the wrong person. Detective O'Neill seems to be quite capable. Perhaps you can let him do his job, and if he asks for input, then pursue the questioning."

Tillie's laugh tinkled in the deepening night air. "I seriously doubt one of the servers is the murderer. We just need to put their answers together to get a picture of Mandy's life. Besides, we have you, young man, to keep us out of trouble."

Randall tipped an imaginary cowboy hat. "I'll do my best, ma'am. But I had to give my safety speech first."

I didn't want to sound negative, but finding the answers seemed next to impossible. "Everyone was in costume, so I have no idea who was even there. Anyone could have snuck into the party, and we never would have known they weren't on the guest list."

"If we can look into Mandy's past, we'll find some answers." Tillie took the last swallow of her gimlet. "Then we'll give the information to the police, and they can collect the evidence. Don't worry, dear. We're just asking questions. What could go wrong?"

Chapter 8

Samantha brought out our plates of pasta then returned with our glasses of wine. After checking to make sure we—well, Randall—had everything we needed, she leaned in, practically brushing her chest against his shoulder. "Talk to Ruby, the sous chef. She had a huge fight with Mandy right before she quit."

"What was the argument about?" Tillie asked in a hushed whisper.

"Kenneth." This time, I noticed the blush spreading over her neck as she stared at Randall. "He was involved with Ruby until Mandy started working here. Then that witch stole him away and broke his heart."

"Is Ruby working tonight?" I asked, figuring that was a valid question that wouldn't frighten Samantha away.

"Yeah, but you can't talk to her until dinner service is over. One of the prep crew called in sick, and they're slammed back there." She looked over her shoulder. "I gotta get back to work."

Tillie reached out to grab the young woman's skinny hand. "Can I ask one quick question? What time does dinner service end?"

"We stop taking orders at eight thirty, but she won't be out of the kitchen until ten thirty."

Before we could stop her, Samantha rushed away from our table and back into the bar.

"I don't think we can hang out here for four hours waiting for Ruby to get off work." I waved my hand over my pasta to cool it off. The aromas of tomato sauce, garlic, and basil rising with the steam coming up from the blue china plate made my stomach growl. I snapped a photo to upload the elegantly presented dish to Instagram later.

"I think we should go home after dinner and then come back." Tillie took a bite of the buttery garlic bread and swallowed. "We can park in the employee lot and wait for her to leave the building. Bring some cookies and a thermos of coffee or tea to sweeten her up while we chat."

I nodded, my mouth too full to answer. I had plenty of cookie dough balls in the freezer, so it would be easy to tempt Ruby with fresh-baked treats.

"Don't forget Vince is coming for breakfast tomorrow morning."

If Vince was dropping by for breakfast, I needed to prep for that too. An overnight sausage-and-egg casserole would allow me more time in the morning. "When should I have it ready?"

"I think nine o'clock will be best." Tillie turned to Randall, who was staring intently at his cell phone, his pasta barely touched. "Would you like to join us for a cookie rendezvous with Ruby tonight?"

"What? Oh, err, sorry." He shot a quick glance my way. "There's an emergency with the security firm, and they want me to fly to San Francisco this evening. A car service is on the way to take me to general aviation."

I racked my brain trying to recall what he had said about the new company he was working for. His job was why he had stayed in Florida much longer than he expected as he worked on details to expand the company. He had moved back to Southern California to open new branches of the security firm. Other than that, he had been vague about what his work entailed. I had assumed we would have lots of time to talk about him, his life, and career once he was here permanently. Instead, I was in the middle of a murder, and he was in the middle of an emergency.

"You'd better eat your dinner, then." Tillie wiped her mouth with her linen napkin. "Or would you prefer to take it in a to-go box?"

"I've learned to eat fast whenever there's an opportunity."

I stared in amazement as huge forkfuls of pasta disappeared into his mouth in rapid succession. He washed them down with several gulps of ice water, while his glass of wine remained untouched.

"I apologize for not being able to stay and spend time with you ladies. It's been an enjoyable evening." Randall took another bite, reached into his pocket, and pulled out his wallet. "May I pay for our dinner and drinks? It's the least I can do for running out on you."

"Absolutely not. The pleasure of your company is payment enough." Tillie's eyes twinkled. "Or you can repay me by taking Emory out to dinner when you get back."

I choked on the sip of wine I had just taken, struggling to catch my breath without coughing all over the table. "That's unnecessary, Randall."

"I'd love to take her to dinner." He winked at me. "Thanks for the suggestion."

They were ganging up on me. *Oh boy.*

When Randall's plate was empty, his phone dinged. He glanced at the screen then stood and leaned down to peck Tillie on her cheek. "Thank you for a lovely evening. Next time it's my treat."

"Anytime, dear."

I stood up, too, and wondered if I should shake his hand

or pat his arm. Instead, I clasped my hands behind my back. "Safe travels. I hope everything goes well."

"I'll call you when I get back into town. It could be a couple of days."

I nodded. And then, without warning, his warm lips were on mine, and my arms wrapped around his waist. I was breathless when he stepped away.

"Stay safe. Don't get into any trouble with Tillie." His voice sounded husky in my ear.

I watched him walk through the doorway and into the clubhouse. The place felt emptier than it had before.

I sat back down, and Tillie left me to my thoughts while we finished eating. She probably thought my mind was on Randall. Instead, I was musing on how best to solve the murder and what we'd learned so far. Aside from Thomas being blackmailed by the victim, the rest of the suspects seemed to be women who'd been fighting over the bartender, Kenneth.

I just couldn't see his sex appeal. He had looked and acted goofy in his jester costume at the party. He was short and had thin sandy-blond hair. I guess his face was nice-looking—though a bit too tan for my tastes—and it looked like he worked out. I hadn't talked to him much at the party, so perhaps he had a charming personality that attracted women.

WE SAT in my well-used Honda in the dark employees' parking lot, waiting for Ruby to get off work. The fragrance of lemon cookies filled the small space, and my stomach growled. Since I had gorged on the baked ziti at dinner, I had no idea how I could be hungry again already. I had meant to take some home to share with my sister so that she could figure out the recipe. But instead, I had eaten every last morsel on my plate. I hoped Ruby would share the ingredient list with me, and I could pass that along to Carrie.

Tillie nudged my arm. "They're coming out. Do you see her?"

"I don't know what she looks like."

"Good point. My eyes aren't what they used to be so look for a short, young woman."

There was only one thing to do, and that was get out of my car and approach the group of employees who were headed toward theirs. As I walked, Tillie stayed close behind me.

"Excuse me, I'd like to speak with Ruby." My voice sounded weak.

A woman's alto voice cut through the dark. "Yeah? And who are you?"

The parking lot was too dark to see much. *Where are the security lights?*

"I have Mrs. Skyler with me. We have a couple of things we'd like to talk to you about."

"Sure thing, Mrs. Skyler." The voice broke away from the pack of people who had stopped walking at my first question.

Ruby stepped closer to us. She was about my height—just a couple of inches over five feet—and it was obvious she also enjoyed sampling her own cooking because, like me, she was a bit on the chubby side. Her dark hair was cropped close to her head, and a row of ear piercings glittered in the faint light.

"Would you like some lemon cookies and tea?" I showed her the small plate I held in my hands.

"Sure." She looked at me warily. "I know Mrs. Skyler, but who are you?"

"Oh, sorry." I moved the plate to my left hand and thrust out my right. "I'm Emory Martinez."

Ruby shook my hand, her grasp firm, then took the offered plate of cookies. "Where've I heard that name before? You're not a member of the club. Have we met?"

I shook my head. She had likely heard my name

mentioned as a suspect in my ex-best friend's murder, and I didn't want to remind her.

Tillie gestured toward my car. "We can sit in Emory's car and chat. If that's okay with you?" She rubbed her arms as if she were cold. A breeze had sprung up, and ocean fog was creeping over the small western hills separating us from the beach.

I placed my hand on Tillie's arm to give her some warmth. "I have a sweater in the car if you need it."

"If I get out of the breeze, I'll be fine."

Ruby followed us and chose the back passenger seat. I noticed she had already consumed a few of the lemon cookies.

Tillie settled in on the opposite side of Ruby, so I got back in the driver's seat. I had to twist around to see the two women.

"Can I offer you some tea?" I held up the thermos.

Ruby waved away my offer. "Naw, I'm fine. I'm assuming this has to do with Mandy?"

"How did you know?"

"Gossip around the club is she was killed at your party, Mrs. Skyler." Ruby studied my face. "I remember now—you killed that woman who cheated with your husband."

"No!" I squeaked. "I didn't kill her. I only found her. And then I found the murderer."

"Hey, chill out. I wasn't judging. She probably deserved what she got."

I shook my head. No one deserved to have their life taken away from them, but I didn't want to discuss the worst experience of my life.

Tillie interrupted my thoughts. "Now Ruby... what can you tell us about Mandy?"

"Are you trying to find the killer again?"

"No," I said, not wanting her to get any ideas. "We're just asking a few questions."

"Shouldn't the police be doing that?" asked the incredulous sous chef.

"Well…" I stalled, trying to figure out what to say. "It's complicated."

Tillie barged in, taking control of the conversation. "Emory's brother-in-law is the prime suspect. He's innocent, so of course we're investigating."

Ruby raised her eyebrows. I noticed she had a small hoop piercing on her left eyebrow, and in the dim light of the car, I could see that the tips of her hair were magenta. She lifted another cookie to her mouth, revealing a prominent tattoo of a whisk and mixing bowl on her forearm.

I shrugged. "We're just asking a few questions about Mandy's life and will let the police take it from there."

From the shadows of the back seat, Tillie snorted.

"Come on, Tillie, this new detective seems to know what he's doing," I said. "He'll find the killer."

It dawned on me then that maybe we were sitting in a car with the killer in a very dark, very deserted parking lot. I glanced out the window. All the other employees had left, and it was just the three of us. I shivered, wondering why I'd agreed to this unsafe situation. We should have met Ruby for coffee, surrounded by people in a popular coffee shop.

"So, what did you want to know?" Ruby's tone made it clear she was annoyed. "I'd like to get home sooner than later, if you don't mind."

My mind whirled with the questions I should ask. I worried I would offend her and she would stomp off, leaving us with nothing but cookie crumbs in the back seat. Before I could say anything, Tillie's voice cut through the darkness.

"How long did Mandy work here?"

"Just a few months. Long enough to make some enemies and steal my boyfriend."

"So you'd consider her an enemy?"

Ruby laughed, but it wasn't a cheery, funny laugh. "Let's

cut through the crap and answer the question you really want to ask. No, I didn't kill the witch."

"But you might have wanted to, along with several other employees?" I probed.

That elicited a real laugh. "I was so angry when she stole Kenneth away from me, and I'm sure you heard about the fight we had. But he finally came to his senses and dumped her a few weeks ago, and we're back together now."

I really, really wanted to ask what was so special about Kenneth. I also had to wonder if Ruby knew Kenneth had been with Mandy the day of our party. *Was he two-timing them?*

Tillie's voice sliced through my thoughts. "Who else at the club got into altercations with her?"

"Let's see…" Ruby took another bite of cookie. "There's Samantha, the server. She told Mandy that she'd get even if that was the last thing she ever did. And several of the 'ladies who lunch' hated Mandy with a passion. They thought she was after their husbands—which she was."

Oh boy. Now we had more suspects to track down and talk to. I wasn't quite so intimidated about talking to the employees at the country club, but I couldn't imagine questioning any of the "ladies who lunch." Still, I would do whatever it took to help my sister and brother-in-law.

"Do you have the names of these ladies?" I asked. "I saw a woman at our party getting into a fight with Mandy."

"Which woman?" Tillie asked. "I'm sorry I missed that."

"It was Madonna. Elton John had to pull her away from Mandy."

Ruby's eyebrows almost touched her hairline, and her mouth dropped open. "You… you mean you had Madonna and Elton John at your party? Wow… just wow!"

I giggled. "No, sorry for the confusion. It was a costume party, and the woman was dressed like Madonna, with the pointy-cone outfit. She had on a wig and loads of makeup, so

I couldn't tell you who she was, just that she had an awesome body."

And that would be the crux of the problem as we tried to talk to the people who had come to our party. The costumes had hidden their true identities, and anyone could have snuck in without us knowing.

Ruby sighed. "Too bad it wasn't them. That would have been so cool."

I agreed.

Tillie got us back on track. "We've kept you long enough, but do you remember the names of the 'ladies who lunch' who disliked Mandy?"

Ruby's guffaw was loud in my small car. "Oh, Mrs. Skyler, it went way beyond dislike. I came out to talk to a member about a gluten-allergy issue one time, and when I walked by their table, those ladies were talking about how to get away with murdering her."

Chapter 9

"What?" I yelped. *Could finding the murderer be this easy? Could the murderer be a perfectly manicured, perfectly coiffed country club lady?*

"Oh, yeah." Ruby wiped a cookie crumb from the corner of her mouth. "I'm sure I was talking gibberish to the table about the gluten issue because I was trying to hear what the ladies were saying."

"And?" I was getting impatient.

"They talked about types of poison and how to get Mandy to eat or drink it. I didn't hear much, since I couldn't hang out in the dining room."

"Who were the women?" Tillie prompted.

There was a long, silent pause. I held my breath.

"I'll lose my job if anyone finds out I gave you the information."

"We won't tell anyone you told us about them," Tillie reassured her. "And if it comes out and you lose your job, I promise I'll find you another one that pays even better."

Ruby still hesitated.

"Most likely, these ladies were at our party, so we can say

we figured it out from our guest list." I hoped that would ease her mind.

Ruby shook her head then sighed. "I'll regret this, but the main instigator was Vivienne Gainer."

Tillie thought for a moment. "Yes, Vivienne attended the party. Although I don't recall what her costume was."

Since I didn't know most of the people Tillie had invited, I couldn't help. Then I remembered Brad had been taking photos with his iPhone. "I'll text Brad and have him email the photos he took. Hopefully, we can figure out if Madonna and Vivienne are one and the same."

"Who were the other ladies sitting with Vivienne?"

Again, Ruby sighed. "I guess you'll find out anyway. Chloe Martin and Shannon Dexter were with Mrs. Gainer."

Tillie sucked in her breath. "That's not good."

"Why? What does it mean?" I was at a loss. I wasn't familiar with any of the people they were talking about.

"Shannon Dexter is married to California state senator Zach Dexter." Tillie looked at Ruby for confirmation. "He's up for reelection and doesn't need a scandal like this."

Ruby snorted. "If he doesn't want a scandal, he should keep his hands to himself."

"Really? How is it even possible to get away with that kind of behavior now?" I was glad women were finally saying enough was enough and no meant no.

"Don't get me wrong—he doesn't force himself on anyone. But let's just say certain women find him attractive, and he takes advantage of it... and them." Ruby pursed her lips together.

Tillie frowned. "I saw him canoodling with Vivienne at a cocktail party last month. I'm surprised Shannon remained friends with her after that."

"Did Shannon and..." I had forgotten the other woman's name. "The other friend attend our party?"

Tillie thought for a moment. "Chloe? No, neither of them

could make it."

We said goodbye to Ruby, and, while Tillie climbed into the front passenger seat, I sent Brad a quick text asking if he could email the party photos to me.

He responded right away. **Playing investigator again? Count me in!**

My fingers flew as I typed in my answer. **No! Even if we were, u can't risk ruining things w/ your Adonis.**

Might be able to get inside scoop on what police r thinking.

He had a good point. **I'll keep u posted.**

Coffee tomorrow am? The usual?

I sent him the thumbs-up emoji. **Gotta run, I'm driving. xoxo**

Vince was coming for breakfast, but Brad's idea of "a.m." was eleven, so I figured there would be plenty of time to do both. Brad owned a software development company, and he created a lot of games too. He was a night owl who spent a lot of time in online chat rooms to watch for gaming trends and customer input on his products. I had never quite understood the appeal of computer games, but he was very successful and seemed to enjoy what he did.

Before I could even make it out of the parking lot, my phone chimed with the photos. I handed it to Tillie and told her to scroll through and look for Madonna. The more I thought about it, the more likely it was that she and Vivienne were the same person.

Tillie located Madonna in one of the photos and zoomed in on her face. She then logged in to Newport Cove Country Club's member roster and found the photo of Vivienne. I pulled to the side of the road and compared both pictures. I was right—Vivienne Gainer and Madonna were a match.

"We need to have a chat with her tomorrow." Tillie took the phone back from me. "We should take her some cupcakes or muffins."

I shook my head. "You don't have a body like hers and eat cupcakes or muffins. Flowers might be better."

"You're right. We can pick up a bouquet on our way."

"What time do you want to visit her?" My schedule for the next day was getting busy.

"Around one thirty? Right after lunch?" Tillie put the phone away. "I think dropping in unexpectedly is the best thing. It gives her less chance to make excuses to not see us or concoct a story about her altercation with Mandy."

I yawned and pulled back onto the road. "Sounds like a good plan."

FUELED by several cups of coffee after not much sleep, I slid the overnight sausage-and-egg casserole out of the oven. The bread had puffed up and turned golden brown, and the tantalizing smell of maple sausage scented the air. I popped a tin of mini blueberry muffins into the oven and started a fresh pot of coffee. Just as the timer dinged to alert me that the muffins were done, the doorbell rang. I heard Tillie's voice as she greeted our breakfast guest.

A few moments later, she poked her head in the kitchen. "I settled Vince on the patio. Do you want me to take anything out?"

I handed her a carafe of coffee. "Take this, and I'll bring the muffins out before I plate the casserole."

"I can take the muffins too." Tillie flexed her bicep. "I'm no eighty-pound weakling."

"The warming insert still needs to be heated for the muffin basket. You can entertain our guest. I already have orange juice on the patio table."

"Maybe we should serve mimosas to loosen up his tongue." Tillie mimicked tilting a flute to her mouth. "It's not too late to offer."

My schedule for the day had become extra busy, and I

didn't want to be slowed down by alcohol, nor did I think Tillie needed to start her day off with champagne. The last thing I needed was for one of her grandsons—Theodore, especially—to find her tipsy first thing in the morning. "I think we're good with juice and coffee. We both need to keep a clear head while we question him."

After expressing her disappointment, Tillie left with the coffee carafe. I busied myself by placing the hot muffins into a breadbasket with a clay warming insert and plating the breakfast casserole. With the dishes perched on a large serving tray, I carried it to the patio overlooking Newport Bay.

Even though it was late October, the warm Santa Ana winds made it pleasant to sit outside. Sparkling clean glass half walls surrounded the large flagstone area, so if the winds became gusty, we had protection. The sun warmed my face, and not one cloud shadowed the deep-blue sky. Earlier I had placed a large covered bowl of cubed melon and glistening berries on the table. I had also arranged turquoise placemats along with the silverware, coffee mugs, juice glasses, and crisp white napkins on the wrought iron glass-topped table.

"Good morning, Vince." I slid the plate of breakfast casserole in front of him and placed the breadbasket in the center of the table. "Help yourself to some blueberry muffins and fruit."

"This smells amazing. Sure beats my usual bowl of cornflakes."

As Vince ate and Tillie chitchatted, I observed our guest. His wavy dark hair still flopped over one of his eyes, and I fought the urge to smooth it back. He had dressed in casual khaki cargo shorts, flip-flops, and a vivid red-and-yellow Hawaiian-print shirt. I noticed he skipped buttering the mini muffins and instead popped one after another into his mouth.

"Oh my god, these muffins are amazing," he said after he had consumed at least five of them. "The eggs and sausage are killer too."

Tillie and I shared a look. We needed to find out what Vince knew about an *actual* killer.

"Thanks. I'm glad you're enjoying breakfast." I fussed with the melon on my plate for a moment. "What can you tell us about Mandy?"

Tillie shot me a disapproving glare that indicated I should have let her take the lead with a more indirect approach, but I figured Vince knew why he was here.

"She was a real piece of work." The bartender's eyes darkened, and he placed his fork back on his plate. "One of those women who has to stir up drama. She spread so many rumors that almost every employee hated each other by the time she left. It took a long time before our team rebuilt their trust in each other."

"Why did she quit?" Tillie asked. "My understanding is that she only worked there a few months."

Vince snorted. "She worked just over six months and quit after claiming she was being poisoned at work."

"What?" I yelped. Surely it couldn't be this easy to prove one of the club's employees had been trying to kill Mandy months before our party. If so, how appropriate that they used the Poison Apple Cake Pops. "Who did she think was trying to poison her?"

"Oh, that would be me." His sly grin caused a dimple to appear in his cheek. "I got her the job because we were, uh, dating, and then she dumped me for Kenneth."

"Were you trying to poison her, Vince?" Tillie's voice was quiet.

I choked on my orange juice and coughed. Where was the subtlety that Tillie had touted before? I didn't want to think about how we might be eating breakfast with a killer. I shivered and coughed again. Vince wasn't one of our suspects. He was just supposed to tell us who he thought had a motive to kill Mandy. He wouldn't confess and then kill us… would he?

Once I got my coughing under control, Vince answered

with a laugh in his voice. "Oh, Mrs. Skyler, you are such a hoot."

Tillie looked at me with her eyebrows raised. We had both noticed he didn't deny it.

She wouldn't give up. "Well, if you weren't trying to poison her, who was?"

"No one was." His voice hardened, and his dimple disappeared. "That tramp was trying to stir up trouble. She even tried suing the club for the 'poisoning,' hoping they'd just settle and give her money. But after talking to us employees, management threatened to countersue, and she let it drop."

"So, when she dumped you for Kenneth, she stole Kenneth from Ruby?" Tillie prodded. "Is it possible Ruby might have tried to poison her?"

"Naw, Ruby's one of the good people. Not a mean bone in her body. Besides, Ruby and I hooked up for a while after we were 'dumped,' as you so succinctly put it. It was fun while it lasted."

"Ruby's back with Kenneth now?" My head spun as I tried to keep up with the back-and-forth relationships that had gone on among the employees. And at what point did Brian date Mandy? If he was still trying to avoid her, it couldn't have been that long ago. One thing was certain—Mandy had played everyone.

"Yeah. Ruby's an idiot for taking him back." He rubbed his jaw. "He doesn't deserve her."

"If Mandy was such a witch, why did Kenneth stay with her so long?" By my guesstimate, their relationship must have lasted five or six months, off and on.

"Mandy was sweet when she wanted something, and she knew how to have fun." Vince slid a hand through his hair and pushed the strands away from his eyes. "I think she hid her real self from Kenneth because she was using him to blackmail several employees and club members."

Chapter 10

Tillie tapped her manicured nails on the tabletop. "How do you know that?" she asked.

"Because she tried blackmailing me." Vince's face turned red, his eyes narrowing. "When we were together, she found out about an, uh, indiscretion I'd had my senior year in high school. I blew her off because of the statute of limitations, and besides, I was a stupid seventeen-year-old. I'd done my penance and made amends long before Mandy came around. Her threats didn't scare me."

I was skeptical. "And Kenneth was okay with the blackmailing?"

Vince snorted. "He was clueless. He still doesn't realize the extent of how she played him."

"How did she play him?" Tillie asked.

"I'm not one hundred percent sure, and I'm only going on my experience with her." He thought for a moment. "I believe she used Kenneth's laptop and signed up for a free email address with his name. Probably trying to cover her tracks, so to speak."

I interrupted. "So it might have been Kenneth trying to blackmail you?"

"No. Mandy made sure you knew it was her. I think she was laying groundwork for Kenneth taking the blame if something went wrong."

I stared at him in horror. "Why didn't you tell your friend what Mandy was doing?"

"My reward for that good deed was a black eye. Kenneth punched me. He said I was lying." Anger clouded Vince's eyes. "Mandy keyed my car later. I might not have any proof, but I'm sure it was her."

"After they broke up, did Kenneth ever acknowledge Mandy's blackmail?" Tillie asked. "He had to have been angry with her."

"We don't talk, and I've made sure I'm never around when he's working." Vince grinned. "What I have heard is that he almost choked her to death when they broke up."

Tillie and I exchanged a glance. If that was the case, why had Kenneth acted like Mandy was his girlfriend at the party? Or was Vince trying to throw suspicion onto Kenneth to cover his own tracks?

After he departed, taking the leftover blueberry muffins with him, Tillie sat in the kitchen and chatted with me. I took the opportunity to stir together chocolate cake mix with eggs and vegetable oil for my nieces' Halloween cookies. Our talkative bartender had seemed adamant that Kenneth should be our prime suspect. I suspected Vince's judgment was clouded because Kenneth had stolen his girlfriend and then punched him. I couldn't get past the fact that Kenneth and Mandy had acted like a couple while working together at the party.

"I have a very strong feeling about Vivienne Gainer." Tillie started ticking off her reasons on her fingers. "One, Ruby overheard her talking about poisoning Mandy. Two, she was seen getting into a fight with the victim at our party. Three… was there a third reason?"

"It's hard keeping the suspects straight." I laughed then

sobered. "I can't believe how many people hated her. How terrible to be remembered for being an awful person."

Tillie grabbed her iPad. "I'll compile a list of everything we've found out. It might help us see a pattern."

"Great idea." I placed scoops of cookie dough onto a parchment-lined baking sheet and slid it into the oven.

The easy cake-mix cookies would turn into Halloween black cats at my nieces' after-school decorating session. I took a packet of homemade dark chocolate buttercream out of the freezer and stuck it in the refrigerator to defrost. The girls could spread the frosting over the tops of the cookies then use an assortment of candies and sprinkles to create the cats. I pulled open the container holding my stash of candies and retrieved candy corns, mini M&M's, mini jelly beans, and shoestring licorice strings. From the storage racks hanging on the inside of the walk-in pantry, I retrieved heart-shaped sprinkles and chocolate and rainbow jimmies.

Past experience indicated the girls would want to pile frosting onto the cookies then cram on as many candies and sprinkles possible. Never mind how cute my sample of the black cat cookie was—they would want to do it their way, with no thought to the season. I had tried to enforce a rule that they could decorate two crazy cookies each if they did the rest in a more appropriate manner first. It usually worked... but not always. What mattered most was that the girls had a blast experimenting, and I loved the memories we were creating.

Tillie's voice interrupted my recollection of all the cookie and cupcake crafts I had enjoyed making with my nieces. "I just received a text from Marge. She'd like to come pick up the serving ware now, if that's convenient."

"Sure. I put them in your butler's pantry." I took some of the frozen chocolate buttercream from the refrigerator and defrosted it in the microwave for ten seconds. "Too bad we gave Vince all the leftover muffins. I suppose I can offer Marge a Halloween cookie instead."

Tillie twisted her lips. "Well… Vince didn't actually get all the muffins. I kind of hid a few to keep for myself."

A giggle burst from my mouth. "Keep them. You don't have to share with Marge. I'm sure a warm cookie with melty dark chocolate buttercream will be fine for her."

"That sounds delicious." Tillie smacked her lips. "Maybe I should try that too."

"There's more than enough for all of us and for the girls to decorate. I'll put a fresh pot of coffee on."

While the coffee brewed, Tillie tapped on the screen of her iPad. "Here's the list of suspects I have in order of probability: Vivienne, Kenneth, Vince, Ruby, Shannon, and Thomas. Did I miss anyone?"

"Thomas shouldn't be on that list," I sputtered. "We know he's innocent. What about Samantha? The server at your club."

"Of course he's innocent. I just thought with his experience, we might see a pattern emerging."

"We've already seen a pattern. Mandy was a blackmailer." I groaned. "The killer is probably someone who's not even on our list yet. We need to narrow the names down. Can we find out who worked at the club that night? It would at least give them an alibi."

"Not necessarily. The employees are all given dinner breaks, and someone could have driven to my house, killed Mandy, and returned to work within thirty minutes. Risky but doable." Tillie tapped on her iPad again. "We still need to consider everyone, but I'll take Thomas off and put Samantha's name on the list. She may have had issues with Mandy, but I don't see her as the killer. She's too sweet."

"Maybe, but sometimes looks can be deceiving." I put the mixing bowl into the dishwasher. "We need to talk to her again and find out why she threatened Mandy."

"Let's plan to go to the club for dinner tomorrow night. I'll find out if Kenneth and Samantha are working, and if we're lucky, we can talk to them both."

The security gate buzzed, and I went to let Marge in. She was standing by the gate, checking her phone while waiting for me. The random strands of silver that streaked her short brown hair glinted in the sunlight. Her face was pasty, giving the impression she never spent any time outdoors. She had on the bulky orthopedic shoes that she always wore while working, but she was dressed in baggy blue jeans and a teal-colored T-shirt. With Mr. Skyler out of town, she apparently dressed in a more casual manner.

I opened the gate and gestured toward Tillie's house. "Would you like to stay for some warm cookies and coffee?"

"I'd better not." She glanced down at her phone. "The window washers will be at the Skyler residence soon, and I need to be there to supervise."

"I'm sorry you had to make the trip to pick up the serving pieces." I felt bad that Marge had not only delivered the pieces for us to use but also had to return for them. "If you didn't need them right away, I could have dropped them off tomorrow."

"It's not a problem. I had to come this way to pick up some dry cleaning and do a few other errands."

Marge was usually chatty and friendly with me, but today she seemed subdued. I worried she was annoyed with me for not following through on my promise to return the serving ware, or perhaps she had other things on her mind. I motioned for the older woman to follow me into the house. "Let me get the dishes, and you can be on your way."

Marge sniffed the air. "The cookies do smell delicious."

"I can send a couple home with you for later."

"No thanks." She tapped her tummy, which looked flat to me, and laughed. "I'm trying to watch my weight."

I grabbed two large, reinforced tote bags that contained

the cushioned boxes of crystal serving pieces from the butler pantry. The bags were heavy, so I passed one off to Marge, who lifted it effortlessly from my hands. I carried the second bag as I followed her outside to a pristine Land Rover. She had parked in front of the garage entrance, which made me grateful. My arms were complaining at the weight of the crystal I carried, and I wouldn't have wanted to walk a block or two. Marge seemed to barely notice the heft of the crystal and used one hand to lift the bag into the cargo hold before she took the second tote from my arms. I wondered how much Mr. Skyler paid his housekeeper for her to afford such a nice vehicle.

Once we stowed the totes in the back of her vehicle, I told her I planned to come to the office the following day. After she drove off, I realized Marge hadn't said one word about the new Mrs. Skyler. *Does she even know he remarried? Or is she trying to be discreet?*

Inside, Tillie played Candy Crush on her iPad while I hurried to clean the kitchen. I glanced at my watch. "I've got to run and meet Brad for coffee. If I'm back around twelve forty-five, I should have enough time to freshen up before we visit Vivienne."

"That's plenty of time." Tillie's eyes twinkled. "Give him a peck on the cheek for me. I just love that boy."

I DID as Tillie had asked, plus I gave Brad a big hug when I saw him. As soon as I had found out he wasn't interested in me romantically, our friendship had blossomed back to the closeness we had shared in high school.

"How is your new detective doing with the case?" I took a sip of the macchiato he had waiting for me on the table then contemplated the ocean view. The water always brought a sense of calmness to me.

"He's frustrated as heck," Brad said, rubbing the back of his neck. "No one is talking to him, and while Thomas is a good suspect because of the blackmail, there isn't any physical evidence to link him to the crime. You didn't hear this from me, right?"

"Of course not." I felt a weight lift from my shoulders. Thomas wouldn't be arrested right away. "Perhaps Tillie and I can help Detective O'Neill out a little. You'd be amazed at how people open up and spill their secrets when a sweet little eighty-something-year-old lady chats with them."

"Do tell." Brad leaned in, his eyes glinting with anticipation. "I'll figure out a way to drop hints to my detective."

I glanced around to make sure no one else was within hearing distance, leaned in closer, and told Brad everything we had learned. Once finished, I took a gulp of coffee and settled back in the chair.

Brad whistled. "Who would have thought Tillie could accomplish all that?"

"Hey, I was there too," I sputtered. "It was my idea to ask questions and then bake goodies to sweeten up Ruby and Vince."

He laughed. "Cupcake, I doubt you would have gotten half that information on your own. You and Tillie make a good team, though."

"The problem is I shouldn't let Tillie get involved. We'd have some serious problems if her son and grandson find out. Can you pass the information to Detective O'Neill without letting him know where you got it?"

"I'll do my best, but it'll be a hard sell with these bombshells you just dropped." Brad ran his fingers through his hair. "A senator's wife talking about poisoning Mandy? I mean… wow."

"I know, right?" I took another sip of coffee. "Tillie and I will chat with Vivienne this afternoon. Hopefully, we'll find more clues."

"Just be careful, Em. If she's the killer, it could be dangerous."

Chapter 11

"We won't accuse her or anything." My voice was a little more forceful than I'd meant for it to be. "Besides, there will be two of us and only one of her."

Brad lifted his right eyebrow but said nothing.

"Okay, we'll be careful."

"Call me as soon as you leave her house." Brad held up his little finger for a pinkie promise. I relented and hooked my finger to his.

After we finished our coffee, we meandered through several ocean-view shops and admired the local artists' canvases and sculptures. Even though it was autumn, the sunny, warm day had brought throngs of people to the beach and the surrounding stores. We shoved the discussion of murder and suspects aside and instead chatted about upcoming holiday plans and looked for gifts for our loved ones.

Brad purchased a small handblown vase for his mother and talked me into doing the same for mine. The swirls of white floating through the clear glass would go well with any decor, but it was the whimsical shape that captured our attention. Once the vases had been tightly wrapped in bubble packaging and placed in artsy paper bags, Brad kissed my cheek and headed to work.

I decided I had time to grab lunch before I needed to pick Tillie up to visit Vivienne. I crossed the street and walked along the boardwalk bordering the expanse of sandy beach. The vibrancy of the ocean lifted my spirits even more, and I breathed in the salty sea air while waiting in line for a hot dog. Once the hot dog, topped with grilled onions and bell peppers, was in hand, I added chopped tomatoes and pickled jalapeños. I sighed in bliss with my first bite... and sputtered and choked when a piece of spicy jalapeño adhered to the back of my throat. My eyes watered while I coughed. I tried to chug the cold bottle of water that had come with my lunch but choked even more when hit with another coughing fit.

"Here, take a bite of this." Someone shoved a tube of string cheese into my hands. "It'll cool the burn."

Even though I couldn't see much more than a blurry male figure through the tears in my watering eyes, I did as directed. I tore back the plastic wrapper and bit into the rubbery cheese. It took a couple of tries to swallow and then a couple more bites before I stopped coughing. I finally had the chance to inspect my rescuer—Brian Skyler. My cheeks flamed even hotter than from my coughing fit. He was dressed in colorful board shorts that were sun-faded, and his chest and feet were bare aside from the sand that clung to his tanned skin. His blond hair was salt and sand encrusted from time spent in the ocean. It was hard for me not to stare at his perfectly toned body.

"Thank you." My voice still sounded like a frog trying to croak. "A pepper got stuck in my throat."

"I figured that's what happened after I saw you piling on the jalapeños." He grinned. "Most people try to calm the capsaicin burn with water, but that only inflames it. Dairy, on the other hand, cools the burning sensation."

I swiped at my wet eyes, and black streaks smeared my fingers. Why hadn't I applied waterproof mascara? I could only guess how ridiculous I looked. *Probably like a raccoon.* "I suppose as a chef, you'd know stuff like that. Thanks for rescuing me."

"That's my job. Rescue damsels in distress." He reached over and wiped a trail of moisture from my cheek with his cool hand. Instead of pulling away, he let his fingers linger in a gentle caress.

My cheeks burned even hotter, and I moved back half a step. I didn't need this kind of complication with Tillie's grandson, especially now that Randall was back in town.

Brian let his arm drop to his side. "So, that guy's back in town."

"You mean Randall?"

He nodded. "Is it serious?"

Serious? What does he mean by that? Is he hitting on me? "Um, I don't know. We're just, um, having dinner, I guess."

Brian looked down the walkway toward the pier. "I was wondering if you'd go out to dinner with me sometime."

"Like on a date?" I couldn't believe it. Brian had waited until Randall was back in town to ask me out. "Um, Brian… I'm sorry…"

"No problem. I get it." He wouldn't meet my gaze. "I waited too long to ask you out."

"It's not that. Randall and I clicked from the moment we met. I don't want to date anyone else, no matter how great they might be. Like you." I couldn't tell Brian that I wouldn't ever date a player like him. My ex had been more than enough for one lifetime. "But thanks for asking."

"You can't blame a guy for trying."

I held up the half-eaten piece of cheese. "Did I eat your lunch? Can I buy you a hot dog or something?"

"Naw, I'm fine. It was one of my extra snacks to hold me over until I meet my brother for lunch. Surfing always makes me ravenous, so I bring snacks, which I'm happy to share with you."

"Lunch with Theodore?" The two men were not prone to hanging out together, so I wondered what they were meeting about.

Brian laughed. "You're an open book, Em. The curiosity is killing you, wondering why brother dear would want to have lunch with his surfer-bum sibling."

"No, not at all." I lied. "It seems odd, since Theodore is rather vocal about his dislike for most people in your family."

"I doubt our dear Teddy has use for anyone who doesn't advance his career or kiss up to him," Brian practically snarled. "But to answer the question you won't ask, he wants to 'strategize' about what to do with our new mommy. It doesn't take a rocket scientist to figure out she married our father for his money."

I gulped. There was no love lost between these people. Tillie seemed to be the only sane one of the bunch, and her family was trying to prove she had dementia. To be fair, Brian was a huge supporter of his grandmother, but I worried he might secretly hope to get his hands on her fortune. It would go a long way toward cutting his dependency on his father and rescuing his struggling restaurant.

"What can you do? I doubt your father would listen to either of you."

"My brother already has a private investigator digging into her past. So far he's found nothing."

"So maybe she's squeaky clean."

"No, that's not it at all. He's finding she didn't even exist until ten months ago." Brian ran his fingers through his salty hair, still not meeting my gaze. "You'll be working for her later this week. We want you to go through her things and see if you can find out anything we can use against her."

"No way!" I lowered my voice when I noticed beachgoers turning their attention toward us. "I absolutely cannot afford to lose this job. Mr. Skyler would fire me in a heartbeat if he thought I was spying on Mrs. Skyler."

"I don't think you have to worry about getting fired. You always have your mom and Tillie to beg him to reconsider." Brian glanced at me from the corner of his eye. "What is going on with Dad and Addie?"

"Nothing," I squeaked. "Nothing is going on. They're old friends, and he did a favor for her and hired me."

"Uh-huh." His lips curved into a mischievous grin. "My dad doesn't do favors for anyone. Ever. Something's going on there, even if he has remarried."

"No, I'm sure they're only old friends." I cringed, remembering the reaction my mother had had when I told her about his new marriage. "Besides, it's none of my business."

"All I'm saying is that it would help us out if you could spy on the new Mrs. Skyler when you're working for her." Brian bent down and gave me a peck on my cheek. "Please?"

"No! Just no." I wouldn't allow them to manipulate me. "I'm sure your private investigator can find something for you to use more than I can. Besides, she won't trust me, since it's obvious I'm friends with Tillie... and you."

Brian threw his hands up in the air, palms facing me. "Don't get so upset. I thought I'd ask, since we're all in this together. Mark my words, she'll fire you sooner than later, and then my grandmother's going to be left defenseless."

He had a good point, and I thought Tillie might be worried about the same thing. I sighed. "Okay, let me see what I can do. Have you heard when they're returning?"

"Yeah, I got an email summoning my brother and me to meet him Thursday afternoon." He groaned. "Why can't they stay away for a year or two?"

"I haven't heard from Mr. Skyler yet, so I guess I'd better catch up on his mail tomorrow." I crossed my fingers. "Hopefully, Mrs. Skyler will want to settle in and won't ask me to work anytime soon."

"Good luck with that," he answered. "I don't think she can wait to get her claws into anything and everything that's part of my father's life."

Chapter 12

I rushed home to get ready for our meeting with Vivienne Gainer. Because I had tossed my hot dog into the trash to avoid another coughing episode while talking with Brian, I downed some yogurt while slapping on fresh mascara, even though my raccoon eyes weren't nearly as terrible as I had worried they were. Despite having turned down his invitation to dinner and not being interested in dating him, I still didn't want to look ridiculous.

Tillie had her driver, Andrew, take us so we would "make an impression." "Vivienne is all about image," she had said. "And if we don't live up to her standards, she won't give us the time of day."

I decided on wearing the Lilly Pulitzer dress my mother had given to me for my birthday last year. The distinctively colorful wrap dress was not only comfortable, but it also complemented my plump figure. I paired the look with imitation pearl earrings and a matching necklace, along with summery wedge sandals, and I was ready to present myself to one of the "ladies who lunch."

Tillie, dressed impeccably as always, leaned close to me in the back seat of the town car and whispered in my ear, "Let me take the lead on this. I don't think we can bombard her, or she'll clam up and we'll never get another chance to talk to her or her friends."

Since I felt overwhelmed and out of my element, I was only too happy to comply. As the car climbed up into the hills south of Newport Beach, the houses got larger, and it didn't take long for Andrew to come to a stop in front of an Italian villa–inspired McMansion. I gulped. Even though I had kind of gotten used to Tillie's wealth, her taste wasn't ostentatious like this home. A large bubbling fountain sat in the front courtyard while an expertly trimmed lawn and hedges bordered the ornate brick walkway. Wide steps led up to the largest glass-and-wrought-iron arched door I'd ever seen.

I dropped back and stayed a step or two behind Tillie. She marched up to the door, her Burberry handbag clutched beneath her elbow, and rang the doorbell. After waiting a few moments, the door swung open, and an older stocky woman wearing a black dress with a white half apron greeted us. I almost giggled but then stifled it by pretending to cough. I had thought uniformed maids only existed in movies. Tillie was right—these people were pretentious.

"Yes? How can I help you?" The woman spoke slowly, with a thick Eastern European accent.

Tillie handed the maid an embossed card with her name on it. "We're here to call on Mrs. Gainer. Is she available?"

"Please come in, and I will check with her." The maid opened the door wide enough for us to follow her in.

I shook my head. It was as if I'd stepped onto a movie set. If I had thought the maid act was over the top, the entryway just about made my jaw drop. The polished cream-colored marble floor held elaborate inlaid scroll patterns, which had to have been painstakingly installed. Eight enormous marble columns rose up to create a rotunda effect, while a huge ornate crystal chandelier hung from the domed ceiling.

"Wait here, please. I'll see if Mrs. Gainer will see you."

The maid trundled off to find Mrs. Gainer, though I thought it would have been easier for her to text the woman, since the house was so enormous. I almost giggled again but settled down when Tillie shot me one of her "you'd better behave" looks. I'd seen her give that look to Brian often enough, even though he'd never paid attention to it.

Wrought-iron stairways led up on both sides of the entry hall. One set of stairs led to a small landing area that held a glossy black grand piano, while the other set led to the second floor. Everywhere I looked, fresh floral arrangements were situated on small tables scattered around the rooms and along the area leading to the main room. The flowers alone looked like they had cost a small fortune. I tried to keep my mouth from dropping open at the sheer opulence of the home.

"Mrs. Gainer will see you now." The maid's voice was brusque. "Please come."

We followed her down the towering, wide hallway toward the back of the house, where bright sunlight flooded a great room and a restaurant-sized kitchen. She led us through French doors that opened onto a sunroom. Mrs. Gainer sat on an overstuffed sofa covered with a bright yellow French provincial print. She rose when we entered the room, gesturing for us to sit in the overstuffed armchairs on either side of the sofa that faced the center of the room, her long bloodred nails glinting in the sunlight.

"Please have a seat, and Aurora will bring us some tea." She sat back down as soon as we had made ourselves comfortable and gave me the briefest of looks before she focused her icy-blue eyes on my friend. "To what do I owe this pleasure, Matilda?"

Tillie's tone was conciliatory. "We're sorry to drop in on you without calling first, but I thought it was important to talk about Mandy. The police questioning has been dreadful, and I wanted to see how my party guests are doing. I hope they haven't been causing you too much trouble, Vivienne."

"Police? Why in the world would they want to talk to me?" The socialite's voice pitched on the word "police." She brushed her platinum-blonde bangs from her eyes.

"Oh, dear me." Tillie tsked. "I was under the impression they were talking to everyone at my party. Such a tragedy. A young life cut short by violence."

"I don't know anything about what happened, so there's no need for me to talk to the police. In fact, I left before they even arrived since I don't need my name associated with something like that." Vivienne's voice sounded pinched, as if maybe her skinny jeans were too tight on her skinny body.

"Perhaps you saw something or someone that can help them solve the case," Tillie persisted. "Don't you think it's your civic duty to give them any information you might have?"

"I don't know anything."

"What about the fight Mandy had with 'Madonna'?" I asked, my voice dripping with sarcasm. Tillie scowled at me, and I instantly regretted it. But I was tired of skirting around the real reason we needed to talk to this woman. Plus, I didn't much like her. She reminded me of those mean-girl school bullies who made fun of you because they had the latest designer attire, while you wore bargain-rack or thrift-shop clothes. I was probably more sensitive to the haves and have-nots, since my family had gone through a rough patch before my mother married Lars.

Vivienne shot me a look of pure disdain. "I know who you are. You're that woman who killed her husband's lover. You have no right to come snooping around my home. Aurora will see you out."

Just then, Aurora came in, carrying a tray with three glasses of iced tea and a plate of shortbread cookies that looked like they had come from a package.

I inclined my head toward the tray. "I'll see myself out,

but Tillie will stay and enjoy your hospitality. And for the record, I didn't kill anyone."

I let myself out of the house and sat in the car, fuming. I shouldn't have let Vivienne get under my skin like that, but I was fed up with people like her who thought they were so much better than everyone else just because they had money. Hopefully, Vivienne would commiserate with Tillie over my rudeness and open up about her argument with Mandy.

I chatted with Andrew for a bit then turned my attention to my phone after he glanced down at the popular thriller lying open on his front seat. I googled Vivienne but didn't get any hits other than pages of her attending this or that event. *Blah, blah, blah.* Next, I researched Senator Zach Dexter. I scrolled through the usual **PR** fluff and campaign minutiae, but buried three pages deep on the search engine was a small segment in an op-ed piece published in a small regional newspaper. The bottom line was that he was a womanizer, but he only got involved with wealthy women who contributed heavily to his campaigns. Although there was nothing illegal about it, I felt there was something morally sketchy about the man.

After we'd been sitting for almost thirty minutes, Andrew jumped out of the car and opened the door for Tillie.

"Thank you, Andrew." She handed him a slip of heavily embossed paper with an address written on it. "I think we'll drop by and chat with Mrs. Dexter."

She slid into the back seat next to me and grinned like the Cheshire cat.

"What did you find out?" I demanded, yet I couldn't help but grin back at her.

She drew her eyebrows together and wrinkled her nose. "You need to control your temper, Emory," she said. "However, she opened up after you left when we commiserated on the bad manners of youth these days."

I must have had a horrified look on my face because

Tillie patted my cheek. "Don't worry about it. She deserves your scorn. I'd prefer to steer clear of these self-centered, manipulative women, but being on several philanthropy committees with them, I have to act like I enjoy their company."

"Well, are you going to tell me what she talked about aside from my bad manners?"

"Basically, she thinks Senator Dexter had several reasons to kill Mandy, and she's certain Shannon Dexter will give us the scoop."

My mouth dropped open. *Another suspect? And one who is so famous?*

Tillie tapped my chin. "Sensational, isn't it?"

I snapped my mouth closed, still stunned. "Did Vivienne say why she thought that?"

"Oh yes, in great detail." Tillie's eyes sparkled, knowing she was dragging this on. My curiosity was whetted.

"You're killing me, Tillie." I whined just as the car slid up to the curb in front of another impressive mansion. Senator and Mrs. Dexter lived large. "Should I wait here or try to contain myself this time?"

"You can come. Shannon is expecting us both."

I followed Tillie up the flagstone walkway to the massive front door. Instead of a maid, Shannon Dexter herself opened the door. It was obvious she had tried to use makeup to conceal her red-rimmed eyes and blotchy face, but she couldn't hide the fact she had been crying. I almost felt pity for her.

"I have coffee brewing in the kitchen. We can chat there." She turned around and gestured for us to follow her toward the back of the house. The layout of her home was a close replica of Vivienne's, but Shannon's color scheme was whites, grays, and black tones. It felt cold and uninviting. Shannon was also dressed in the same color palette as her home: white skinny jeans and a black silk tunic that clung to her model-slender body. Her white-blonde hair was cut in a stylish short bob that followed the curve of her chin.

The cabinets in the kitchen were black, and the counters and floor were white marble. A breakfast nook held a white marble table and black wrought-iron chairs without chair pads. I guessed they didn't linger over coffee or tea in this house.

Shannon motioned for us to sit, and she brought us white china cups filled with black coffee. She settled herself at the table, and I looked to see if she had milk or a sugar set out on the counter, but it was bare. Tillie must have noticed my inspection, because she shook her head imperceptibly before sipping her own coffee.

"Thank you for coming to talk with me, Matilda." Shannon ran a well-manicured finger around the rim of her coffee cup. "I've been so upset and don't have the slightest idea what to do."

"Now, now, dear, things can't be all that bad."

And then the formidable Mrs. Dexter burst into tears. Tillie rummaged in her handbag, pulled out a pack of tissues, and placed them on the table. I squirmed in my seat, the taste of bitter coffee lingering in my mouth. The raw emotions of the woman made me uncomfortable, and I was sorry we had intruded on her. I wondered if I should leave and let Tillie have a private talk with her, but I didn't want to draw attention to myself. I tried to stay as still as I possibly could.

"My husband had an affair with that awful woman. She was blackmailing him." Shannon dabbed at her cheeks with Tillie's tissues. "You probably think I killed her. I swear I didn't, but I'm terrified Zach did and now he wants me to lie about his alibi."

Chapter 13

I forgot I was trying to be invisible. "What makes you think he's guilty?"

Shannon turned her aquamarine eyes toward me. Her brows furrowed, and she stiffened her back. Her tears disappeared. With a sigh, she fluttered her hand in the air. "It's only a figure of speech. He would never harm anyone, but it looks bad when he won't tell me where he was that evening. I'm afraid it's only a matter of time before the police ask questions, so I'm begging you to help us out."

Tillie crossed her arms. "I can see where it's a huge concern with elections coming up."

"It's all about reputation. Even a whiff of scandal could affect his career for years to come." Shannon sniffed. "I don't understand why he had to jeopardize everything for that tramp."

"Do you have any idea where he was that evening?" I asked.

"We planned to meet up with friends for dinner, but Zach told me to cancel on them earlier in the day. He mentioned something about needing to meet with someone who would help him secure a big campaign contribution."

"But you don't know who he met with?" I probed.

"We've barely been on speaking terms ever since I found out about this affair, even though we have to pretend in public that nothing is amiss between us." Shannon dabbed at her eyes again. "You probably think I should leave Zach, but I love him, despite his issues with other women."

I remembered Tillie saying the senator had been cozy with Vivienne, so apparently Shannon forgave everyone who took advantage of her. I wondered how someone in her position could lack self-appreciation or self-confidence. I didn't get it. "How do you expect us to help?"

"Everyone knows you're both nosy busybodies. You can steer clear of my husband and point the police in the direction of other suspects." Shannon leaned in and lowered her voice. "I'll make it well worth your effort."

Tillie snorted. "Are you trying to bribe us, Mrs. Dexter? My family's fortune is on par with yours, so I don't see what you could possibly offer to compensate for my 'effort' of obstructing a police investigation."

My mouth fell wide open. No one had ever tried to bribe me before, and I didn't know what a socially appropriate response should be. Tillie nudged my leg beneath the table. I snapped my mouth shut and decided to let her answer for us both.

"That's where you're wrong, Matilda." Shannon lifted her chin and crossed her arms. "I do have something priceless that you'd sacrifice your principles for."

"I can't even imagine that being true." Tillie pressed her lips together and tilted her head.

Shannon turned her scorn toward me. "And you, Miss Charity Case. Your ex left you beneath a mountain of debt. I'll pay it off and bequeath you a house of your own so you're not forced to live in a pool house."

My breath caught in my throat. What she said was true. I was deeply in debt thanks to my no-good ex, but I loved living with Tillie, and the pool house was perfect for me. It was a charming refuge, and I couldn't imagine living anywhere else in the foreseeable future. I couldn't be bought, but I held my tongue to see what the arrogant woman would say next.

Tillie wrinkled her nose and shook her head. "Frankly, I don't have the patience to listen to your pathetic attempts to protect your philandering husband."

I wondered if Shannon was using her husband as a scapegoat when, in reality, she was the one without an alibi and needed to make sure the police didn't suspect her.

"Matilda…" Shannon's voice oozed seduction. "What would you say if I had information that would put your new daughter-in-law away for a very long time and would keep your greedy son and grandsons from trying to take away your freedom? Isn't that priceless? And all you have to do is steer the police away from us. It's more of a sin of omission than lying. Simple, isn't it?"

It was Tillie's turn to drop her mouth open. All color drained from her cheeks. I had no idea "society" had even heard about the marriage. How did Shannon already have something on the new Mrs. Skyler? Was she making it up?

Much to my relief, Tillie straightened her back, took a sip of coffee, and then leaned toward Shannon. "My dear, let me make something clear. I cannot be bought nor, in good conscience, alter the truth. If you know something about the murder of Mandy, or if your husband knows anything about it, then I suggest you go directly to the police. It will look more suspicious if you try to cover it up."

"You're going to ruin everything!" Shannon stood up so fast she almost knocked over the heavy chair. "Get out of my house and stop prying into our personal lives."

I jumped up and bumped the table. Coffee sloshed over the sides of the china cup. I wanted to apologize for the mess, but more than anything, I wanted to get out of there. Tillie rose slowly, with much more grace than I had.

My friend stood erect, her chin held high. "We'll see ourselves out. But don't forget, things will go easier for you if you voluntarily talk to the police."

I walked as fast as I could toward the front door, turning every so often to make sure Tillie was right behind me. I worried that Mrs. Dexter would try to attack us. I yanked open the door and stepped out into the fresh air, relieved to see that Andrew was waiting beside the car. It was now three against one should Mrs. Dexter try anything violent.

As soon as the house was out of sight, my hands started to shake. I turned to Tillie. "That was intense. What does she have on Mrs. Skyler? Do you think she killed Mandy?"

Tillie rested her palm on my leg. Her warm hand settled my nerves. "It is all very interesting, isn't it?"

"How can you be calm? How can she even know about Mr. Skyler's new wife?"

"This is a small community. Gossip spreads like wildfire. Most likely one of my grandsons complained to a friend or asked for a recommendation for a private investigator, and it went from there."

"Brian told me Theodore already hired an investigator to find out about Mrs. Skyler." The speediness of his response in finding an investigator had surprised me. Neither of them had given their father's new wife even one day to prove herself.

"Perhaps you should tell them to look at when Barbara's life and Shannon's life could have intersected."

"I doubt that will be easy, since Mrs. Skyler doesn't seem to have existed until a few months ago."

"Shannon's life is splashed all over the internet. A good investigator will find the link, and I'm sure my grandson is paying for the best." Tillie grimaced. "Probably with the money he thinks he'll inherit from me."

My heart broke for the woman sitting next to me. She had everything but the confidence that her son and grandsons weren't after her fortune, and she deserved better than that.

I sent Brian a quick text about Shannon Dexter's alleged connection to Barbara Skyler. He didn't respond, so I sent a text to Brad letting him know Tillie and I were safely on our way home. I reminded him I had honored our pinkie promise. He didn't respond, either, so I tucked my phone back into my purse.

"We'd better head home so you can get to your cookie-decorating party with your nieces."

"I forgot about that." I glanced at my watch and sighed with relief when I saw I wouldn't be late. I hated to disappoint them when they had been so excited about our project. "You're more than welcome to join us."

"Thanks, but I'll pass." The elderly woman looked tired and weighed down with stress. "I've scheduled a hair appointment, and I might nap before I go."

I often forgot Tillie was in her eighties. She exuded more energy than I did and had a zest for life that kept her going. But today, she seemed like she felt her age. "I'll have the girls each decorate a cookie for your dessert tonight."

"I'd like that. Be sure to post some pictures of them decorating to Instagram. I'll be looking for them."

WHEN I PULLED UP, the girls rushed to the curb with Piper close on their heels. All three were excited to see me, and Piper's barks and wagging tail convinced me she had missed me as much as I missed her. The girls helped carry in the cookies and all the decorating paraphernalia while my dog pranced beside them. I had learned early on to divide the cookies equally into two containers, along with two containers of frosting, two sets of sprinkles, and two sets of candies. Carrie always rolled her eyes and told me the girls could share, but my nieces enjoyed having something to call their own. As a twin myself, I could relate.

We carried in the cookies and decorating boxes and spread

them out over the butcher paper—covered table. It amused me to find that my sister still spread plastic dry cleaning bags, reused from her husband's shirts, beneath the table and chairs to capture the wayward sprinkles and frosting that inevitably went flying. Still, I had to admit it was a speedy way to clean up after these sessions without having to scrub the floor.

Sophie and Kaylee had decorated with me often enough that they had a routine and didn't need a lot of input, although that didn't stop them from hamming it up and demanding I take pictures with my phone or asking me to pull up Pinterest and show them other cat decorating ideas besides the sample I had provided. They arranged candies and sprinkles on top of the frosted cookies, experimenting with positions and colors. Piper sat beneath the kitchen table, waiting for one of the girls to drop something so she could snatch it up. In a quiet voice, so my nieces couldn't overhear, I filled Carrie in on what I had found out so far about the murder investigation.

She kept her voice to a whisper. "This may sound awful, but I'm relieved so many people wanted to kill Mandy," she said. "Not that she deserved to die, but at least this takes the pressure from Thomas looking like the only suspect."

I agreed. "Every time I turn around, it seems like Mandy crossed someone else. The hardest part is narrowing down the suspects."

"What did Shannon Dexter mean by being able to put Barbara away for a long time? Do you think she has a criminal past?"

"I'm not sure." I bit my lower lip. "Maybe she's grasping at straws and thought making something up was the best means for getting Tillie to comply."

Carrie snorted. "The nerve of that woman, trying to bribe you. She has to be aware that your own brother-in-law is a suspect and you'd never do anything to keep the attention of the police on him."

While I agreed with my sister, I didn't add that if I believed Thomas was guilty of the murder, I wouldn't shield him from justice. Fortunately, I was one hundred percent certain he was innocent. I changed the subject. "Has Mother mentioned anything about Mr. Skyler's new marriage?"

"No. Why do you ask?" Carrie turned her attention away from me. "Kaylee, don't feed Piper frosting. You'll make her sick."

I called Piper away from the table and absentmindedly rubbed her head and back. "She just had a very un-Addie-like reaction when I mentioned Mr. Skyler remarried. She actually dropped her teacup. It shattered everywhere."

"It could have just slipped from her hand."

"It wasn't just the teacup. You should have seen the look on her face, like she'd just heard some devastating news." I paused and let Carrie soak in my words. "Could something have gone on between Mother and Mr. Skyler? Tillie has hinted, but then she tells me it's not her story to share."

Carrie shook her head. "No, there's absolutely nothing going on. Mother and Lars are devoted to each other."

"I agree that they love each other, but things happen—"

"Stop it, Em," my sister snapped, scowling at me. "Don't look for intrigue where there isn't any."

She clearly didn't want to even hint about any improprieties between our mother and my boss, but I couldn't ignore my curiosity. "Maybe they were involved a long time ago?"

"No. Just… no." Carrie's voice came out louder than she must have intended. She dropped it back to a whisper when she noticed her daughters had stopped decorating. "You need to focus on clearing Thomas's name and stop creating conspiracies about inconsequential things."

I studied my sister's face. Her lips were turned down into a frown, and her green eyes wouldn't meet mine. What did she know that I didn't? Why wouldn't she talk to me? I knew she was closer to our mother. Had she confided in Carrie? I dropped it… for now.

Carrie steered the conversation to other topics, like upcoming catering events, and we brainstormed new cocktail-cupcake flavors she thought I should create. Once my nieces had finished decorating and were properly wired from too much sugar, I asked them each to choose a cookie for me to take home to Tillie. I placed the cookies in individual containers and had them decorate their package with ribbons and stickers. While they were busy, I cleaned up the spilled sprinkles, smeared frosting, and cookie crumbs.

"Would you like to stay for dinner? It's nothing fancy, just leftover mac and cheese." Carrie leaned in toward me and lowered her voice to a whisper once again. "The sauce has a lot of puréed cauliflower, butternut squash, and carrots. Just don't tell the girls."

I whispered back, "Your secret is safe with me, but I'd better get home and start Tillie's dinner. Mr. Skyler's remarriage and this investigation is taking a toll on her, and I want to make sure she's okay."

"Poor lady," my sister murmured. She loved Tillie almost as much as I did. "Let me send some mac and cheese home with you. I made tons of it, and it reheats well."

I thanked her and loaded my car up with all the cookie-decorating supplies. My nieces placed their elaborately decorated boxes into a bag with the mac and cheese and walked Piper to my car with me.

Sophie had tears running down her cheeks as she gave Piper hugs and kisses. "I'll miss you so much, Pipuh," she cried while her small arms encircled my dog's neck.

Her tears kick-started Kaylee's own waterworks. I was at a loss about what to do with the two sobbing girls. Piper sat, wagged her tail, and occasionally licked salty tears that ran down their faces. I stood, frozen in place, and looked helplessly at the house, wanting to cry too. When Carrie stepped out onto the porch, I felt nothing but pure relief. She took in the scene with one quick glance and made her way over to us.

"Too much sugar," Carrie mouthed to me. "Girls, we'll visit Piper and Auntie in a couple of days. If you stop crying, I'm sure she'll even let you go swimming."

It was as if their mother had flipped a switch. No more tears, no crying hiccups… nothing but bright, smiling faces with a trace or two of sticky frosting smearing their cheeks.

Sophie tugged at my shirt. "Can Pipuh go swimming with us too?"

I adored her pronunciation of "Piper." "We'll need to wait and see if Piper wants to go swimming. Sometimes she doesn't like the water. But even if she doesn't, you can still have fun. Right?"

"Yay!" Both girls jumped up and down then raced back to the house.

Piper looked at me, so I opened the car door. She hopped into the front seat, turned around in two circles, then plopped down. I reached in and attached her harness to the seat belt clip.

"Whew, I'm glad you came out when you did."

Carrie laughed. "You looked like a deer caught in the headlights."

"No kidding. I didn't have a clue what to say or do. I envisioned losing Piper forever to your girls."

"Not a chance." Carrie stroked her rounded belly. "Especially with this little one on the way. The last thing I need is another dependent."

After we hugged and said our goodbyes, I headed home, hoping the police had removed the crime scene tape from my cozy pool house.

Chapter 14

I let Piper into the pool house yard and dashed across the alleyway to Tillie's house to chill the mac and cheese. Dusk had fallen, and the inside was dark, so I assumed Tillie was out for the evening. I hoped she was staying out of trouble. I entered the kitchen and froze. A large man was rummaging through the refrigerator, faintly illuminated by the light spilling out from the open door. My heart started pounding. A whimper escaped my lips as I turned to run back the way I had entered.

"It's me. Brian."

My hand flew up to my heart. "Why aren't the lights on? You scared me to death."

He turned and gazed around the dark kitchen as if seeing it for the first time. "I guess I didn't notice how dark it was getting."

"Is everything all right?" I walked over to the bank of electrical switches and pushed a few buttons, and gentle light bathed the room.

Brian closed the door of the refrigerator with a firm push. "Sure, everything's fine."

Only he didn't sound fine. He sounded angry.

"Are you hungry? Can I make something for you?"

"That would be great." He opened the refrigerator again and peered inside. "I was hoping you had some leftovers I could heat up, but you don't have much in here."

"My sister donated most of the leftovers from the party. I didn't want to keep anything to remind us of the... you know..." My voice quivered. "The police confiscated the cake pops for their investigation."

"That makes sense, although it wasn't poison that killed her."

"How did you find that out?"

He gave me a crooked smile. "I have my sources."

His smile didn't reach his eyes, and that had me worried. I pushed my concerns aside. Instead, I focused on the question I didn't want to ask yet needed to. "So, what did your sources tell you?"

"Mandy was first strangled, then the killer shoved your cake pops into her mouth."

I was relieved she hadn't choked to death on my cake pops, but I couldn't get the disturbing image of the dead woman out of my head. I shivered. "Makes you wonder if the cake pops were a message or just a humiliating afterthought inspired by my Poison Apple theme."

"It was definitely a message. Think about it. Mandy was a blackmailer who threatened to expose people's secrets." He scowled. "She had a poisoned mouth."

"I guess that makes sense. It certainly ramped up the drama."

"Yeah, she was known for that too." Brian's voice was bitter, and I saw that his fists were clenched, his knuckles white.

Something was going on with Brian, and I wondered if Mandy had blackmailed him too. I couldn't remember if he had said anything. I needed to distract him and take his mind off her, so I pulled a package of pork chops from the freezer and popped them into the microwave to defrost. I'd serve the mac and cheese as a side dish.

"Are you starving, or can you wait for me to cook the chops?" I pulled a grill pan out from a deep drawer and placed it on the cooktop. Then it hit me. Brian should have been at his restaurant, Oceana, cooking. "Why aren't you working? Or are they finally giving you time off for good behavior?"

He paced around the kitchen, opened a few cabinets to look inside, then banged them shut. "Do you know where my grandmother is?"

"No, I just got home." I watched him out of the corner of my eye. He was acting like a caged animal. "What's wrong, Brian?"

"Some drunk hit a transformer. We lost power at Oceana, and Edison says it'll be hours before they can restore it." His scowl darkened his face. "We had to comp meals for all our customers then throw away most of the leftover seafood. Do you know how much money we lost tonight?"

I gathered it was more than what the restaurant could afford to lose. "I'm sorry. Can you sue the drunk driver and recoup some of your losses? Maybe your insurance will cover some of it."

"I need to talk to Tillie," he said, ignoring my question.

"Did you try her cell phone?"

He slammed another cabinet door shut. "Of course I did. I've been waiting here an hour, but she hasn't called back."

I grabbed my phone from my pocket and opened my calendar app. I didn't see any appointments for Tillie, but then again, she didn't always tell me. I sent Andrew a text asking if he was driving her tonight.

"She'll be fine." I opened the refrigerator and pulled out produce for a salad.

"Except there's a killer on the loose, and you have both been asking questions."

"How did you… does Theodore know?" That worried me more than anything. Well, except their father. He scared me more than Theodore.

"Not yet." Brian glared at me. "I'm warning you. You'd better watch it and keep my grandmother contained."

"As if." I laughed, even though I was certain he didn't think it was funny. It wasn't possible to keep Tillie contained. Her determination kept her young at heart.

"I mean it, Em. Just because you 'solved' a murder doesn't make you an investigator," he said, making air quotes with his fingers. "And you shouldn't be dragging an old woman into danger either."

I sighed. Brian was generally a lot more easygoing than this, and I had never heard him say anything derogatory about his grandmother's age before. I hoped his restaurant survived this latest setback. Just then, my phone chimed with a text from Andrew, who always spelled everything out and included punctuation in his messages.

Mrs. Skyler is dining with Mr. Perkins this evening at his home. She said to inform you to not wait up.

Oh boy. She was with the current beau she kept secret from her family. I quickly deleted the text. I wasn't about to be the one to spill the beans about her love life, which was far more active than my own.

"Tillie is having dinner with a friend, and they might go to the movies." I kept my back to Brian while I checked on the defrosted pork chops.

"What friend?"

"I have no idea, nor is it any of my or your business." My voice was sharper than I had intended it to be, so I turned to give him a smile. "Andrew is driving her, so she's safe. Seriously, you need to let her have a life without always breathing down her neck."

"I guess you're right." Brian looked sheepish. "I'd hate for her to always be asking where I was or who I was with."

I started to give him a smart-alecky remark, but I stopped when I heard a commotion outside. "Is that Piper barking?"

He paused for a moment, listening. "I don't know, but some dog is sure going crazy."

I ran to the front door and yanked it open. Piper sounded like she was in full attack mode, barking her head off for all it was worth. I ran down the steps and across the courtyard. Once I threw open the security gate, I dashed into the alley. Red paint ghoulishly dripped down the front of the garage. Someone had spray-painted in huge letters:

STOP BEING NOSY
OR ELSE

I looked up and down the alleyway, trying to see if the culprit was still there. It was empty. I ran toward the side gate to get Piper, who was still barking ferociously, then stopped in horror. There, on the ground, was an open package of hot dogs with several missing and a spilled container of rat poison.

"Oh no. Oh no." My hands fumbled with the gate latch. "Please be okay."

I lurched through the gate and scooped my dog up into my arms. She wiggled to get down, her tail wagging at a frantic rate. I tried to sniff her breath to see if she smelled of hot dogs, but she wouldn't hold still. I put her back on the ground, and she pranced around my feet.

"Good puppy." I praised her for sounding the alarm and scaring off the intruder then searched the ground, using the flashlight app on my phone, for any hot dogs. My heart fell when I saw a half-eaten one.

The vet was on speed dial, and I connected with the on-call doctor. I had a difficult time explaining the situation. It felt like the wind had been knocked out of my lungs and I couldn't catch a breath.

"Is Piper showing any adverse symptoms?"

"No, she seems fine."

"Do you know the exact poison she's been exposed to?"

I asked the veterinarian to wait a minute, and I ran back to the alleyway. I made sure I closed the gate so Piper couldn't eat any more of the hot dogs still lying on the ground. Brian was on his cell phone, gesturing at my garage door with his free hand. I bent over and looked at the brand name on the box of rat poison and told the doctor.

"That's good news. That kind is easy to treat," Piper's veterinarian said, trying to reassure me. "Symptoms don't show up for two to three days, if any was ingested. We can start her on vitamin K right away to combat the effects, and she'll need to take the pills for thirty days. Don't worry. Piper will be fine."

I gave a huge sigh of relief, tears pricking the corners of my eyes. "Thank you."

"I'll call it in to your pharmacy on record, and you should be able to pick it up within the hour." The veterinarian cleared her throat. "You'd better call the police and report the incident."

"That's the very next thing I'm going to do." I took in a deep breath. "But Piper's safety came first."

I disconnected and gave Piper a hug before putting her inside my house and blocking the doggie door. She didn't need to be exposed to any more danger until we figured out what had happened. When I returned to the alleyway, Brian was still pacing in front of the garage.

"I called the police. Someone should be here soon." He glared at the startling message. "Now do you see why you shouldn't be poking your nose where it doesn't belong? You've put yourself and my grandmother in danger. We should fire you."

The tears that had been prickling my eyes finally trickled over and spilled down my cheeks.

"Who were you on the phone with?" he demanded.

"Piper's vet. Someone threw hot dogs over the gate and left a box of rat poison in the alley." I shuddered. I would never forgive myself if something happened to Tillie or to Piper. This was all my fault.

Brian's face reflected my anguish. "Is Piper all right?"

"The vet seems to think she'll be fine, although she has to take some pills for thirty days just to be on the safe side." I began to think the poison left on this side of the gate had only been a warning, but I wasn't going to take the chance.

Lights from a car suddenly blinded us, and we both stepped out of the alleyway's street. A black sedan came to a stop in front of us. Detective O'Neill sat behind the steering wheel. He didn't look happy.

He stepped out of his car. "Ms. Martinez, just what have you been up to?"

"N-Nothing," I stammered. "Except, I suppose, Mrs. Skyler and I may have chatted to a few people. But that's all."

He scratched at the light stubble on his cheeks. "Chatted as in 'how's the weather today?' or asking people if they were murderers?"

I squirmed. We hadn't exactly come out and accused anyone, but we most likely insinuated it, or else someone had construed our questioning that way. So I didn't answer.

Detective O'Neill sighed. "Did either of you see anything?"

"No, we were in Mrs. Skyler's kitchen when we heard Piper barking."

"How about security camera footage?"

Brian shook his head. "Unless something has changed, my grandmother doesn't want security cameras. She thought of it as an invasion of her privacy."

Tillie hadn't wanted security cameras installed because she

worried it would give her son and grandsons the means to spy on her comings and goings—and the comings and goings of her gentlemen callers. And from what I had seen of her family's behavior, it wasn't an unwarranted concern.

"A pity." The detective looked up and down the alleyway. "Aside from the vandalism, is anything else amiss?"

"Whoever did this also tossed hot dogs over the gate to my dog and left an open box of rat poison." I pointed at where the box lay. "The vet called in a prescription, and they'll start treatment, even though she's not showing any symptoms."

"I'll get a forensics team to take a look." Detective O'Neill's attitude changed from annoyance to one of great concern. "Is your dog okay? Will she let me examine her?"

I gave my consent, but before I led him to the pool house, I turned toward my companion. "Brian, can you call Andrew and tell him what's happened? He needs to let your grandmother know."

"Where is Mrs. Skyler this evening?" The detective tapped a message on his phone.

I heard Brian muttering, but I jumped in before he could say anything. "Dinner and a movie with a friend."

The detective turned his gaze to Brian. "Perhaps it would be better for her safety to stay overnight with the friend."

If Tillie's grandson found out her "friend" was a gentleman wooer, he would throw a fit. But I wasn't going to be the one to mention it. Somehow it would be my fault and added to the long list of reasons the family would fire me.

Brian agreed and made the call.

"Now, Ms. Martinez, let's check your dog. What's her name?"

"Piper. I locked her inside just in case there were more hot dogs or poison I missed."

The detective glanced around my yard. "I don't remember seeing Piper here on Saturday."

"She stayed with my mother. I didn't want her getting

underfoot or to risk her running away, since the gate was wide open all evening." I opened the door to my home.

Piper dashed over to us as we entered, happily prancing and begging for scratches. Detective O'Neill squatted down and murmured calming words to her while stroking her behind the ears. She soaked up the attention, and I was glad to see she didn't appear to show any symptoms of eating the hot dogs. Still, I planned to get to the pharmacy just as soon as possible.

After a cursory examination of Piper and more scratches behind the ears, the detective moved back to the pool area and shined his bright mag light over the ground. He bagged up two more hot dogs he found lying beneath some plants.

"I'll have the lab check for traces of poison, since there aren't any visible granules on the meat. It looks like the perpetrator only wanted to scare you. I hope you take the warning to heart and stay out of the investigation."

"I appreciate your concern, Detective O'Neill, but haven't we given you information that people won't willingly share with the police?"

"Give us time and we'll eventually find the truth." He rubbed a hand over his stubble. "I know it doesn't seem like we'll solve the murder, but we will."

"The problem is that in the meantime, my innocent brother-in-law is a suspect, and it's adding too much stress to his family's life."

"Please trust me, Ms. Martinez, and stop putting yourself and Mrs. Skyler in harm's way."

I nodded, but I wasn't sure I could stop Tillie once she had set her mind to do something. Nor could I stand by and risk Thomas' freedom. We would just have to be more cautious.

It didn't take long for the forensic team to arrive and dust for fingerprints and bag the remaining hot dogs and poison. Tillie showed up a few minutes later, and I hoped her grandson wouldn't notice how she wobbled as she walked. She must have imbibed a little more than she usually did, so I gave her a hug. If she needed, she could steady herself on my arm as I walked close to her side.

Detective O'Neill came over to us. "You should have stayed over with your friend," he told her. "There's nothing you can do here."

"Nonsense. This is my home, and I want to be in my own bed tonight." Tillie lifted her head high. "Em can stay in the house with me."

"I'll stay over too." Brian looked over at me. "You know, safety in numbers and all that."

Uh-oh. I hoped he wasn't getting any romantic ideas about staying here. I needed to nip them in the bud in case my message earlier today hadn't been loud and clear. "You don't need to do that—"

"That would be lovely, dear. Thank you," Tillie said.

Brian winked at me and took his grandmother's free arm. "Let's go have a nightcap. You can tell me all about your date, and I can tell you how a drunk shut down my restaurant."

I froze. How had he found out?

"Oh, Brian, you say the darndest things. It'll bore you to death listening to me talk about a bunch of old ladies watching *Steel Magnolias* while enjoying a couple of toddies." Tillie giggled. "But I'm dying to hear about the drunk."

I almost snorted, but I had to admit that Tillie was quite an accomplished liar. I guessed she had to be to survive in that family. We said our goodnights to Detective O'Neill, and I fetched Piper and put her into the house with Brian and Tillie. Instead of enjoying a nightcap with my friends, I tossed the ruined pork chops into the trash and drove to the pharmacy to get my dog's medication. I prayed the prescription would work and that Piper would come through this with no dire consequences. It would be all my fault if she didn't, and I wasn't sure I was strong enough to bear it.

Chapter 15

After a fitful night of sleep, during which I had nightmares of rats that turned into hot dogs and then chased me, Piper and I decided it was time for a walk. I was relieved to see that my dog was acting like her normal perky self as she danced around my legs, eager for me to get dressed. The sun peeked over the distant foothills and filled the bedroom with soft golden light, promising to be another warm day.

The entryway of the house was still dim in the early dawn, and a scratchy male voice made me jump as I tiptoed toward the front door.

"Morning, Em." Brian stepped out of the shadows and walked toward me. "Sorry, I didn't mean to scare you —again."

I was surprised Piper hadn't warned me he was there, but then again, she was more focused on the walk I'd promised her. "That's okay. I didn't expect anyone to be up this early."

"There are some big swells this morning, so I thought I'd catch a few waves before going to the restaurant." He reached down and scratched Piper behind her ears. "How's the pooch doing?"

"She seems fine. I haven't noticed any side effects from either the hot dog or the medication. She's definitely ready to go for a W-A-L-K." I always spelled out "walk" because if I didn't, Piper would tug on her leash as soon as she heard the word.

"I'm glad to hear it." Brian turned his attention to scratching Piper's belly, which she had displayed for him by flopping onto her back.

"Have you heard any news about your restaurant? Is the power back on yet?"

"My partner told me our power came on late last night, and we have a full seating tonight. Our insurance should cover some of our losses too."

"That's great news." I was glad Brian seemed to have found a more positive outlook on his restaurant.

"Reviews are coming in and generating word of mouth. Hopefully, business will continue to pick up and we can make up for the disaster last night." Brian stood up and opened the heavy front door then guided me onto the front steps, where Piper started pulling me toward the gate. Brian locked the door. "You should bring my grandmother in and let me treat you both to dinner."

"Thanks, but you don't have to do that. We'd love to try your food as paying customers. Just tell us when you're not too busy, and we'll come down."

"I'm happy to do it, and if it makes you feel any better, you can consider it a free meal in exchange for a good review." Brian smirked. "Just keep it a secret."

"Of course." I felt awkward, wondering what I should do if I *couldn't* leave a good review.

Once Brian had disappeared around the corner toward his car, I pulled out my cell phone and took a photo of the garage door, which was still sporting the red-lettered message. I sent the photo along with a text to Tillie's handyman, Paul, begging him to paint over it as soon as possible. Despite being in his late fifties and having a touch of arthritis, Paul was a hard worker and would do everything he could to help us. The last thing I needed was for Mr. and Mrs. Skyler—or even Theodore—to find out about the incident. I glanced up and down the alleyway, hoping no neighbors were out yet. If even one of them saw the warning, our secret would be out.

After prompting Piper to do her business quicker than most days, I opened the garage door. Tillie's garage was pristine, with built-in cabinets and a shiny race car–style floor that was spotless thanks to the attentions of her housekeeper. It made me feel a little guilty every time I parked my car in there, but Tillie always insisted. I rummaged in the cabinets until I found an extra-large painter's tarp and some blue electrical tape. With the garage door lowered, I taped the tarp over the offending letters. People would know something was there, but they didn't need to know exactly what it was. Worst-case scenario, we could tell Mr. Skyler that some kids had tagged the door with graffiti. It wasn't a complete lie.

Once I returned the tape to its proper drawer, I allowed Piper to pull me along for a walk down the main thoroughfare of the Balboa Peninsula. I usually preferred to keep to the small side streets and back alleyways, but considering what had happened the night before, I thought it best to stay where there was plenty of traffic. Despite the early hour, cars were streaming toward Newport Beach as commuters headed to their jobs. Within a few hours, there would be a steady stream of cars returning, bearing tourists seeking sun and sand on a warm autumn day.

My phone dinged with an incoming text, and I sighed with relief when I saw the handyman was confirming he would come to Tillie's house with primer and paint right away. I urged Piper to walk faster and headed home. I was more than relieved to see my dog was her usual energetic self and that our walk hadn't tired her out—though she still wanted to stop to sniff anything and everything we came across, but that wasn't unusual. The vitamin K didn't seem to have caused any side effects so far. With the promise of breakfast dangling in front of her, Piper trotted home at a brisk pace.

Paul's truck was parked in front of the garage door, and I watched him peel the tarp away from the letters. His bulky frame filled the space and made the garage door look smaller than it actually was.

"Good morning, Paul." I pulled Piper up short so she wouldn't nuzzle him. He had once told me he was allergic to dogs.

"Morning." He turned around, pulled a paint roller from the bed of the truck, and wiped his red, bulbous nose on a hankie. "These Santa Anas are making my allergies unbearable."

"The winds have been brutal this season. I hope they end soon." I gestured at the garage door. "Thanks for coming on such a short notice."

"Looks like someone's not too happy with you. Or I s'pose it could be Tillie's stirring up some trouble these days." He chuckled. "I sure hope I'm that feisty when I get to be her age."

I grunted, not willing to agree or disagree. "I'd rather none of the neighbors see this, and it's best Mr. Skyler doesn't find out."

"No worries. I'll have the primer on in a couple minutes, and no one will be the wiser." He bent over and pried open the can of paint.

"Thank you." I looked up and down the alleyway, happy that none of the neighbors were leaving the security of their gated and locked-tight homes. "How long will it take?"

"I have a fast-drying primer, so I should be out of your hair by noon."

"Perfect. I'm baking some muffins, so I'll bring you a few

when they're ready." I was halfway to Tillie's security gate. "Would you like some coffee or tea?"

"I'd appreciate a cup of coffee. Black is fine." He turned his back to me and started to apply the primer over the letters.

With Piper fed and content to lie in the sun that was trickling through the large kitchen-nook windows, I started the coffee and whisked together a batch of banana muffins. I almost added walnuts to the batter but changed my mind. Paul seemed to have so many allergies, and nuts might be a big trigger. I mixed chocolate chips into the batter instead.

Tillie shuffled into the kitchen, looking a little worse for wear. I handed her a cup of coffee liberally doused with milk. "Rough night?"

"Just a little too much fun." She took a sip. "Is Brian still sleeping?"

"No, he left a while ago to catch some waves." I slid the muffin tin into the preheated oven. "He invited us to have dinner at his restaurant. His treat."

Tillie snorted. "More likely he wants us to eat there so he can hit me up for money later to keep his restaurant afloat."

"From what I gather, they've got every table reserved tonight. It sounds like word is getting out that they serve good food."

"I hope so. If his restaurant fails, Brian's father will make him sorry for the rest of his life."

I didn't think I had a very good relationship with my mother, but from what I had seen, it was downright cozy compared to the Skyler family dynamics. It was too depressing to think about, so I changed the subject to murder while I washed the dishes. "I called Paul. He's already here, painting over the graffiti. I thought it best to make sure none of the neighbors or Mr. Skyler have a chance to see it."

"Good thinking. I wouldn't know how to explain it to David, and I'm sure his new wife would use it to benefit her agenda." Tillie shuddered. "What are we going to do about her?"

"I plan to go to Mr. Skyler's house this afternoon and deal with his mail and bills. I'll do a little snooping before they get home." I refilled both our coffee cups then poured some into a disposable travel cup for Paul. "I hope Brian remembers to tell the private investigator to check if there's a connection between Mrs. Skyler and Shannon Dexter."

Tillie yawned and stretched. "Should I come to David's house with you and do my own snooping while you work?"

"No!" I said, my voice loud and too aggressive. "I mean… no, I don't think there's a need for that. I doubt Mrs. Skyler has had time to move much of her belongings in. Otherwise, I would have known about their relationship already."

Tillie sniffed and rolled her eyes. "You're probably right. But please, do me the courtesy of calling that tramp 'Barbara' or 'David's wife' or even 'Trophy Wife Number Four,' instead of giving her my name."

"I'm sorry. You're right." I dried my hands, hugged the elderly woman, and hoped what I had uttered was the truth. "Don't worry. We'll figure this out, and before long she'll be out of our lives and a distant memory."

The timer dinged, and I pulled the golden muffins out of the oven. I transferred them to a wire cooling rack and plated two, which I placed in front of Tillie. "Eat while I take a few to Paul. When I get back, I want to hear all about your nondate last night."

Tillie chuckled. "Brian may be suspicious, but he's no match for his grandmother."

"I was impressed with how you deflected and then distracted him last night."

My cell phone went off with a text from Paul.

I found something in garage u need to see

I sent a thumbs-up emoji, placed four muffins in a paper

bag, grabbed his to-go coffee, and headed for my garage. "Be back in a jiffy."

Tillie waved, her mouth too full of muffin to say anything.

After transferring the muffins and coffee to Paul, I followed him into the open garage. A ladder was standing against the back cabinets, and a long white silk scarf rested on the countertop. Candy apple–red stains were visible in several places, vivid against the brilliant white fabric.

"I think you'd better call the police." He pointed at the scarf. "I think this might be what strangled the victim."

My head whipped around so fast I saw stars. "How? How do you…? I mean, how do you even know about the murder?"

"My cousin is on the investigation team. We had a few beers last night, and he filled me in on some details." He rubbed his jaw. "Please don't tell Detective O'Neill about that. I'd hate for my cousin to get into trouble on account of my big mouth."

Or his cousin's *big mouth*, I thought. "Sure. I'll just let the detective know you found the scarf and I recognized the, uh, glaze color."

"Thanks. I appreciate it." Paul took a sip of coffee and then a bite of muffin, seemingly undisturbed by his discovery.

"Where did you find it?"

He pointed up at the cupboard where the ladder stood. "Stuffed behind a box on top of that cabinet," he said.

"Why were you even up there?" *Is Paul the killer and he's trying to plant evidence? No… my imagination is running away from me again.*

"The last Mrs. Skyler was, well, what you might call a tiger lady. She harped on any contractor that came around and said that if she was paying us, then we'd better make use of every spare second we were here and do something useful. Even if it was only dusting." He looked a little sheepish. "I have two hours to wait for the primer to dry, so I thought I'd dust the tops of the cupboards, since Dorie can't easily reach them. I don't want her to get in trouble when the new Mrs. Skyler comes back."

"Mr. Skyler's wife shouldn't have any say-so on how contractors are treated here," I said, but I was worried, wondering if the new Mrs. Skyler would demand I work longer hours and take on new responsibilities.

"I wish that were the case, ma'am, but it's how it goes." He gestured back toward the scarf. "I'd feel better if you got the detective over here."

"You're right." I whipped my cell phone out of my pocket and called the number from my contact list. When Detective O'Neill didn't answer, I left a detailed voicemail.

"You should probably put the scarf in here until the detective comes." Paul handed me a thirteen-gallon garbage bag. "Do you think I should call my cousin and tell him I found it?"

I shook my head. "Let's make this simple. You found the scarf in a strange place. I saw it and noticed the red glaze and thought it might be important to their case. We don't need to tell them anything else."

"I appreciate it. My cousin has never been good at keeping secrets."

I wondered if his cousin was in the right line of work. "It'll be fine. You probably shouldn't do any more cleaning until we talk to Detective O'Neill. You're more than welcome to come in and eat your muffins inside with us."

"Thank you, but if it's okay, I'll sit in my truck. I need to return some phone calls and tend to business."

"Sure, no problem." My phone dinged with an incoming text, and I rolled my eyes. "The detective is on his way, and he says not to touch anything else in the garage."

Paul chuckled. "Yeah, as if we couldn't figure that one out on our own."

"Guess they have to cover their you-know-what."

After placing the scarf in the bag—while trying hard not

to touch the fabric—I went inside to update Tillie on what Paul had found.

"Don't you think the police searched the garage the night of the murder?" Tillie stood up, coffee cup in hand. "How did they miss the scarf?"

"Maybe the killer planted it last night before they spray-painted the garage door?" I suggested, though Tillie had voiced a good point. How had the police missed it Saturday night? I hoped it wasn't an indication of Detective O'Neill's competence—or lack of.

Tillie motioned me over with her free hand. "Well, aren't you coming?"

"Where?"

"Across the street to search the garage for more clues."

"No. We're not going to willingly mess up a potential crime scene." I shuddered, thinking about what kind of reaction that would get from the detective. "We'll wait right here until the police arrive."

"But I want to be there when they pull up. I can't wait to see their faces when they look at the evidence."

"It might be nothing." I didn't want her to get her hopes up that the case might be solved soon. My expectations were already high enough for the both of us. "It might just be a scarf that has nothing to do with Saturday night."

"Uh-huh." Tillie moved toward the hallway. "And that scarf with the red glaze just happened to be hiding in my garage for no reason?"

I conceded. She had another good point. "Let me put the muffins in a bag and pour some to-go cups of coffee. We might as well share them with the detective and his team."

"Yeah, sweeten them up. Perhaps they'll share some of their secrets on crime scene investigation." Tillie's eyes sparkled, her morning-after malaise forgotten.

I brewed another pot while Tillie impatiently looked on. After placing the remaining muffins in a pastry box, I poured the coffee into an insulated thermos and grabbed some disposable cups with lids. Tillie was halfway out the front door by the time I caught up with her. An unmarked black sedan was parked behind Paul's work truck, and I could see Detective O'Neill talking to our handyman. Neither man seemed happy.

"Good morning, Detective O'Neill." I handed him the pastry box and pointed at the thermos. "Muffins and coffee for you and whoever wants it. Would you like a refill, Paul?"

"No thank you. I'm good."

I turned toward the detective. "Can I pour you a cup?"

"No thanks. I need to talk to you both while we wait for the crime scene team." He handed the pastry box back to me. "We'll take this to go after we finish here."

I walked toward the garage, intending to put the box on the countertop.

"Ms. Martinez, please do not contaminate the crime scene any more than it already has been."

Chapter 16

Detective O'Neill's sharp voice in the quiet morning air made me jump, and I stumbled. I almost dropped the pastry box, and my face flamed as I retreated from the garage. "Oh, sorry. I didn't think about that. Can I put the muffins in your car?"

"Be my guest." He turned his back on me and spoke to Paul in low tones.

So much for sweetening him up. After placing the pastry box on the front seat of his car, I started back for the house to return the coffee. Out of the corner of my eye, I saw Tillie unobtrusively edge closer to the detective and the handyman. Eavesdropping. I gave her a thumbs-up.

I dawdled in the kitchen for a few minutes to give Tillie some time to tune in to the conversation. When I returned, Paul was back in his truck, and Tillie was regaling the detective with stories of her youth. He seemed to have given her his full attention, but his eyes still darted to the garage and back whenever she turned away from him. I liked him even more for that. He was a busy man, but he could still be courteous to my elderly friend.

"Ah, Ms. Martinez." He beckoned to me with his hand. "Might I have a word with you?"

"Sure, but I don't think I have any new information."

"No worries. I'd just like to chat with you." His gaze fixed on Tillie, but she stood firm, almost attached to my arm. "Mrs. Skyler? May I speak with Ms. Martinez in private?"

She huffed. "If you must, but she'll tell me everything anyway."

"It will only take a minute or two, and I'll send her back in for your *kaffeeklatsch*." Detective O'Neill's eyes twinkled, and I noticed laugh lines around his eyes when he smiled. I was liking this man more and more by the minute.

Once Tillie had returned to her house, the detective retrieved a muffin from the box and took a large bite. I wondered why he was stalling. Maybe he was trying to make certain Tillie hadn't hidden behind the security gate in order to eavesdrop. He swallowed then wiped the back of his hand across his mouth. "Thank you, Ms. Martinez. That hit the spot."

"Please, call me Emory." I pointed at a crumb of muffin on his chin then mimicked wiping off my own to send the message. "There's no need for formality, and I'd rather not be reminded of that last name."

"As you told me in great detail the first time we met."

Why, oh, why did he have to remind me of my embarrassing, incoherent babbling the night of the murder? I wanted to melt into the asphalt beneath my feet.

"I didn't mean to embarrass you." He awkwardly reached out to touch my shoulder, but he dropped his hand before he made contact. "It was meant as a friendly tease. I guess I feel like I know you because Brad is always chattering about your friendship."

"It's okay. I know I have a problem with babbling on and on when I'm nervous."

"But in regard to your name, I'd better wait until this

investigation is over to become casual. I would hate for any of my superiors to think I was being partial to my witness, especially since you were the one to find the body." He grinned, and his laugh lines deepened. "Brad's kept me apprised of what you and Mrs. Skyler have found out. I should be upset about civilians interfering, but you've opened some doors for our investigation that would've taken me much longer."

"I'm glad we could help you." A stray lock of hair blew into my face, and I smoothed it back. "People seem to open up to Tillie, and when the right questions are asked, we find answers. We make a good team."

"Hmm, about that…" He paused when his cell phone chimed and checked the screen. "You need to back down and let me handle it from here. It's not safe, and I can't allow you to put yourself and Mrs. Skyler at risk."

"But we've only been asking a few questions from people Tillie already knows."

"And you've already ticked someone off." Detective O'Neill gestured toward the open garage door then lowered his voice to almost a whisper. "Do you know what would happen to me—to my career—if Mrs. Skyler was injured or worse while investigating one of my cases? David Skyler would have my head on a plate, and I'd never find another job, even if I moved to Timbuktu."

He was right. I was probably in the same position. Still, it would be difficult to rein in my friend. "I'll see what I can do. She's one determined lady."

"I'll do my best to minimize the publicity of this murder and the threats on my end. Consider yourself lucky Mr. Skyler is on his honeymoon and not paying attention."

I bit my lip, worried that my boss was going to find out sooner rather than later. "He may not be paying attention now, but someone's bound to tell him about the murder. Things will be pretty rough around here when he finds out."

"I'll do what I can to help you as long as you promise to stay out of the investigation."

I nodded, since I didn't trust my voice, nor did I think I had the choice to sit and wait for the police to find the killer. I didn't want to out-and-out lie. My brother-in-law's future depended on me clearing his name.

"The team should be here any moment to collect forensics. Once they're done, your guy can finish painting the garage door."

"Thanks. I'll let him know." I stood there, not knowing whether I was being dismissed or if he had anything else to warn me about.

He jerked his thumb toward the large house. "Go on. Get back to Mrs. Skyler. I'm sure she's dying to know what we talked about," he said. "I'll let you know what we find out here, but I'm sure this was the scarf used to kill Ms. Graber."

"How did it get in my garage?" I pulled my eyebrows together, trying to remember the last time I'd been in that space. "Didn't your team search everywhere Saturday night?"

"We did and found nothing of interest. I have to assume the killer put the scarf back here when they spray-painted the garage door." He paused and checked the screen of his phone again then looked up. "The big question is why would they take the risk? Why not destroy the scarf or hide it elsewhere?"

I agreed. Those were big questions that needed to be answered. I worried someone had tried to throw suspicion on me by planting evidence.

I walked over to Paul's truck and knocked on his halfway-open window. Engrossed in paperwork, he startled and spilled some of the coffee he had been about to take a sip of.

"I'm so sorry. I didn't mean to scare you." I opened the truck door, not knowing what else to do. "Would you like me to get some napkins?"

"I'm fine." He shook a few drops off the papers he had

been reading. "Won't be the first spill I've ever had, and I'm sure it's not the last."

"I just wanted to let you know that it'll be a while before you can paint the door. The investigators need to go through the garage, and that might take hours." I stooped down and picked up a paper that had floated from the truck and handed it back to him. It looked like an architectural drawing. "You might as well go work on another job, and I'll call you later when they're done."

"Thanks." He shuffled his papers and stacked them on the empty passenger seat. "I juggled some jobs when I got your call, and my clients are getting antsy. But the Skylers always get priority. You know how it is."

Before I worked for Tillie, I hadn't known how it was. But the more time I spent with the family, the more I saw how influential they were in the community. I wasn't sure that was such a good thing, especially if the new Mrs. Skyler was as malicious as I feared. "I'll let you get to your other clients, and I'll call when we're ready. We're not in such a big hurry now that the primer is covering up the spray paint. That was my biggest concern."

"Thanks for understanding, miss." He rubbed his shiny forehead with the sleeve of his work shirt. "I'll make sure it's done before Mr. Skyler gets into town. There's no need for him to know about this and cause trouble for you."

"I should be the one thanking you. Can I get you a coffee or more muffins to go?"

"I'm good, but thanks for the offer. I already had too much caffeine, which is probably why I jumped like I did."

We said our goodbyes, and I hurried into Tillie's house. The cool interior soothed my nerves. I'd had too much caffeine myself, on top of too much stress.

"What did our cute detective have to say?"

I jumped at the sound of Tillie's voice. *Yep, too much caffeine.*

"He's almost certain it's the scarf that strangled Mandy. He's waiting for the forensic team to go through the garage."

"Ooh, *CSI* right in my yard." Tillie rubbed her hands together, and I thought I heard her cackle. "I'd better call my gal pals and invite them over. We can mix up a pitcher of gimlets and watch. It'll be like live TV."

"I don't think that's a good idea," I said, though I hated to put a damper on her enthusiasm. "We need to keep on the detective's good side, and if this turns into a three-ring circus, he'll blame us. Plus, we need to keep this quiet so it doesn't leak back to Mr. Skyler and Theodore."

Her shoulders dropped, and she rolled her eyes. "Why does my son ruin all my fun? But I suppose you're right. I'd hate to make things uncomfortable for the detective, especially if he's going to be one of our new friends."

I hoped that would be the case. Gabe O'Neill seemed like a nice man, and it was obvious Brad was besotted. "There's another thing Detective O'Neill was adamant about. He wants us to stop getting involved, because he's worried about the danger."

Tillie flung her hand out, waving away my concerns. "Oh, posh. We can take care of ourselves."

"Maybe. But he's worried that if anything happens to you, he'll lose his job."

"He's worrying about nothing."

"Really? He thinks Mr. Skyler can ruin his entire career if something happens to you." I let that sink in for a moment. "Plus, I'll be out of a job and probably prosecuted if you're hurt or worse."

"Where did I go wrong with my son? I didn't raise him to scare the living bejesus out of people." Tillie tapped an index finger to her mouth. "I'm calling my attorney, and he'll figure out how to keep him in line."

"Don't do anything drastic." The last thing I needed was

for Mr. Skyler to think Tillie was acting under duress or exhibiting signs of dementia.

"There's nothing to worry about. My attorney won't do anything unless something happens to me and my son decides to place the blame on other people instead of me."

I tried not to let my exasperation color my voice. "You're missing the point. None of us want anything bad to happen to you. We're only trying to keep you safe."

Her eyes became misty. "And *you're* missing the point. I've lived by the rules all my life and did everything everyone told me to do. I don't have many years ahead of me, and I want to have fun. Let me experience whatever life has to offer."

My own eyes stung, and I blinked hard several times to clear them. I put my arms around her shoulders and gave her a tight hug. "I couldn't bear for anything to happen to you, but I understand."

Tillie went to make her phone call, leaving me to worry about whatever plans she was hatching up with her attorney. I had to trust him to give her sound guidance.

Not being able to postpone my job any longer, I grabbed my purse, snapped a leash onto Piper, and headed to Mr. Skyler's house. He lived about a mile and a half away from Tillie, so I figured I would get in some exercise and fresh air by walking and taking the short ferry ride across the bay. I would also get to procrastinate a little longer than if I were to drive.

I rarely minded doing the accounting. With a key and alarm code to the separate entrance of my office in his home, I could come and go as I pleased. Mr. Skyler had traveled extensively since I began working for him, so I was usually by myself. Once in a while, Marge would poke her head into the office and ask if I wanted something to drink or eat, but other than that, I seldom saw her. She always made a fuss over Piper, however, and she kept a stash of dog treats in the pantry. When Mr. Skyler was in town, he would schedule a short meeting to go over any pressing issues and then leave me to my own devices.

The new Mrs. Skyler, though, made me uneasy about my job despite my not having worked with her yet. Plus, I felt guilty about snooping in their private quarters. I wasn't banned from that area, and in fact, Mr. Skyler had asked me several times to express-ship articles of clothing or books to him. But that was different. This time I would be prying, without an invitation, in his private rooms.

Chapter 17

We made our way onto the ferry, and I found a seat beside a handful of colorfully dressed tourists. A fit older couple, dressed in tight biking shorts, held their bikes steady as they were perched on the long bench. There was only one car on the ferry, so I had a clear view of the water. Piper seemed to enjoy the wind that ruffled her fur, and she sniffed the air that carried the scent of hot dogs, seaweed, and sunscreen. She gave a sharp bark when a seagull dived overhead to snatch a piece of popcorn from the deck, and she strained at her leash to follow the bird. I held on tight and returned the smile that a few passengers gave us. The ride across the bay only took about ten minutes, but the closer we got to the dock, the more reluctant I was about going to work. I was worried I wouldn't find anything about the new Mrs. Skyler—but I was also worried about what I should do if I did find something.

After we disembarked from the ferry, Piper pulled me toward our destination at a faster pace than I wanted to walk. She must have remembered the treats Marge always gave her. "Slow down, Piper. You can't possibly be hungry."

She twisted her head and glanced at me before she turned

134

and pulled the leash even harder. Instead of trying to correct her behavior like I knew I should, I picked up my pace to keep up. Once we arrived at the huge stuccoed house painted a light cinnamon color, I pulled the key from my purse and climbed the spiral wrought-iron staircase to the small second-floor balcony. Piper raced by and knocked me off balance, so I grabbed the railing to keep from falling. She seemed to be in a hurry to get inside. I threw the French doors wide open to let the sea breeze blow through the office, and Piper rushed through the office and into the hallway. After barking a couple of times, she plopped down on the fluffy dog bed beneath my desk.

Thinking that maybe Piper was trying to tell me that someone was in the house, I listened at the top of the stairs for a couple of minutes but didn't hear a sound. *What is up with her?* After filling her water dish in the bathroom next to my office, I checked the pile of mail and looked for any notes or phone messages that needed immediate attention. Everything looked straightforward. Once I made sure Marge wasn't in the house, I threw back my shoulders, took a deep breath, and headed to the Skylers' private quarters, trying to ignore the tingling at the base of my skull.

I hollered hello a few times as I walked into the master suite, not wanting to surprise anyone, but the house remained quiet. Flipping on the crystal chandelier lights that hung in the middle of the master closet, I found Mrs. Skyler had moved in a few of her belongings. Several dresses hung on padded hangers. The labels on the dresses confirmed they were all from top designers. A few high-end purses and evening bags rested on a shelf, while several stiletto-heeled shoes were neatly displayed in cubbies. I didn't need to look at the labels on the shoes. My dead ex-best friend had schooled me on how to identify those kinds of shoes at a single glance, not that I'd ever owned a pair. Mrs. Skyler wore nothing but the best.

Worried about leaving behind fingerprints, I used my shirt

to open the built-in drawers, which were all empty. The vanity drawers held several new tubes of lipstick, still in their boxes, along with eye shadow and powder. After I fumbled several times with an elaborate clasp on a purse, I chided myself for not thinking to bring gloves. My shirt wasn't a good substitute, so I returned the purse to the shelf and went downstairs to the kitchen.

Marge was sure to have cleaning gloves I could borrow. After opening and closing cabinets, I finally found a few unopened pairs stashed in the butler's pantry. I went back to the master closet and donned the gloves. This time, opening the purse was a cinch, and the capacious bag finally gaped open. It was empty except for a small card at the bottom.

It was a business card for an attorney up in Los Angeles. I tried to take a photo with my phone, except the camera app wouldn't work while I had the gloves on. I pulled one off a sweaty hand. Not wanting to touch the business card, I wrestled with my shirt to position the card for better lighting before I took a picture.

I struggled to put the rubber glove back on my sticky hand, and prickles of perspiration broke out along my hairline and down my back. This was taking much too long. How would I explain my presence to Marge if she returned? Especially if she caught me wearing bright yellow rubber gloves in the closet. I wanted to give up. I didn't belong in the spy business.

When I tried to arrange the business card at the bottom of the purse exactly like I had found it, my gloved fingers brushed against something stiff and unyielding beneath the liner of the bag. Using my fingers, I felt around the edges of the item. It was rectangular and hard. Its shape reminded me of a credit card.

I propped the purse wide open and placed it on top of the island dresser so I would have more light to see the seams inside. Ever so gently, I pulled the liner up and slid my gloved fingers down the side to look for a hole, but the seams were completely sealed. Next, I ran my fingers around the bottom seams and, in a corner of the lining, found where a few inches of the seam had been pulled out. The seam had been put back together with thin Velcro to hold it in place. Unless you pulled the lining up like I had, no one would ever notice.

I separated the Velcro and wiggled two fingers into the gap. I grasped the card between my index and middle finger and gently slid it out from beneath the liner. With the rubber gloves encasing my hands, it wasn't an easy maneuver, and my face felt even stickier with the effort. It wasn't a credit card. Instead, it was a New York driver's license with Mrs. Skyler's picture. Only instead of "Barbara," it indicated the woman's name was Benicia Morray.

Chapter 18

I almost dropped the driver's license in my haste to take a picture. The rubber gloves weren't making it any easier, and I had to remove one, again, to get my camera app to work. Sweat trickled down my cheek. I took the photo, struggled to get my hand back into the glove, then carefully wedged the driver's license back into the slit in the fabric and secured the Velcro, all the while fuming at how long it was taking me to snoop. I needed to finish and get back to my office before I was caught.

I had just placed the purse back onto the shelf when I heard the alarm panel chime, alerting me that an external door had opened. Could Marge be coming back? What if Mr. or Mrs. Skyler was home early? Panicked, I froze in place for a moment. I shook my head, glanced around, and then sprang toward the light switch. I needed to get away from this wing of the house.

With the closet in pitch darkness, I stepped out and swung the oversize mahogany door closed. I cringed when the latch caught, the sound booming in my ears. I tiptoed to the master suite door while taking off the rubber gloves. If I met whoever had just entered the house in the hallway, I wouldn't be able to explain the banana-yellow accessories, so I stuffed them beneath my shirt.

I had just made it to the top of the stairs on the side of my wing when Piper barked.

Marge hollered below me on the first floor. "Is that you, Emory?"

I leaned over the wrought-iron railing and saw the house-keeper/cook standing in the gigantic open space below. "I'm here for a while, catching up on the mail before Mr. Skyler returns tomorrow."

"Didn't he tell you? They're coming back this evening." Marge brushed her bangs back from her forehead. Her mouth turned down at the corners. "The new missus called this morning with detailed instructions on what she wants served for dinner. I had to visit three markets to find the ingredients."

I groaned. Why couldn't my boss stay away longer? Why had they cut their honeymoon so short? "I'll let you get to work, then. I heard the chime and thought I'd better see who it was."

Marge didn't leave. Instead, she walked toward the stair-way. "Are you feeling okay? Your face is so red."

"I got a little overheated walking Piper here." I slid my latex-scented hand across my still-damp forehead. "I opened the doors to my office, and it's starting to cool off."

"Let me bring you a glass of iced chai. That always cools me off." Marge turned toward the kitchen on her bulky ortho-pedic shoes.

"You don't need to wait on me. I can come down and get it."

"I should air out the master suite and cool it down before they return. Go on. Get back to your work, and I'll bring you the chai."

I expressed my appreciation and walked toward my office. I looked down at the ultraplush carpet, where I could clearly see my footprints leading to the master suite. It was a dead giveaway I had been where I shouldn't have been. My stomach plummeted, and beads of sweat gathered along my hairline. Marge would notice, but would she tell the Skylers? It was too late to do anything about it, so I went back to my office and buried the rubber gloves in the bottom of my purse.

Ignoring the dread over being caught out, I had sorted all the opened mail into piles by the time Marge walked into my office with the iced chai. Piper sprang to her feet and alternated between barking at the housekeeper and wagging her tail while she nuzzled the woman's free hand.

"Piper, back to your bed." I grabbed her collar and pulled her away from Marge. "Sorry about that. I don't know what's gotten into her."

"I've been to a couple fish markets this morning, so maybe she smells something on me." Marge shrugged her broad shoulders then smiled. "Or it's her way of telling me I neglected to bring her a treat."

Piper let out a low rumble in her throat as if she agreed. I shushed her, and she lay back on her bed and closed her eyes. I turned around and took the drink Marge held out to me. The multifaceted glass contained a reddish-hued liquid with crystal-clear cubes of ice. She had drizzled cream over the top, and tendrils of milky white swirled their way down to mix with the tea.

"You've spoiled both of us too much." I took a sip while Marge looked on. "This is amazing."

"Thanks. I've been experimenting with the spice blend and brewing my own tea." She handed me a napkin. "My chai latte habit was getting too expensive. I was visiting the tea shop every day."

I took another sip. An explosion of sweet spices with a hint of heat filled my mouth. The coolness of the iced drink and the richness of cream lingered on my tongue. My mind whirled with possibilities of duplicating the flavors in a cupcake. "This is, by far, the best chai I've ever had. Would you mind sharing your recipe with me? I'd love to try these flavors in cupcakes."

"I made chai-flavored snickerdoodles a couple weeks ago. I would have saved a few for you, but Brian dropped by, and between the two of us, we polished them off."

Marge had known Brian since he was a teen, but I hadn't realized he spent time with his father's housekeeper. "Oh? Did he stop by to see Mr. Skyler?"

"No. He had a problem he wanted to discuss with me before making a decision."

Raising one eyebrow, I wondered if she would elaborate. She didn't, and I decided not to pry. For all I knew, he was trying to get her to invest in his restaurant. "If you're willing to share, I'd love to have your chai recipe and the cookie recipe too."

Marge blushed. "I'm glad you like it, but honestly, it's just some spices thrown together with black tea. You know, a little bit of this and a tad of that."

"Whatever your combination is, it's perfect. I'd love to know what it is." Marge still appeared reluctant, and I could see her biting the corner of her lower lip. "But I understand if you want to keep your blend a secret. I think you have a huge seller on your hands if you ever market it."

"Oh, it's not that." She swept her hand in the air as if dismissing my suggestion. "I haven't written anything down, so I'm not sure of the exact measurements."

"Can you make a few notes the next time you mix up a batch?"

Marge looked down at the blond bamboo that covered my office floor and furrowed her brows. She remained silent.

"Is something wrong?"

Her neck started to turn a mottled red. "I don't think I'll have the chance to mix up another batch anytime soon."

"Why not?" Had there been a worldwide cinnamon or spice shortage I wasn't aware of?

"Because the new Mrs. Skyler has all but accused me of mismanaging the household funds and using their food and belongings for my personal use." She still wouldn't look at me, and she twisted her hands together. "Mr. Skyler has always told me to prepare enough food so I can eat what I'm fixing for him. He's even told me he would pay for the groceries when I housesit during his travels. And you know I always cook something for you when you work. That's been at his request."

Mr. Skyler had told me about his agreement with Marge, and I had a similar arrangement when I prepared meals for Tillie. I made a mental note to replace the rubber gloves this afternoon in case Mrs. Skyler had taken inventory before they left for their honeymoon. "I'm sure she can't fire or even reprimand you, since we both have the same arrangement with Mr. Skyler. He'd never allow that to happen. Right?"

"She's got him under some kind of spell." Her hand-wringing increased. "Before they left on their trip, she was screaming at me for not having the berries she wanted for breakfast, and Mr. Skyler just put his coffee cup down and left the dining room. I've worked for him for over fifteen years, and I've never been treated like this."

My sense of foreboding increased drastically. Mr. Skyler expected a lot from his employees, but he always treated us with respect and courtesy. I had never heard him raise his voice toward Marge, and he certainly had never shown exasperation with me. "Oh, Marge, I am so sorry."

"I've been using their spices to make the blend because I can't afford to keep buying them myself. Not with my mother's medical bills and my daughter's college tuition." Her eyes turned shiny as moisture gathered along her lower lashes. "I can't afford to lose this job. What am I going to do?"

Piper, sensing emotional distress, got up from her bed and nudged Marge's hand. I was relieved she had stopped her barking. I stood up and wrapped my arms around Marge's shoulders. "Let me talk to Tillie. You're too valuable to lose or be treated this way."

She sniffed. "I keep hoping Mr. Skyler will rein her in and keep control of the house himself, but I don't see that happening."

I shared her pessimism. We had a bumpy ride ahead. "Do you know why they're coming back so early?"

She grimaced and rolled her eyes. "I have no idea. I received a text from her, telling me to have their driver meet them at general aviation at five tonight and then a long list of what she expects me to serve for dinner. She even had the nerve to type 'fresh sea bass' in caps. Like I'd serve them frozen or old fish."

I wasn't sure I should confide in Marge about my investigation of the new Mrs. Skyler. However, she was in the perfect position to keep her eyes open for any incriminating evidence, if there was any… aside from the fact that the new missus was a witch. I took a chance, hoping it would keep Marge from becoming so distraught. "I need to tell you something, but you have to promise to keep it confidential. Okay?"

She agreed.

"We all think there's something strange going on with Barbara Skyler, so we're investigating her."

"Who's investigating?"

"The boys have hired a private investigator, and I've been doing a little snooping." My cheeks warmed. "You can't tell anyone about this because I'll get fired, the boys will be disowned, and Tillie will get locked up in a senior home."

"I think we're all in this together. From the moment she stepped foot in this house, I got the feeling she's been scheming. I'll keep my eyes open for anything we can use against her." She took my hand into her rough one. "Why can't Mr. Skyler see what she's like?"

"We've all wondered the same thing. I, um, looked through Mrs. Skyler's closet and, um, left behind footprints in the carpet. If you need me to, I can vacuum for you." I squeezed her hand before releasing it. It didn't feel right telling her what I had found. I would text the license and business card to Brian and let his private investigator take it from there.

"I already noticed that and wondered what you were up to. When I air out their room, I'll need to vacuum up my own marks." Her chuckle was music to my ears. I had hated seeing the tears that had glittered in her eyes earlier. "We can't have her highness annoyed by footprints in the carpet. Do I need to wipe down fingerprints?"

I laughed but inwardly cringed. No matter what Marge and I did, I suspected we would be an annoyance to the new Mrs. Skyler. I bent down and retrieved the yellow rubber gloves from my purse. "I borrowed these, but I'll buy a brand-new pair and replace them this afternoon. There's no need for you to get in trouble."

"Don't worry about it. I can still use these. Besides, I don't think she's had a chance to take a detailed inventory of the household items… yet." She took the gloves from my hand.

"Are you sure? I don't mind replacing these with a brand-new package."

"I'm sure. If you need gloves again, I have disposable food-prep gloves stored with the plastic wrap and tin foil in the kitchen island top drawer."

"Thanks, but I hope I won't ever have to do this again. My nerves are shot." I lifted my hand parallel to the floor and saw I was still shaking. Of course, it could have been because of the jolt of caffeine from the chai.

"I'd better get back to work. I have a mile-long list now that they're coming home this evening." Marge paused at the door. "Is a turkey sandwich okay for lunch? I'm not sure I can prepare a hot meal."

"You really don't need to fix me anything. I'll be fine." I had said these exact same words a few times a week for the last three months and could repeat verbatim what she would say back to me.

"It's no trouble. I have to eat, too, so it doesn't take any extra time to fix two plates instead of one."

"Thank you. I appreciate it, especially when you're so busy."

"No worries." She padded down the hallway, the thick carpeting muffling her steps.

I went back to my piles of sorted mail and paid the bills from an account Mr. Skyler had set up for me. After setting aside society-event invitations for him to look at, I compiled and copied information his accountant needed for a report. I stopped for a few minutes to inhale the sandwich Marge brought me, along with another glass of sweet chai. I wanted to make sure I was long gone before the Skylers returned. After washing my hands, I responded to the many charitable donation requests he'd received.

By the time I had finished work midafternoon, my back was stiff. I realized I had put off too much of the paperwork while preparing for the Halloween party and then investigating with Tillie. From the beginning, Mr. Skyler had told me to work whenever it was convenient for me, unless he needed to schedule a meeting to review something. So far, I had stayed on top of the paperwork and responded quickly to requests from his accountant and company. Not once had I given him cause for complaint. Still, I worried my work habits might have to change once Mrs. Skyler took charge. I shuddered and hoped she didn't expect me to show up at eight every morning. I treasured my morning-coffee-and-breakfast chats with Tillie each day.

I found Marge in the professional-sized kitchen, laboriously stirring risotto. She ladled a scoop of hot broth into the pot holding Arborio rice and stirred until the liquid was absorbed before adding another scoop of broth. The smell of the onions and garlic sautéing in a skillet on another burner filled the air, and my tummy rumbled. It was so loud I was sure Marge had heard it.

"I wish I had this finished so you could taste it for me. I tend to go a little too light on salt." Marge scooped another ladle of broth into the pot, and it hissed as the liquid hit the hot surface.

"It smells divine." I stepped closer to the stovetop and admired the creamy rice mixture. "Have you ever tried making risotto in a pressure cooker? It turns out amazing and sure saves your arm from all that stirring."

"I've seen recipes making it that way, but I've always been too worried to try."

"Trust me, no one will ever know you took a shortcut." I patted her arm and felt her sinewy muscles flex beneath my hand. "You're getting a good workout, but you'll need a massage after this."

Marge rolled her eyes. "As if that'll happen anytime soon. I'll be lucky to get out of here by midnight tonight. The new missus sent me a text and said to prepare a cheesecake with strawberry sauce for dessert. She wants it served at nine tonight to their six guests."

"I wonder who they're entertaining so late." I also wondered what the rush was to come home and cut the honeymoon short. Was it her idea or his? "Do you need help with anything?"

"Thanks, but I've got it under control." She fell silent while she skillfully stirred the risotto and the skillet of aromatics at the same time. "If I find out anything interesting about their mystery guests, I'll call you."

Chapter 19

I left Marge to the whirlwind of dinner and dessert prep and collected Piper. I double-checked to make sure I had locked the door then headed for the ferry. After dozing most of the day, Piper was frisky and full of energy. I picked up my pace and extended our walk through the Balboa Fun Zone. I thought that perhaps I would even treat myself to an ice cream waffle cone. Carnival-type noises drifted on the sea breeze, and the closer we got to the Fun Zone, the harder Piper pulled on her leash. I decided I would have to invest in more doggie training, but for now I gave in and trotted to keep up with her.

Established over eighty years ago, the Fun Zone had been a family-friendly place to go to for carnival rides, arcade games, beach-side eats, and an area to board boats for fishing or whale watching. Over the years, ownership had changed hands a few times, with upgrades added each time. The newest owner had brought in an ocean science museum, with traveling exhibits and hands-on experiments for young visitors. I avoided the place during the summer, but once kids were back in school, it was an entertaining place to stroll through and allow the fun memories of my youth to surface. It still stayed busy during the school year with some tourists, but it wasn't as frantic as the summer months.

I had just taken a big lick of my double-scoop mocha-almond-fudge cone when I received a text from Tillie.

We need 2 go 2 club for dinner to talk to staff. What time will u be home?

I groaned. I had completely forgotten about eating out that night.

Home in about 20 min or so.

I took my ice cream-filled waffle cone back inside the charming shop and asked for a to-go cup. They graciously transferred my scoops into the cup, snapped a lid on it, and wrapped a fresh waffle cone in a bag for me to eat later. I left another tip and headed home.

I was pleased that the police were gone and the handyman had finished painting the garage door. No one would ever suspect something had been spray-painted in that spot. Once I fed Piper her dinner and refreshed her water bowl, I sent Tillie a text telling her I would shower and change clothes. She responded by saying she had gimlets chilled, and she would be over in twenty minutes so we could have a cocktail and discuss our strategy. Andrew would drive us, of course. She knew I spent little time on makeup and hair. There was almost nothing I could do to tame my frizzy red locks aside from pulling them back into a ponytail or a messy bun.

I dressed in stretchy black slacks and ballet flats. My flouncy cream-colored tunic would cover any expansion my waistband might have after I consumed Tillie's cocktails on top of dinner and drinks at her club. My mouth watered as I thought about the baked pasta dish I had ordered the last time. I still needed to get Carrie to recreate the recipe. Maybe Tillie and I could use that as an opening when we talked to Ruby.

Just as I applied the last swipe of mascara to my lashes, Randall sent me a text.

Flying home tonight. Are u up for a nitecap?

I checked the time and decided Tillie and I wouldn't be too late getting home as long as dinner didn't last more than a couple of hours.

Having dinner with Tillie. Should be home after 8:30.

I'll swing by around 9:30 if that works for you.

I sent him back a thumbs-up emoji just as Tillie knocked on my door. Piper was beside herself with joy at seeing her friend. She acted like it had been weeks since she'd been petted instead of mere hours. I plated some cheese and crackers while Tillie poured the gimlets into two cocktail glasses. We carried our libations out to the patio so Piper could romp in the yard in the waning light.

"Well, did you find out anything about that woman? The suspense is killing me."

The confusion must have shown on my face. I had been thinking about how to approach Ruby and the young server, Samantha. "Um…"

"You know, Barbara. My idiot son's fourth wife." She knocked back the rest of her gimlet. "The more I think about her, the madder I get. We have to do something about her."

"Oh my gosh! I completely forgot—I found a driver's license with another name she might have used." I opened my camera app, pulled up the photo, then handed my phone to her. "Let me grab my laptop, and we can search for this name. I didn't want to use Mr. Skyler's computer in case they try to retrieve deleted browsing history."

She let out a low whistle. Piper must have thought she was being called for, because she bounded up and nudged Tillie's hand for pets. "This proves she's hiding something."

I agreed and went into the house and got my laptop. After

opening a search engine page, I typed in "Benicia Morray, New York" and didn't find one thing. I tried typing in the license number and the name. Again, nothing. Tillie's shoulders drooped as she scratched behind Piper's ears. We were both disappointed.

"This doesn't mean there isn't anything to implicate her," I said. "Let me text the photo to Brian, along with the attorney's business card. His investigator can check it out. I'm sure there are all sorts of people-finding websites he subscribes to that can track down her identity using the driver's license." I sent the photo and card to Brian, along with a lengthy text explanation. When I didn't receive a reply back, I figured he was in the midst of busy dinner preparations at his restaurant.

"I wanted some answers now." Tillie looked dejected, and I knew exactly how she felt.

To take her mind off our strikeouts, I told her about my snooping. She hooted over me getting found out by Marge and was happy we had an inside spy.

"I hope Marge doesn't get so fed up she quits." She fingered her drained glass. "I wouldn't blame her one bit, but it would be hard to replace her. My son had better rein his wife in."

Once again, I agreed. "What time is Andrew picking us up for dinner?"

She glanced at her watch. "He should be here in about twenty minutes. That should give us enough time to work out a game plan on how to approach the staff."

"Ruby might be harder to question, especially if the kitchen is busy. We might be able to use the excuse to chat if I tell her I want the recipe for the baked ziti."

Tillie's eyes twinkled. "I've already taken care of how to question Ruby. I talked to the general manager and said I'd like Ruby to cater a party for me after the new year. Since we're dining there tonight, I asked if it were possible to talk to her during her break. He's arranged it for about the time we finish eating."

"That's a great idea. I hope she's not suspicious and doesn't try to ditch us before we can chat."

"That'll be hard for her to do, since the manager will be there to see she complies." She twirled the empty cocktail glass between her manicured fingers. Her fuchsia nail color matched her flowing kaftan and turban-style head covering. "Kenneth's working the bar, so I'll use the excuse I want to hire him again."

"He'll run screaming from the room. Who in their right mind would take another job in the same place their girlfriend —or even ex-girlfriend—was murdered? I think we need a better plan."

Neither of us could figure out a sneaky way to start our interrogation without him knowing that was happening. We decided to wing it and hoped we wouldn't get thrown out of the club.

A few minutes later, Andrew walked into the pool yard to let us know he was ready whenever we were. Piper, thinking she had another friend to play with, dropped a tennis ball at his feet, and we chatted while Andrew threw the ball again and again for my pup. He paused for a moment to take off his tailored suit jacket, and I admired his broad shoulders. The early-evening sun made his blond hair gleam, and once or twice, he reached up to brush a lock off his forehead between throws of the tennis ball. After a few minutes of play, I stood up and called Piper into the house. I knew she would be more than happy to collapse into her bed and rest while Tillie and I went out to dinner.

I pointed at Andrew's hands. "Would you like to come in and wash your hands? I know that ball is slobbery."

"Thanks. I think I'd better."

I pointed the way to the bathroom then refreshed Piper's water dish. Once Andrew retrieved his jacket and was ready to go, I fished a treat from the freezer, defrosted it for a few seconds in the microwave, and put it in the dog's food bowl. I think she inhaled it without even chewing. I closed her doggy door and made sure she was securely locked inside the house. Neither of us needed a repeat of the night before.

When we checked in for dinner with the hostess at the club, Tillie told the young woman we would have a drink in the bar first. She slipped the hostess a folded green bill and asked that she seat us in Samantha's section when we were ready to dine. I trailed behind Tillie as we made our way to the lounge and once again found seats at the polished wood bar. I couldn't help but muse about the fact that before I had met the woman sitting beside me, I would only drink a glass of white wine when I was out with my BFF—no, make that ex-BFF—Tori. Now, I sipped cocktails before sipping more cocktails, and when Tillie ordered wine with dinner, I would always have another glass. I kind of liked the new not-so-uptight me.

Kenneth glanced our way, and I thought I saw him roll his eyes. After he placed two glasses of white wine on a waiter's tray, he ambled our way. "Uh-oh, here comes trouble with a capital *T*. What can I get for you ladies?"

Tillie ordered a gimlet, and I asked for a glass of red wine, since I hoped the baked pasta dish would be on the menu again. Once he delivered our drinks, I took a sip of the fruity wine and decided that since there was a lull in orders at the bar, I should ask him a few questions. Still, it seemed rude to just dive in. "We're really sorry for your loss, Kenneth."

"I was shocked at first, but I'm finding out I didn't know the real Mandy." He shrugged. "I'm thinking she got what she deserved."

Surprise must have registered on my face, because Tillie kicked my shin. Fortunately, Kenneth had turned away to fill another order of wine. I waited for him to turn back before I continued, "Still, it must be hard to deal with. Do you have any idea who could have wanted to kill her?"

He snorted. "You'd have a shorter list of people not wanting to murder that witch."

Could Kenneth have done the deed himself? I wondered. I had noticed he left the bar at the party for a short time, but I didn't know how long he was gone. To be honest, I'd paid little attention because I was too worried about Thomas and his argument with Mandy. "I heard you were dating her."

This time, the eye roll was obvious. "It was an on-again, off-again thing. We happened to be on again the day of your party."

Tillie tapped her nails on the bar. "Did you speak with Mandy after she went into Emory's house? We noticed you weren't at the bar around that time."

"No, I did not speak with her." He banged a wineglass onto the bar so hard the stem broke. He tossed the pieces into the trash, grabbed another glass, and made a white wine spritzer. "I've heard you're both nosing around, looking for trouble. Let me set the record straight. I did not kill Mandy, and I don't know who did."

"If you weren't in the pool house with Mandy, then where did you go?" I needed to cross names off our suspect list and confirm alibis, despite how bad I felt for pushing Kenneth.

"I don't have to tell you anything. I've already spoken with the police twice." He glared at me for a long moment. "But if it'll get you off my back, I'll tell you what I told them: I walked to Mrs. Skyler's house and used the restroom. After that, I went into her kitchen and got more of the Poison Apple cocktail mix from the refrigerator. Your sister can verify I was there."

"Why didn't you use my bathroom?" This puzzled me because I had shown him where it was when he arrived to set up for the party.

"You just won't let up." He turned his back and made a

margarita while a server hovered close by. Once the waiter had taken the frosty drink to a waiting table, Kenneth came back to us. "Mandy was making a fool of herself, flirting with all those rich, married men. She was looking for a sugar daddy, and I decided I'd had enough of her. I didn't want to get into a fight at the party, so I went to the main house to avoid being around her. Read my lips: I did not kill her."

Chapter 20

Tillie placed a fifty-dollar bill beneath her cocktail glass and stood up. "Thanks for being honest with us. I realize it hasn't been an easy time for you."

Personally, I thought a twenty-dollar bill would have sufficed, but that was Tillie— almost generous to a fault. I followed her as we headed over to our dinner table without saying another word. I hated being pushy and felt bad we had made Kenneth feel so uncomfortable, but I would do anything and everything I could for my family.

Once seated, Samantha walked over and warily handed us menus, looking like she wanted to run away. "Would you like to order drinks before dinner?"

Tillie looked at me, and when I shook my head, she told Samantha she would take a glass of the house red.

"I'll bring that right out with hot sourdough rolls. Our special tonight is eggplant Parmesan served with crusty garlic Italian bread." Having given her spiel, she spun on her heels and made her way to the bar at double the speed I'd seen her move before.

"It doesn't look like she wants to talk to us." Tillie gazed around the dining room and saluted the table across the room, where several of her blue-haired friends were sitting. "I wonder if she's hiding something."

"Either that or someone is threatening her to not talk to us."

"Oh dear, I hadn't thought of that. I hope we haven't endangered her."

I hoped not either, but before I could say so, my comment was choked off by one of Tillie's friends, who charged up to our table.

"You've really stirred up the hornets' nest," she said.

Tillie raised her eyebrows. "Oh? What is it I'm supposed to have done this time?"

"That Shannon Dexter woman is lobbying to have your membership revoked." The tiny almost-birdlike woman rubbed her hands together, and her eyes sparkled with mischief. "The board will need to consider it, given the senator's status here at the club."

"I assure you, I don't know what you're talking about." Tillie held her lips in a flat, thin line.

"I knew you'd cross the wrong person one of these days. What in the world did you do to make her so irate?"

Our server saved Tillie from having to answer, maneuvering around Tillie's friend to place a glass of wine and a basket of warm rolls on the table.

"If you'll excuse us, Frances, I'd like to enjoy my dinner and finish my conversation with Emory," Tillie said.

"Of course. I'm sure Shannon and her coterie will share what transpired." Frances turned to leave then looked back at Tillie. "Enjoy your dinner… while you can."

I noticed Samantha had darted back to the kitchen the second the wineglass and breadbasket hit the table. I didn't blame her. Frances seemed like quite the vindictive woman. "Why was she so nasty to you?" I asked Tillie.

She dismissed the question with a flutter of her hand. "She's not worth bothering about. Frances is known for being spiteful and a gossipmonger. I never liked her, and I'm surprised that group of ladies over there has put up with her for all these years."

"Who knew so much drama and angst would exist in a country club? It seems like you would all be great friends."

Tillie's laugh caused the diners at the next table over to look at us. "Honey, it's practically a bed of vipers here."

Samantha returned with two plates of steaming eggplant Parmesan. She cautiously placed the dishes onto the table and glanced over her shoulder at the dining room manager. When he looked our way, she turned back to us.

"Please be careful. The plates are hot." She looked over her shoulder again then directed her gaze over our heads. "Would you like some fresh-grated Parmesan?"

"Yes, please." Tillie placed the linen napkin on her lap. "That would be nice, dear."

"None for me, thanks," I said. The dish was already laden with cheese.

Samantha excused herself. Tillie leaned over and half whispered to me, "Take the cheese. That'll give us another minute or two to talk to her. She's acting awfully skittish for someone who's innocent."

"Either that or someone doesn't want her talking to us. Or she believes whatever gossip Mrs. Dexter is spreading about us."

Samantha returned with a rotary-style cheese grater holding a block of Parmesan. She bent over Tillie's plate and whirled a stream of cheese onto the hot food.

"Do you have any new information to tell us about Ruby or anyone else as it pertains to Mandy's death?"

Tillie's question must have startled the young woman, because she jerked, and cheese flew onto the snowy-white tablecloth. "Uh, no, Mrs. Skyler. I haven't heard anything."

She turned to leave, and I placed my hand on her arm. She jumped at my touch. "I changed my mind. I'd like some cheese too. Can you tell me if it's made in the US or imported from Italy?"

"No idea," she muttered, almost too soft for us to hear.

"Did someone get mad at you for talking to us before?" I studied her face, looking for a reaction to my question. Her cheeks lost the little color she had, which wasn't much.

"No."

"We don't want to get you into trouble," I said softly. "Can you tell us what's wrong?"

She smashed her lips together and whirled cheese onto my eggplant. "Nothing's wrong. We're just shorthanded tonight. I gotta get back to work."

She didn't even take the time to ask if she had given me enough Parmesan cheese before she bolted for the kitchen. Although, when I looked down at my plate, I saw she had shredded about a thousand extra calories onto it. I suspected she had been too distracted to notice how much cheese she had added.

"Is everything to your satisfaction, Mrs. Skyler?" The manager was suddenly standing at my elbow.

"Everything is lovely. Thank you for checking on us, Stephen," Tillie answered.

"If you need anything else, feel free to let either myself or Samantha know." He walked back to the hostess station. I thought he looked distinguished, with black hair that had turned silver around his temples. He was dressed in a sharp black suit and a crisp white buttoned-down shirt with a gold-striped tie, which fit the formality of the dining room.

"New manager." Tillie pointed at Stephen with her fork then plunged it into the gooey entrée. "They fired the last manager after they caught him pilfering several bottles of expensive wine."

Once I had enjoyed several bites of my dinner, I put my fork down. "Someone has frightened Samantha. Did you see the way she kept looking over her shoulder? It was like she was trying to make sure no one saw her talking to us. Or do you think the new manager is creating the unease?"

"Good question. Stephen seems to keep a close watch on the employees. Perhaps he's trying to increase their efficiency and table turnaround." She dabbed her lips with her napkin. "Service was terrible under the last manager. It wasn't unusual to wait thirty minutes for a drink and another twenty minutes to get a salad or hors d'oeuvres. This guy must've heard all the bad stories and doesn't want to repeat them."

I took another bite of cheesy deliciousness, still unsure. Samantha had been uneasy when we tried to ask her questions. There had to be a way to question her away from the club and away from prying eyes. "Does she go to school or hold another part-time job?"

"I'm not sure. We could follow her home after dinner service then visit her tomorrow."

"It's not a bad idea, but I don't want her to think we're stalking her."

"It's not stalking if we bring cookies when we visit."

I conceded. "Good point. But if someone finds out or if she complains, that'll be another nail in the proverbial coffin in terminating your club membership."

"I'm not the least bit worried. Shannon's overreaction to our questions has me thinking we need to snoop around her life a little more." Tillie drained her wineglass. "Our young server looks like a lemon fan rather than chocolate or cinnamon. Do you have any more lemon crinkles in the freezer?"

"I certainly do. I'll bake them first thing in the morning, and then we can drop by her house around ten."

Once our table had been cleared by a busboy, the manager brought our check. Tillie took the small leather folder. "Where's Samantha?"

"She went home sick." Stephen licked his lips and appeared nervous. "It was a migraine. Nothing contagious, so you need not worry."

"Poor kid. I hope she feels well enough to go to class tomorrow." Tillie handed the signed receipt back to him.

"I didn't realize she's attending college. I should have guessed, since she's only available for weekend and evening shifts." Stephen gave a slight bow to Tillie. "I hope you had a lovely dinner and join us again soon."

"Thank you. It was delicious." Tillie stood up. "I asked the general manager if I could speak with Ruby tonight about catering an event. Is she available right now?"

"I'll check and send her to your table. Or would you rather meet in the bar?"

"Right here is fine."

After the manager was out of earshot, Tillie hissed while she picked her purse up from the floor and sat back down, "Drat! Samantha must have guessed we were going to follow her."

"Our reputation has preceded us."

It didn't take long until Ruby was headed our way. She carried an ice-filled glass and a can of Coke, which she banged on the table before she sat in the empty chair next to mine. "I'll give you two minutes, and then I'm outta here to take my break. You didn't come to talk about any catering job."

Tillie leaned forward. "How do you know that?"

Ruby inclined her head toward me. "Her sister's a caterer. You'd use her company instead of someone else. There's one minute and forty-five seconds left on the clock."

"Why did Samantha ditch us?" I ignored Tillie's glare. "She seemed like she was afraid of something or someone when we walked in."

"She had a migraine. Maybe she's worried about making a bad impression on the new dining room manager. He's already fired a couple servers." The sous chef looked at her large-faced Minnie Mouse watch. "Is that it?"

Tillie cut me off before I could ask another question. "How long do you usually get for your dinner break?"

"Thirty minutes, unless we're swamped or shorthanded."

"Were you shorthanded the night of my party?"

"I don't recall."

"Isn't it true you could have left work on your break and made it to my house, harmed Mandy, and made it back to work without anyone realizing you'd left the premises?"

"Theoretically, it could have happened that way, but I didn't do it. Besides, I don't even know where you live." Ruby examined her watch again. "Bzzzzz… time's up, ladies. Please don't bother me again with your silly investigation, especially if you can't even bother to bring cookies."

I stared at her back as she marched across the dining room and through the swinging doors that led to the kitchen. "That wasn't very productive."

Tillie freshened her lipstick. "More than you might think. We'll talk about it on the way home."

Once we were in the backseat of her car and Andrew began the drive home, she leaned close to me. "Ruby has been to my house before. She was lying."

Chapter 21

"What? When was that?"

"A few years ago. I had reservations to host some out-of-town guests for lunch at the club. A water pipe burst and flooded part of the dining room, so the club offered to deliver the meals to the house, since their kitchen wasn't impacted." She waggled her eyebrows. "Guess who that delivery person was, before the club promoted her to the sous chef position?"

I wanted to believe that was the "smoking gun," but truth was, I wasn't sure I would be able to remember an address or directions to a person's house I had visited once two or three years before either. Heck, I could see forgetting that I'd even been there at all. I said as much to Tillie.

"But she has access to my address from the club directory, and with GPS available on any and every electronic device these days, it would be a piece of cake to find my house."

"You might be right. She also could have just forgotten. That was a long time ago."

"I doubt she would have forgotten the house where she received a hundred-dollar bill for a tip—along with the full-on charm-and-flirtation treatment from Brian."

Tillie had a point. Ruby wouldn't have forgotten Brian. He had an irresistible appeal I'd had a hard time ignoring, despite knowing he was a player. Still: "We need proof before we can make an accusation."

"We need to talk to Vince. I'll bet he can get us Samantha's address." Tillie picked up her handbag. "I have a feeling she knows something."

After we arrived home, I left Tillie safely locked inside her house and went to bake a dozen chocolate chip cookies from my stash in the freezer for Randall's visit. As fit as he was, he still indulged his sweet tooth when given the chance. Just as I had placed the last cookie on the cooling rack, he sent a text letting me know he was at the gate. I smoothed down my hair and tried to soothe the butterflies that jumped around in my stomach before I opened the gate.

We hadn't even reached the French doors that led into my home when Randall sniffed the air. "Is that chocolate chip cookies baking?"

"I just took them out of the oven," I said, suppressing a delicious quiver when he lightly placed his hand on my lower back before I stepped through the doorway. "Would you like some milk or coffee with your cookies? I think I'll have some herbal tea."

"Milk would be great." He walked to the cooling rack and lifted one of the hot cookies. "Mind if I have one? Dinner was a tiny bag of pretzels on the flight down."

"Help yourself. They're all for you." I poured milk into a frosty glass I had removed from the freezer and handed it to him. "Would you like a sandwich or omelet? I'm happy to make something for you."

"Cookies and milk are perfect." His words jumbled together as he took another huge bite of cookie.

"I thought you took the corporate jet up to San Francisco. They didn't bring you back home?"

"It wasn't available until tomorrow morning, so I got a

seat on a commercial flight this evening—which is how I ended up with pretzels for dinner." He studied my face with his mesmerizing sapphire-blue eyes. "I've been away too long and don't want to waste any more time getting to know you."

"Uh, thanks. I've missed you too." My face blazed, and my tongue twisted into knots. He wanted to get to know me, and all I could think of to say was *uh, thanks*? I cringed when he laughed, but before I realized what was happening, he wrapped me in his arms and the taste of chocolate was on my lips.

OVER BOWLS of steel-cut oatmeal with fresh blueberries for breakfast at nine the next morning—and two cups of coffee for me, since Randall hadn't left until midnight—Tillie and I tried to cobble together a plan. We needed to figure out how to reach Samantha since Vince hadn't answered her text. I realized Brian hadn't confirmed receiving my information on the new Mrs. Skyler either. I shuddered, remembering she was now in residence. We lingered over another cup of coffee, and I listened, distractedly, to Tillie gossiping about the minor Newport Beach celebrities while I thought about Randall. Just as I had taken a huge swig of coffee, my phone rang. I recognized the number as Janelle Frankel's, Mr. Skyler's executive assistant at his office in Irvine.

I swallowed and pressed the button to connect the call. "Hi, Janelle."

Her overly loud deep alto voice filled my ear. "Good morning, Em. I'm sorry to bother you, but Mr. Skyler wants to know where you are."

"I'm with Tillie. Fixing her breakfast. Same as every morning." I came across a little snippy and defensive. I didn't mean to take it out on Janelle, but deep down I think I had expected an intrusion into what had become my normal schedule.

"Don't take it out on me. I'm only the messenger, okay? Mrs. Skyler expected you at the house at nine sharp this morning." I could picture her twisting her curly raven-black hair around her index finger. It was a habit she did when something annoyed her.

My eyes snapped wide open. "What? No one told me that. I haven't spoken with her or Mr. Skyler since they dropped the bombshell on the family last Friday."

"Yeah, apparently one of our new job requirements is to be clairvoyant." Her sarcasm practically oozed from the phone. "I was chewed a new one because I didn't have his office correspondence waiting at their home last night."

"Oh no. That's not like him." I was puzzled because Mr. Skyler had always treated both of us with respect. While not exactly laid-back, he had never gotten upset or angry, even when I had made mistakes while learning the ins and outs of the job in the first few weeks.

"I think he must be between a rock and a hard place. With the missus pushing the hardest, obviously you and I will take the heat so he can keep peace with his new bride."

I had feared as much. "What am I supposed to do? Go to their house as soon as I can?"

"That's a good idea, but you'd better prepare yourself."

That didn't sound good at all. "What do you mean? What do I need to know so I'm prepared?"

"First, you'd better leave Piper at home and dress in business attire."

Mr. Skyler didn't care how I dressed, so I was most often in shorts, a T-shirt, and flip-flops, though I tried to dress in nicer resort-casual clothing when I met with him. "Did he tell you that, or is it coming straight from her?"

"Marge has sent me several texts this morning, so I'm passing on my interpretation of what she's said."

"Why didn't she text me?" It wasn't uncommon for the three of us to text one another to keep apprised of the household and work things to make sure Mr. Skyler's life ran smoothly.

"It's a madhouse over there this morning, and she has her hands full." Janelle must have covered the phone receiver with her hand, because her voice became muffled as she barked an order to another person in her office. Then back to me: "Keep your phone silenced and take your own snacks, lunch, drinks. Whatever you're used to Marge providing, don't count on it."

"You know I never asked for food or took advantage of him, right?"

"I know. Mr. Skyler has been incredibly generous to all his employees, but there's a new boss now. And it's not going to be pretty." Janelle groaned. "Gotta go. That witch is calling my cell phone again. Get over there as soon as you can."

Tillie must have overheard part of our conversation thanks to Janelle's booming voice, because her eyes were as big as saucers, and the only color on her face consisted of the coral swipes of blush she had applied earlier that morning. "What are we going to do about that woman? She'll drive all of you away from me so she can get her hands on my property."

"No one's going to abandon you, no matter what happens. We'll find a way to stop her. I promise." I didn't feel nearly as confident as I sounded. In fact, I was downright terrified. I couldn't afford to lose my job or the place I called home.

"You'd better run along and get ready. Piper can stay with me today," she offered.

As if she had sensed the elderly woman needed some comfort, Piper came over and placed her head in Tillie's lap.

I tried to reassure Tillie once more before I rushed to my pool house to prepare for work. While I tried to decide what to wear, I sent Brian another text, including "URGENT" at the top.

He responded right away.

Sorry. Big nite and celebrated till wee hrs. Will forward info to PI.

I sent an immediate text back.

Need answers asap. Big trouble now that she's back.

He sent back the okay emoji, and I threw my phone onto the bed. I dressed in a midcalf-length floral summer dress with cap sleeves. I wore a pair of flat, strappy white sandals, which made the outfit more casual, but I didn't do heels. I couldn't see having to dress up more than that to work in a bayside home office where I didn't interact with anyone most of the time. After adding a banana and a muffin to my purse, I picked up my cell phone and keys. To save ten minutes, I drove to Mr. Skyler's house instead of walking. Before I backed out of the garage, I sent Marge a text saying I was on my way. She didn't respond.

Traffic was fairly light that time of morning, so it took less than twenty minutes to get to the house. Someone had blocked all the parking spaces close to the house with large orange traffic cones. I couldn't see a reason, and as much as I wanted to remove a cone and steal a spot, I drove down the street to find parking. Unfortunately, the only open space I could find was half a block away, and it was a parallel parking space... of course. After trying to ease my car into the toy car-sized space for what seemed like five minutes, I gave up and drove farther from the house, on the hunt for a larger parking space. I located one a block over, and since it was right on the edge of cross streets, I could pull straight into it. *Yay for me*, I thought. But by the time I had hoofed it over to Mr. Skyler's house, I was hot and sweaty, and the sandals were killing my feet.

I climbed the stairs to the outside door of my office and inserted my key in the lock. It wouldn't turn. I twisted it, and still nothing happened. I pulled the key out and examined it to make sure I had the right one—I did. Perplexed, I climbed back down the stairs, headed to the main security gate, and punched in my code. Nothing happened. I tried again. The gate remained locked. I punched the video intercom bell and gave a sigh of relief when the gate unlocked with a buzz. I pushed through it and, once inside the courtyard, made sure it relocked behind me. Marge opened the massive front door and waited for me to climb the few steps to reach her.

"Sorry about that. My key wouldn't open the office door." The words were barely out of my mouth when she yanked me inside the house then closed and locked the front door.

"Follow me." Her voice was so quiet I almost couldn't hear her. She led me through the kitchen and into the huge walk-in pantry then closed the door once we were inside. "That woman is a nightmare. What have you found out? We need to do something to get rid of her before I kill her."

Chapter 22

I finally noticed that Marge was wearing a navy blue maid's dress, complete with a frilly white half apron. She also had on nylon pantyhose, and the kitten-heeled navy blue pumps on her feet looked brand-new. "What the heck are you dressed in? I didn't know they even made pantyhose anymore."

"No kidding. I haven't owned a pair since the eighties." Marge blew a raspberry. She was clearly exasperated. "My costume is the least of our worries."

"What else is going on? And why are we hiding in the pantry?"

"So Dragon Lady can't hear us. Trust me, you need to walk on pins and needles around her."

"Where's Mr. Skyler? Surely he won't put up with her abuse." I hoped I was stating a fact.

"He left right after breakfast for a meeting." Marge massaged her temple. "He's not looking so good. He was abnormally quiet at dinner last night. Kind of withdrawn and pale. I think she's poisoning him."

"No! I can't believe that could happen. Could it?"

"Just wait until you see him. He's like a different man and

not in a good way." She put her ear to the door and listened a moment before turning back to me. "I need to make this quick before she finds us. Dragon Lady has changed all the locks and key codes. Everything, and I do mean everything, has to be approved by her. She canceled your bank account, fired the gardener and the pool guy. My salary has even been cut in half and my insurance benefits canceled. Although she still expects me to be at her beck and call eighteen hours a day. I think she's doing everything possible to make us so miserable we'll quit. But don't do it. You won't get unemployment benefits."

"Can she legally reduce your salary and take away your benefits?"

"Sadly, yes. Mr. Skyler is—or was—a generous employer and always paid a livable wage." She shook her head. "I'm not sure how I'll manage to pay rent now, much less help my daughter with her college tuition. But I refuse to give her the satisfaction of quitting."

This couldn't be good. I worried about what the "Dragon Lady" had in store for me. The sound of a clanging bell came from the intercom system speaker. I raised my eyebrows and thought I heard Marge curse under her breath. "What the heck is that?"

"That, my dear, is the Dragon Lady summoning me. We are now at her beck and call whenever she clangs her bell." Marge opened the pantry door and motioned for me to follow her.

We walked up the winding staircase, entered the master suite, and made our way to Mr. Skyler's personal office. Mrs. Skyler sat behind his desk. Stacks of file folders, filled with papers, covered the surface. Even though it was warm, she wore a tailored cream-colored long-sleeved silk blouse. The largest diamond-stud earrings I'd ever seen sparkled on her earlobes. She had pulled her golden-blonde hair in a tight chignon, which made the earrings seem more dramatic.

Marge practically curtsied. "Mrs. Skyler, Emory Martinez is here, as you requested. Is there anything I can do for you?"

"Where's my Earl Grey tea? It's ten already, and you haven't brought it to me." Her voice was shrill, like a spoiled child's. The garish red of lipstick against her pale skin made it nearly impossible not to stare at her unnaturally plumped lips as she berated Marge.

"I apologize, but I wasn't aware you wanted tea. I'll bring you a pot right away."

"Make sure it's loose leaf. Don't pass off any of your cheap tea bags to me."

I remembered Janelle saying our new job description included being clairvoyant. She hadn't been kidding. Marge hurried from the room like a fire had been lit beneath her. I felt Mrs. Skyler's gaze focus on me, and I tried, unsuccessfully, to suppress a shudder. "Dragon Lady" seemed like an appropriate nickname, especially with her makeup, which was more appropriate for an evening out. Thick black liner ringed her eyes, and long fake eyelashes practically touched her bold swooping eyebrows as they arched with disdain. I stood as still as possible in front of the desk.

"Ms. Martinez…" She looked at my body, from the top of my frizzy red hair to the sandals on my unpedicured feet. "Exactly what are you wearing? Why aren't you dressed appropriately for your position in this household?"

I drew my eyebrows together. *Is this a trick question? And what in the heck do I call her?* I didn't think she'd appreciate Dragon Lady. "Um, since I don't interact with the public and I rarely see any people outside of household help, I dress in business casual attire. Which is appropriate for Southern California."

"This is my household, and one of your job requirements will be to dress appropriately. Effective immediately, all employees of the Skylers, both household and in the company, are to wear full business attire. Women will wear nylon stockings, and shoes must have a heel between one to two inches.

Nothing lower, nothing higher. No plunging necklines, no bare shoulders. Skirts must fall to the knee or no more than four inches below. Slacks must be pressed. No denim is allowed. Men will wear neckties at all times, with buttoned long-sleeved shirts."

I gulped as she recited her long list of rules. Was she trying to take us back to the fifties? But what could I say? "All right."

"I've been reviewing your employment file. I notice you haven't filled out a job application." She handed me a three-page document. "I want that completed in its entirety by the end of the day."

"But I'm household help." I scanned the document, horrified to see the information she wanted—like my Social Security number. Mr. Skyler's company paid me, and human resources had my personal information already. I didn't trust this woman, and I certainly didn't want her to have access to my private information.

"Yes, but it's the new policy. I also need to address your salary. You've been taking advantage of Mr. Skyler's generosity for several months without providing adequate services for his benefit. Effective immediately, your salary will start at the hourly minimum wage rate, and your insurance and 401k benefits will be suspended. Monthly rent for the pool house will be deducted from your paycheck, along with back rent for the time you've lived there. I will review your performance after three months and evaluate if you deserve a raise." Dragon Lady paused for breath then told me the rent she proposed. "Also, you will be required to be here, in your office, from nine sharp to five, Monday through Friday, and available on weekends if we have events."

As an accountant, I could do sums in my head pretty fast. Minimum wage would just cover the absurd rent she wanted to charge me for a house she didn't even own. My face heated to a boiling point. I bit the inside of my cheek to keep from saying something I would regret. I wanted to give this woman a piece of my mind, throw down her absurd application, and stomp out of there. But I had to somehow keep my job and find out something incriminating in order to protect Tillie and Marge.

I clasped the application to my chest. Marge was right. This woman wanted to make us quit. Now, if I could only remind myself of that fact every time I wanted to throttle her, which seemed to be about every time she opened her mouth, I might just keep my job.

Mrs. Skyler handed me another piece of paper with two signature and date lines at the bottom. At the top, in bold, were the words "Acknowledgment of Warning."

"Sign and date this to acknowledge your first infraction on the job. If you have three infractions, you will be fired immediately."

I tried to scan the typed paragraph beneath the words, but the text blurred together as my anxiety rose. "I don't understand. What did I do wrong?"

"Mr. Skyler specifically told you to schedule luncheons and committee meetings to introduce me to the society women in Newport Beach." She swept her hand over the desk. "I see no invitations, nothing scheduled on my calendar, no indication you've done anything to facilitate his instructions."

"Unfortunately, these things take time." I hedged and lied a little. "I've put feelers out but haven't gotten return calls yet. It's difficult because I, myself, am not a society person."

"But your mother is."

"And my mother doesn't work for you or Mr. Skyler."

"If she wants her daughter to keep working and have a place to live, she'd better get busy."

I exhaled and counted to five. "She understands what you want, but we've had a little family emergency. My mother has been caring for my five-year-old nieces and hasn't had a moment to do anything with her committees. Please be patient. It won't take long for your social calendar to fill up."

"I don't tolerate excuses either." She pointed at the paper I clutched in my sweaty hands. "Sign and date."

I did as told and handed it back to her. This was becoming unbearable, and I wondered how long it would take for me to lose my temper and take this woman down. I prayed Brian's investigator was giving his full attention to Dragon Lady.

"I'm busy the rest of the day, so go home and change. You can take the time to speak with your mother and my mother-in-law and have them schedule events to introduce me to the women in their clubs." She lowered her head and studied the files on the desk. I assumed she was looking for other employees to screw over.

"Yes, Mrs. Skyler." I backed out of the room, feeling like a bowing supplicant, just as Marge entered, carrying a tray with a teapot and a plate of shortbread cookies.

"Well, that took long enough." The Dragon Lady went back to badgering Marge.

I turned and fled to my office. I tried to control the tears that stung my eyes and took deep breaths in and exhaled slowly. The woman was intolerable, and I vowed I would do everything in my power to ruin her. I gathered my personal belongings that had collected in the office over the last three months and placed them in a bag. I didn't want the woman going through my photos or to give her any other reasons to write me up because I had a paperback mystery sitting on my desk. When I tiptoed into the kitchen, I found Marge banging skillets onto the stovetop. She turned when I walked in. Her face was flushed, and her eyes glittered.

"You have to do something about her." She slammed another skillet down. "This is insane. I've worked for Mr. Skyler for fifteen years and have been through two of his other wives. But this, by far, is the worst. I don't know how much longer I can take it."

I moved closer to her so I could whisper. The last thing either of us needed was for the new mistress of the house to overhear us conspiring. "As soon as I leave the house, I'll call Brian and find out what his investigator has found. There has to be something we can use against her."

"Mark my words—she's trying to poison Mr. Skyler and take over." She leaned toward my ear. "I overheard her on the phone telling someone there's no prenup."

I gasped. What had Mr. Skyler been thinking? "I truly hope she was making that up."

"I don't think so. There wasn't a prenup with the last one, either, but at least she died before she could steal from him."

I shook my head. I couldn't fathom someone savvy enough to run a megamillion-dollar company but incapable of protecting his wealth for his sons. Perhaps he'd felt he'd done enough for his kids, and he didn't care what happened to his money after he was gone. I'd have to ask my mother about it. "Maybe that's why she's putting us in penury. She sees our wages as money being taken away from her."

The clanging bell sounded again, and Marge cursed. "How does she expect me to cook a three-course lunch, clean the house, and prepare for dinner if she keeps summoning me? She's going to be the death of me."

When she stomped off toward the stairs, I scurried to the front door and ran as fast as I could. I wanted to be long gone before the dragon lady summoned me again. Once I was a block away from the house and certain no one would call me back, I called Brian. It went directly to voice mail. I looked at the time and figured he was surfing before going into work. I disconnected and sent a brief text. A text would get his attention more than a voice mail, which he rarely listened to.

Urgent! Call me asap!!! Life or death!

Chapter 23

I f that didn't get his attention, then nothing would. Next I sent my mother a text asking if I could come by. Given her last reaction to my announcement over Mr. Skyler's new marriage, I thought it best to talk to her in person about what the new wife required of her. Plus, I needed to find out what the real story was between my mother and Mr. Skyler. She was hiding something from me.

By the time I reached my car, sweat trickled down my back, and my hair frizzed even more. I pulled it up into a messy bun to allow my shoulders and neck to cool off in the blasting air-conditioning of my car. Even though my Honda was fifteen years old, it still ran well, and the AC worked like a charm. My phone chimed as I pulled out of the parking spot. I glanced down at the text. Mother. I was tempted to stay right where I was and read it, but a jerk impatiently tooted his horn while he waited for my parking spot. Parking was always a premium this close to the beach, but I still thought the guy could've been a little more patient.

I eased my car into the traffic lane and headed for the central road that led toward the Pacific Coast Highway. My eyes roamed the curb, looking for a parking space or a business parking lot where it was safe to pull over to read the text. Nothing. Every space was full, and it wasn't even summer. When I came to a full stop because of a red traffic light, I snuck a glance at my phone's screen. I couldn't read the entire message, but I could grasp the gist of it that yes, my mother was home and I should drop by.

Seated at my mother's kitchen table and nursing a cup of oolong tea sweetened with a touch of honey, I launched into my tale of the new Mrs. Skyler. I watched her face go from the palest white to splotchy red to full-on angry red. I was mortified that I'd had to ask my mother to intervene and save my job, but desperate times called for desperate measures.

"That witch expects me to introduce her to my friends and my committee members?" Her voice sputtered with indignation. "That'll happen over my dead body. Honestly, where does David find these tramps? Where was he when she gave you these demands?"

"Some meeting, somewhere else. Definitely not at the house." I paused and took another sip. "He told me to get you to schedule some things for her last Friday when he introduced her."

My mother shook her head. "I'll have a heart-to-heart chat with him. That witch will not threaten you or your job. And she certainly can't throw you out of Matilda's house. She owns it outright, and David can't touch a penny, even if she's found incompetent."

I had been certain Mrs. Skyler had been trying to bully me even though she had zero legal authority over my living arrangement with Tillie. "You seem to know an awful lot about David and the family. How is it you can influence him and overrule his new wife's demands?"

I emphasized my boss's familiar first name, which I never used, and waited for a reaction. My mother didn't disappoint. Her face blushed a pretty pink.

"He was a good friend in the past." She picked up her teacup and studied the pattern on the delicate bone china.

"But something went on between you two? Is that why he's taken me in?"

She closed her eyes and lifted her face toward the ceiling. She exhaled then looked at me. "Oh, Emory. Can't the past remain in the past?"

"I need to know. Somehow I've gotten dragged into the middle of something I don't understand."

She fingered the edge of her teacup and blew out a loud sigh. "David and I went to high school together, although he was a couple years ahead of me. When I entered USC, we dated and, well, one thing led to another."

Silence filled the air, and I dared not make a peep. I didn't want her to change her mind and leave the story unfinished.

"I got pregnant. Long story short, his grandmother—that would be Tillie's mother-in-law—whisked him away to Boston under threat of disinheritance and found him an appropriate debutante. I agreed to give up the baby, and they would pay my college tuition." She sighed. "You have to remember in those days, there was a huge stigma if you were an unwed mother. Joel—your, ah, father—had been a close friend in high school and offered to marry me. I agreed. We considered keeping the baby, but in the end, I realized I wasn't ready to be a mother. Plus, I didn't want a reminder of David's aban-donment."

A buzzing noise filled my ears. I wasn't sure I had heard my mother correctly. "So you're saying I have a sibling some-where out there? A brother? Or a sister?"

"A sister. She would be thirty-two now."

"Whoa." My mind was going a million miles a minute in a hundred different directions. "What happened to her?"

"The adoption agency assured me she found a home with a lovely couple who had the monetary means to give her a good life."

"So that's why David owes you..." I still had the feeling she wasn't telling me everything. Something niggled in the back of my brain—something about the way she'd said my dad's name. "Is David my father?"

She didn't make eye contact. "Good lord, no."

"Is Joel my biological father?"

Complete silence. She smashed her lips together and still wouldn't look at me.

"I have a right to know the truth." I was actually torn over finding out the truth. My dad's abandonment was something I still struggled with. But when I looked beyond the hurt and anger, deep down I knew I would always love him. Still, if he wasn't my biological father, it would go a long way toward explaining his betrayal to our family. I said as much to my mother.

She heaved a long sigh. "I've never told another soul. It was an agreement Joel and I made with each other."

"But it's time your daughter knows the truth, especially since it impacts me."

Mother took a sip of tea then placed the cup down with shaky hands. The saucer rattled. "Our marriage was one of convenience for both of us. Joel had his own secrets to hide, and our marriage put any insinuations to rest. You have to realize those were different times back then."

I puzzled a moment before a light bulb clicked on in my head while I pulled memories of my dad from childhood. He was an expert at doing our hair in elaborate braids and styles. He was the one who took us clothes shopping and painted our nails. Sometimes he pranced around, which made my sister and me laugh. We thought he was doing it on purpose, but maybe he wasn't, or maybe it made him feel good. "Dad was, or is, gay?"

"Yes. Please keep this in confidence. Despite our fallout, there are many people around here who respect his reputation."

"So…" I had no idea how to broach my next question.

"How did I get pregnant with you and Carrie?" She rolled her eyes, and her cheeks grew pink again. "I visited a clinic and had a couple rounds of donor IUI."

"Why? Why did you decide to have children, given your nonmarriage?"

"I really wanted to have a child, and at that point, Joel supported me." She picked up her teacup and sipped. I was glad to see she wasn't as shaky as she had been moments before. "He really did love you girls, and it broke his heart to leave."

"Then he shouldn't have left." The bitter words sprang from my lips before I could stop them. "There's no reason he couldn't have been a part of our lives, even if you got a divorce. Lots of families do it. Lots of fathers stay around so they can help raise their daughters… biological or not."

"What you're overlooking is that Joel deserved love and real companionship too. He couldn't have that around here without it tainting you girls."

I tried to stifle the tears that threatened to gather in my eyes. "He should have at least said goodbye or kept in touch or visited once in a while."

"You can place the blame entirely on me. I forced him to choose between us and his companion." She nervously tapped her index finger on the tabletop. "And while I'm being honest, I was such a harpy at that point, I don't blame him for leaving."

"So he never tried to contact us after that? Where is he?" I was disappointed and unhappy with my mother, but getting mad at her wouldn't keep her talking.

"Joel called a few times, but I always slammed the receiver down when I heard his voice." She looked a little embarrassed. "He, um, sent you birthday cards and other letters the first couple of years, but I always put 'Return to Sender' on them without opening them. I see now I shouldn't have done that."

"No, you shouldn't have done that."

"I was trying to protect you, but I now see I owe you and your sister an apology." She finally looked up from her cup of tea and gazed into my eyes. "I owe you several apologies. I know I've been hard on you and distant. It wasn't fair to take my own insecurities about being a terrible mother after giving up my first child out on you. And when Joel left, I floundered, trying to be a single mother and earn a living while raising you and your sister. By the time Lars was a part of our family, I didn't know how to connect with you girls."

"Didn't Dad at least pay child support?" I was angry at my mother and getting angrier by the minute at my supposed dad for abandoning us.

"He offered both spousal and child support. I was too proud to accept, which in retrospect was a mistake."

The silence lingered between us while I let her bombshells sink in. There were so many more questions I wanted to ask, so many answers I needed. "Where is Dad now?"

"I have no idea. Once Lars and I got married, I tried to forget it ever happened."

"Does Lars know the truth about Joel? About us?"

"Yes. I didn't want to start a marriage with lies and half-truths." She got up and refilled our teacups. "Lars has been one hundred percent supportive."

He had been and was still supportive of us. Lars treated my sister and me like his own daughters. "What about Mr. Skyler? You act really weird around him. Are you still in love with him?"

She waved her hand dismissively. "Does anyone ever get over their first love?"

That wasn't the answer I wanted to hear. Poor Lars.

She must've interpreted the look on my face, because she reached over and patted my hand. "I love Lars, and nothing will change our relationship. David brings back memories of youth and the innocence of a first love. Nothing more than that. Head on home and leave David and his dragon lady to me. It'll get better. I promise."

I couldn't keep this new revelation about our family to myself, and since my mother hadn't commanded me to keep it a secret, I headed to my sister's house. The second she answered the door, I pulled her along to the kitchen and heated a kettle of water for herbal tea.

"What's got you so worked up?" Carrie plopped down in a chair and rubbed her growing belly.

"Where are the girls?" I didn't want to spill family secrets around little ears.

"At a friend's house, thank goodness." She pointed at the half-full cookie jar on the counter. "Hand me the cookies. They were in a mood this morning and didn't want to go to school until I told them about their playdate. It didn't help that their father was cranky too. Must be the shorter daylight."

I thought my brother-in-law's mood probably had something to do with being a suspect in a murder investigation. But I didn't tell her that. "I just came from Mother's house, and you'll never believe what I found out."

Carrie listened raptly, letting out small gasps every now and then, while I told her about our family history, our half sister, the progress Tillie and I were making on the investigation, and the new dragon lady inhabiting the Skyler residence. By the time I finished talking, we had drained our tea mugs, and there wasn't even one cookie left in the cookie jar.

Carrie peered inside the empty container. "Oops. Guess that was lunch. I have a checkup tomorrow, and the doctor hasn't been very happy with how much weight I've gained already."

I eyed her rounded belly. "You're not carrying twins, are you?"

"Bite your tongue. I never want to go through that again." She plucked a stray chocolate chip from the bottom of the jar. "Just one baby boy this time around. Thomas is thrilled. The girls are disappointed they won't have a little sister, though."

"Speaking of sisters, what are we going to do about ours? Should we try to track her down?"

"What did Mother say about it?"

"I didn't broach the subject with her. I wanted to find out what you thought of the idea."

"We could do one of those DNA tests and see if we get any matches then take it from there." Carrie hunted for another stray chocolate chip in the empty cookie jar.

I pulled my cell phone out and searched online for a DNA kit. "Should we both take a test? Or would one test be sufficient, since we're twins?"

Carrie stared off into space and didn't answer me.

I touched her arm. "Are you okay?"

"I had a mind-numbing thought. If we take a DNA test, it's probable we'll end up with lots of half siblings, depending on our mother's, err, donor. Will we be able to tell which is our mother's daughter?" She shook her head back and forth. "Do we really want to open the proverbial can of worms?"

"Oh my, I hadn't thought of that." Did I want to know about a bunch of half siblings from an anonymous father? My life was complicated enough as it was. "How about this: One of us takes the test, and I'll see if there's a way to keep it private until we decide what to do?"

Carrie raised her gaze to meet mine. "You do it. I've got more than enough to manage right now. We can talk about it once you get the results back."

I added the test to the shopping cart and hit Purchase. Once I received a confirmation, I put my phone down. "I should have it within a couple of weeks."

"Did you see any of those news reports where an anonymous donor fathered over fifty children?" She looked like a deer caught in headlights. "I'm not sure I can deal with something like that."

"We won't do anything with the results until you're ready." I reached out and grasped her hand. "What do you think we should do about Dad, er, Joel?"

Carrie closed her eyes and didn't answer for a minute. "I don't know. How would we even go about trying to find him?"

"Maybe start with an online search? He was a math professor before he left, so we might luck out and find his profile on some university website."

"I'm feeling overwhelmed with all of this. First the murder and Thomas being questioned then finding out we have a sister and that our dad isn't really our dad." My sister rubbed her palms over her face. "Do you think he would even want to reconnect with us?"

I didn't need to stop to consider her question. Our dad had loved us, even though we weren't his biological daughters. "Absolutely. Can you imagine how heartbreaking it must have been for him to have our mother completely sever his ties with us? It would be like you disappearing with my nieces and not allowing me to see them or even communicate with them. There would always be a hole in my heart where they belonged."

She nodded. "You're right. Can we put it on hold for now and wait for my husband's innocence to be proven? I feel like I can only handle one thing at a time."

"I think that's a good idea." I had to agree with her, and I had more reasons than ever to clear my brother-in-law's name.

Chapter 24

I left my sister and headed back to Tillie's house. My feelings—something like emptiness and longing for an unknown sister—surprised me. I shook off my musings and focused on the more pressing problem at hand: Tillie needed to be warned about the trouble her new daughter-in-law was making. It bothered me that Brian hadn't called me back about the results from the driver's license I had found. I called him again, using the speaker feature on my cell. This time, he answered just as I thought it was going to voicemail.

"I wanted to wait on the investigator for information before I called you." Brian jumped straight into the conversation without social niceties like "hello."

"Well, hello to you too," I mumbled as someone cut me off from the lane I wanted to merge into. "They're back home, and it's dire. I need answers soon."

"The driver's license is a very sophisticated forgery." Brian pulled away from his phone to yell at someone in the background. He came back. "Sorry, we're prepping for dinner service."

"What does the forgery mean?"

"It means it won't help us find her true identity. It's a dead end."

"Oh no! What do we do next?" I worried about what kind of revenge Mrs. Skyler would take out on me now that I had involved my mother. Surely Mr. Skyler hadn't mentioned his history with Addie.

"The PI suggests getting ahold of a water glass or something he can lift her fingerprints from." He yelled again to his kitchen crew. Then: "I've got to go. Send me a text when you have the glass, and I'll pick it up from you."

My phone went silent. As soon as I parked, I sent Marge a text asking her to call me when it was safe to do so. She called me almost immediately.

"Emory, where did you disappear to?"

"Mrs. Skyler didn't approve of my attire and sent me home." I didn't mention her other commands to assign my mother the task of introducing her to society. "Sorry to leave you there on your own."

"What did you need? I don't have much time."

"Can you bag a glass she's handled so the PI can lift her fingerprints?"

"You bet. I haven't had time to wash the lunch dishes yet. I'll bring her wineglass to you this evening."

"Great. Call me when you're on your way so I can make sure I'm here." I opened my car door and stepped out.

Marge lowered her voice to a whisper. "I need to run, but I'll bring it just as soon as I can."

For the second time in under a dozen minutes, I listened to dead air. Could there be any connections between Marge and Mandy in the past, aside from Brian dating the victim? I shook my head. I didn't need to create imaginary suspects. There were enough real suspects already. Besides, I had a more immediate problem to deal with in the form of a dragon lady. Piper met me at Tillie's front door and covered my face with kisses when I lifted her up for a hug.

"You're home earlier than I expected," Tillie called from the patio. "Come on out and tell me about your first day of working for She Who Must Not Be Named."

I laughed at her reference to the Harry Potter character. She wasn't far off the mark. Piper led me out to the patio, where I found Tillie sitting beneath a bright turquoise-striped sun umbrella. She had a cozy mystery novel resting on her lap and a glass of iced tea sitting on the patio table.

"I'm doing some amateur sleuth research." She showed me the colorful book cover. "Would you like some tea?"

"No thanks. I just need to relax for a bit." I sank down into one of the soft patio chair cushions that matched the sun umbrella and lifted my face to the afternoon sun. "It's been a heck of a day."

"I've been on pins and needles. What happened?"

"Let's just say I had to call in the big guns..." I peeked at Tillie between half-closed eyelids then burst out laughing at the look of impatience on her face. But then I remembered my sister, who was somewhere out there, missing out on being part of our family. I turned somber. "My mother. She's going to straighten out your son. Why am I just now finding out about a sister?"

"Ah... It's about time she told you the truth." Tillie reached out and held my hand. "My heart broke when I found out my husband and his mother had forced Addie to give up my grandchild. They hid the pregnancy from me, and by the time David confided in me, it was too late. Back then adoption agencies permanently sealed the records. I couldn't find a trace. I would have loved to have raised your sister. It was also the beginning of the end of my marriage to David's father. The sight of him turned my stomach after I found out what he'd done."

"I'm going to submit a DNA sample and see if we can locate her on the ancestry sites." I hesitated to tell her how my sister and I had been conceived and why Carrie wanted to hold off on the search. In the end, I decided it was better to be open about it. There had been too many secrets in our families for far too long. So I explained the complications of tracking down my half sister.

Tillie tapped her manicured finger against her rose-colored lips for several seconds. "I think we need to tell Brian. We can use his DNA instead of yours, since he's also her half brother. Unless my son has been hiding something from me, he only has the three children, which will make it less complicated."

"Do you think it's safe to tell him? My mother and Mr. Skyler have been keeping this a secret for thirty-two years, and I'm sure they won't be happy if this becomes public." That was an understatement. My mother thought reputation was everything.

"We can trust Brian. Definitely not Teddy. He'll make a stink of this and try to torpedo the entire search if he finds out. He won't want to risk even a penny of his inheritance." She took a sip of the iced tea. "Leave it up to me to deal with your mother and my son. I think I can guilt them over robbing me of my granddaughter for all these years. It's a benefit of being this old."

I spent the next thirty minutes telling Tillie about my time at work and all the changes the dragon lady was forcing on the Skyler employees. We also talked about the bogus driver's license and other ways to discover her identity. After I thought I had covered all the new things that had happened to me that day, I gave Tillie a peck on the cheek. "I hope we find her."

I took my leave after I promised to bring Randall back at seven for gimlets and to cook dinner for the three of us. Randall and I had planned to go out to dinner, but with everything going on in Tillie's family and my own, I felt we should spend time with her. Right now, though, I had an order of chai cupcakes that I needed to bake for delivery the next day.

Disappointed that Marge hadn't been able to give me the recipe for her chai blend that had inspired my cupcakes, I decided to wing it with the spices I had on hand.

With the warm weather continuing, I propped open the French doors that led out from my pool house and onto the patio and pool deck. I wanted Piper to romp outside while I could keep an eye on her as I baked. I was still worried about the intruder who had thrown the hot dogs over the gate. Fortunately, my dog had shown no signs of poisoning and tolerated the prescription without any issues.

I collected the pre-ground spices for the chai: cinnamon, ginger, cardamom, allspice, cloves, nutmeg, and freshly ground white pepper. After mixing them together, I took a heaping tablespoon of the blend and whisked it, along with salt and leavening, into flour. Next, I creamed butter, granulated white sugar, and a little brown sugar together and added eggs with vanilla. When I mixed the flour blend into the sugar, alternating with buttermilk, the heady scent of warm spices and zesty pepper filled the air. Once the filled cupcake tins were in the preheated oven, I went to work on the frosting.

I had forgotten to take the cream cheese out of the refrigerator, so I cut it into small pieces and beat it on medium-high speed in my KitchenAid stand mixer until creamy. Next, I added butter and a level tablespoon of the chai-spice mix and beat it until well blended. I let the mixture sit while the cupcakes cooled on a wire rack.

After a search on Pinterest, I was inspired to garnish the cupcakes with cinnamon sticks that had been cut in half. I found my coping saw, used exclusively for food, and sanitized the blades. With a silicone chopping mat protecting the counter, I carefully held a stick of cinnamon firmly to the mat and sawed with firm strokes across the reddish-brown stick. Any small pieces of cinnamon that fragmented off were placed into a Ziploc plastic bag. I would use them later in potpourri mixes to simmer on the stovetop when I wanted to scent the house.

Once the cupcakes were completely cooled, I added confectioners' sugar to the butter-and-cream-cheese mixture and beat until smooth. With vanilla and splashes of heavy cream added to the concoction, the frosting became spreadable and fluffier the longer it whipped. Once I was happy with the consistency, I piped swirls of the sweet spiced frosting onto the cupcakes. After I stuck the half pieces of cinnamon sticks into the tops, a fine dusting of chai-spice mix sprinkled on top completed the garnish.

I set three cupcakes aside for dessert and boxed the remaining up and placed them in the refrigerator. Frosting with cream cheese worried me if it sat out too long, so I liked to keep it refrigerated until a few hours before serving. I set a reminder on my phone to deliver the cupcakes to my sister first thing in the morning. Since I was required to be at the Skylers' residence at nine, Carrie would have to see that my client received the cupcakes before their luncheon started. It wouldn't be much of an inconvenience, since she was catering the event anyway.

TILLIE, Randall, and I had almost finished our dinner of seared scallops with a citrus-butter sauce when my phone chimed with a text from Marge. She was at the gate. I scurried out the front door and opened the security gate to find her standing with a brown paper bag clutched in her hand. Moths fluttered against the overhead lamps that shone in the dark night.

"Sorry I forgot to text you before. I was in a hurry to get out of there. The dragon lady and Mr. Skyler had one huge fight. She stomped out of there, and I hope she never comes back. But we probably won't be so lucky."

"I can't begin to imagine how awkward that must've been."

"I'll tell you about it another time." She handed the bag to me. "I wrapped it in paper towels to cushion it. I didn't want to risk breaking the glass. Do you think I can have it back? I don't want to be accused of stealing their crystal."

"No worries. I'll tell Brian to give it back just as soon as possible." I was curious about the argument between Mr. Skyler and his new wife. "Would you like to come in for a glass of wine or some dinner? I have a few scallops left."

"No thanks. I've got bridge this evening." She peered at me in the glare from the lights. "How did you get Mr. Skyler to stand up for you? That's what the argument was about."

My mother hadn't wasted any time in protecting me, but I wasn't about to spill her story about why she had that kind of sway with my boss. "My mother and Mr. Skyler go way back. If anyone can get him to listen to reason, it would be her. Besides, I'm sure he didn't know what Mrs. Skyler was up to, nor will he tolerate abusing employees the way she's been doing. Hopefully you'll find your working conditions better too."

"I hope you're right." She batted a moth away from her face. "I'm dead on my feet. I'll see you tomorrow."

Once she had driven away, I secured the gate and went back to the patio. I caught Tillie feeding Piper a morsel of scallop from her hand. I cleared my throat, which made Tillie jump. A whole scallop fell from the fork on her plate and onto the stone patio. It only took a microsecond for Piper to scarf it up.

Randall roared with laughter and poured wine into Tillie's glass. "I'm glad she caught you feeding Piper and not me. I'm still on probation."

"At this rate, you're both going to be on probation for a long, long time. You're spoiling her too much." I had worked hard to train Piper to not beg for food while we were eating, even though it was hard for me to tell her no myself.

"I can't refuse those big brown eyes." Tillie ruffled Piper's ears. "Did Marge bring the glass?"

I held up the paper bag. "Yep, and she said that Mr. Skyler was having a huge argument with She Who Must Not Be Named over her treatment of employees."

"Good. We can only hope he'll see the woman for what she is and get rid of her."

Randall had politely listened as Tillie and I discussed everything that had happened with Mrs. Skyler, even after we rehashed everything two or three times. I appreciated the concern and respect he showed to Tillie and that he didn't dismiss our issues. Instead, he offered some coping skills he had learned to deal with a multitude of unpleasant situations.

I had my doubts that Mr. Skyler would get rid of his new wife anytime soon, just as I had my doubts that Randall's coping exercises would help. But I didn't voice my concerns. Instead, I grabbed my phone and sent Brian a text telling him he could pick up the glass from Tillie. It didn't surprise me when my phone remained silent.

"I have to be at work at nine tomorrow, so I'll leave the glass with you, Tillie."

I began to clear the dinner dishes, but Randall put a hand on my shoulder and guided me back into my chair. "You cooked dinner, so I'll clean up."

I was a little flustered. "That's not necessary," I told him. "You're our guest. The kitchen's a wreck. You really don't need to do anything."

"I'm perfectly capable of washing dishes." He held up his wine goblet, the stem gripped between his long, tanned fingers. "I can even wash and dry delicate crystal without breaking anything."

I started to argue, but Tillie cut in. "Let the man show his appreciation, Em. I think it's his way of making sure he gets another invitation for dinner."

"You caught me." Randall winked at Tillie and expertly stacked the dirty plates and flatware. "Now, if you ladies will excuse me…"

Once he was out of sight, Tillie fanned her face with both hands. "That man is hot, hot, hot."

I couldn't disagree. I wanted desperately to grab a dish towel to dry the dripping dishes while I watched him wash. My ex never helped, even when we had dated.

"Drop Piper off here in the morning. She can stay with me until you get home." Hearing her name, Piper flopped onto her back, and Tillie complied by giving the dog a belly rub. "I don't think she should be left in your yard on her own until we find out who tried to poison her."

"Thanks. I was worried about that, since I won't be able to bring her to work with me." I mentally calculated what time I had to leave to drop the cupcakes off and get to work. It was too early, and I groaned. "I'll bring her over at seven thirty and leave some muffins and fruit salad for your breakfast. You don't need to get up that early."

She waved away my concerns. "We old people wake up at the crack of dawn. It'll give me a reason to get out of bed instead of lying there, texting my friends."

I thought of her latest date and hoped she wasn't doing anything more than texting. Her sexting escapade while walking—and falling—down her stairs a few months before had been what instigated my coming to live here. Her son thought her fall was due to being elderly and feeble. Besides Tillie and her beau, I was the only one who knew the truth, and her secret was safe with me.

After Randall finished cleaning up the dinner dishes, he gave Tillie a peck on the cheek and walked me to my pool house, Piper prancing alongside us. He gave me a toe-tingling kiss goodnight and headed home with the promise he would see me soon.

Before I crawled into bed, I took a half dozen strawberry muffins from the freezer and set them on the counter to defrost. I checked the fruit salad left over from that morning's breakfast and determined it was still fresh. Sleep didn't come easily, and when it did, it was fitful. I dreaded having to face the dragon lady the next day.

Chapter 25

I woke a few minutes after six thirty, just as it was getting light outside. I found two texts on my phone. One was from Brian, stating he would pick the glass up around ten. The other was from Marge, warning me that Mr. Skyler had caught an early-morning flight for the East Coast. I wondered how early Marge had to go to work, since her text came in at six thirty. It looked like we would have to face Mrs. Skyler without our boss providing a buffer. Unsure I would be allowed to have a cup of coffee from the Skylers' kitchen, I brewed a pot and downed a mug while getting ready. I filled a travel mug and poured the remaining coffee into a carafe that would keep it warm for Tillie.

I let Piper out into the yard and threw a ball for her to chase several times to give her some exercise. While I used to work a full day in an office, I had grown accustomed to setting my own pace and hours. I would need to readjust and fit in walks for my dog either before or after work. Once Piper was panting, I led her to Tillie's house across the alleyway and quietly let myself in. The alarm was already off, and Tillie was halfway down the stairs. Piper started to run up to greet her friend, but I held her collar tight. I didn't need her knocking Tillie off-balance and making her fall.

"Good morning." I held up a tote containing the muffins, fruit, and coffee carafe. "I'll put your breakfast in the kitchen."

"Thank you, dear." Once she reached the bottom of the stairs, she ruffled Piper's ears. "Do you have time to sit and eat with me this morning?"

"Not today. I have to drop the cupcakes off for Carrie." I opened the refrigerator and took out a container of orange juice and poured a glass for Tillie. "Until She Who Must Not Be Named settles into a routine, I'd better not be late for work."

"Brian sent me a text and said he would drop by around ten this morning. He'd like to talk to you about your half sister."

"I'll call him and see if we can meet for lunch sometime this week." I placed the bowl of fruit on the kitchen table along with two muffins. "Can I get you anything else before I leave? There are two extra muffins in the bag if Brian is hungry."

Tillie's laughter filled the air, and Piper looked up at her and tilted her head. "That boy is always hungry. It's a wonder he stays so trim."

"He spends a lot of time at the gym and surfs." I filled the water bowl and food dish that Tillie had bought to keep in her house for Piper. She spoiled my dog. We were both lucky in that way. I bent down and gave her a kiss on her cheek. "I've got to run. Call me if anything comes up. I might be able to use it as an excuse to get out of there early."

On my way back to my house to pick up the cupcakes, my phone dinged as a text came through. It was from Marge.

I'm shopping for lunch and dinner. Should be back in a couple hrs. I left office door unlocked. Don't tell her!

With a thumbs-up emoji sent, I headed to my sister's house.

Once there, I waited for her critique as she sampled one of the cupcakes—five stars. She refilled my travel mug with more coffee, and I made my way to Balboa Island. I was lucky to find parking reasonably close to the Skylers' house, since I was already five minutes late. Would I get another written warning? I scurried as fast as I could on the two-inch heels I had dug out from the back of my closet. The pantyhose made my legs itch, and I knew I would be sweating by the time I reached my desk.

Unaccustomed as I was to wearing heeled shoes, I ignored the view and instead watched where I put my feet as I climbed the stairs to my office. As promised, the door was unlocked, and the house alarm chirped when I opened it. I glanced at my watch. Seven minutes late now. The alarm had given my arrival away, so I couldn't lie and say I'd been there since nine sharp.

Papers and file folders littered my desktop, along with instructions, written in a feminine hand, on brightly colored sticky notes. I saw several loose pages ripped from catalogs, with large red Sharpie marks circling items and noting "order asap." Was I supposed to become her personal shopper? Did she expect me to use my own credit card? I didn't want to go find Mrs. Skyler to ask, since I wasn't sure what kind of protocol she expected.

Perspiration dotted my forehead, so I opened the office door for fresh air. I stepped out onto the balcony to admire the view while I caught my breath. I would never tire of it. My gaze swept around then stopped on the Skylers' pool. It looked like Mrs. Skyler was swimming—or floating. Face-down. Her blond hair circled around her head, and she wore a red bikini. I wondered what she found so interesting at the bottom of the pool.

After a couple of moments, my heart plummeted when I

realized she wasn't moving. I kicked off my shoes and ran down the stairs. Small pebbles dug into my feet, and I almost slipped on the wet concrete leading between the shrubbery and house to the pool area. It looked like their irrigation system had trickled all the way to the pool, and the incomprehensible thought that it was wasting water flitted across my mind.

I pushed the notion away as I came to the edge of the pool. Close up, I could see a long piece of white fabric floating close to Mrs. Skyler's head. She hadn't changed positions, so I was certain she was unconscious or even dead instead of practicing some weird water meditation or something. I plunged into the pool, gasping when the cold water hit my hot back.

Grateful she was close to the shallow end so I could stand, I rolled her over and tried to remember CPR instructions. Her unmoving eyes stared straight up, and her skin was ice-cold. She was beyond CPR. I pulled her toward the pool's edge and saw that the white fabric was a silk scarf tied firmly around her neck.

The sight of the scarf chilled me to my bones, and I shook uncontrollably. This was too much of a coincidence between Mandy's murder and now Mrs. Skyler's. *How does the killer know both victims? What could the connection be? Could it be a copycat murder?* A million questions were running through my mind. The details of the cause of death in Mandy's case hadn't been reported in the news yet, so a copycat wasn't likely.

After I pulled her body out of the pool, I tried to get into the house to call 911. The French doors leading out were all locked. I retraced my steps back to the office to retrieve my cell phone and went to open the security gate after reporting the emergency. It didn't take long for sirens to fill the air, and I led the EMTs to the pool area. The youngest medic, a man looking barely old enough to grow facial hair, bent down and checked for a pulse. He shook his head then straightened before stepping away from her body.

The oldest of the three men approached me. "I'm sorry, miss. There's nothing we can do. It looks like this is a matter for the police."

I was afraid of that. "Can you contact Detective O'Neill? He needs to be notified of Mrs. Skyler's death."

"I'll let the responding officer know." He turned away just as another siren split the air. "That should be the police. I'll go talk to them."

Between the shock of having found another body and the chill from the cold pool, I started to shiver. Another EMT—with a smattering of freckles across his nose—wrapped a silver Mylar blanket around my shoulders. My legs felt rubbery, and I sank onto one of the cushioned chaise lounges that were arranged around the pool deck.

Minutes later, several officers dressed in black uniforms with shiny gold badges arrived. The oldest officer, with a graying walrus-style mustache, made his way over to me. "Are you the one who found the body?"

I nodded, unable to speak because of my chattering teeth.

"Do you know the identity of the woman?"

I somehow squeaked out Barbara Skyler's name. I thought I heard the officer suck in a sharp lungful of air, but I wasn't sure, since my pounding heart was echoing in my ears.

"Can you tell me why you're at the Skyler residence?"

I squeezed my hands together and turned to look up at the officer. He towered above me, and I wished he would sit down. "I work here, along with Marge. She's the cook and house-keeper, but I think she's buying groceries right now."

"What time did you arrive this morning?"

I knew I would need to answer that question repeatedly, but I only wanted to talk to Detective O'Neill. "Is Detective O'Neill on his way? He's been investigating a death that occurred at Mrs. Matilda Skyler's residence last week. I think he'll want to interview me."

He looked a little put out with my passive-aggressive

request. But instead of asking me any further questions, he turned away and mumbled something into the radio that had been attached to his utility belt. A female voice squawked something back. I wondered if they'd had to take classes on how to decipher radio talk. He turned back to me. "He's en route. He'll be here in about five minutes."

"Thank you."

The officer left me and went to check the French doors. I watched as he donned gloves and tested each handle then determined they were all locked. I was puzzled. How had Mrs. Skyler gotten to the pool? She wouldn't have carried keys out there to lock the door behind her. Had the killer left through the house, or could they still be inside? I shivered. I needed to call Marge and Tillie, and OMG, who would tell Mr. Skyler his new bride was dead? Two wives killed in less than six months. I didn't want to be the one to make that call, but I didn't see Marge being the one to do it either. I shivered again. Maybe this house was cursed.

Detective O'Neill arrived shortly after. His calm demeanor settled me down a little, and my shaking subsided.

"Ms. Martinez, I'm sorry we're meeting under these circumstances again."

I was relieved he didn't call me a murder magnet. "Me too. I rarely work this early, and I wish I hadn't been the one to find her."

"There's a housekeeper who's usually here?"

"Yes. Marge. She sent me a text earlier this morning. She had errands to run."

"Do you know where Mr. Skyler is?"

"According to Marge, he caught an early-morning flight to the East Coast. But that's all the information I have." I thought for a moment and wondered if the trip was why the honeymoon had been cut short or if this was a last-minute trip after their argument the night before. Was that why Mrs.

Skyler hadn't gone with her husband? "Contact his assistant at his main office. She'll have his flight information."

"Can you think of any reason someone would want to kill Mrs. Skyler?" He stared at me for several moments, and I wanted to squirm. "Can you shed any light on her connection to Mandy Graber, given the method of the murders?"

There were about a million reasons someone might have wanted to kill Mrs. Skyler, but I couldn't bring myself to say that. Instead, I shook my head. "I'm not aware Mrs. Skyler knew Mandy."

"Are you sure? This is too much of a coincidence."

"I only met Mrs. Skyler last Friday. That was the first I'd heard Mr. Skyler was even seeing someone, let alone considering marriage. It was a shock to his entire family."

Detective O'Neill's sandy-red eyebrows shot upward. "Did any of his family members have reasons to resent his remarriage?"

Every single one of them was unhappy with his new marriage and hated his new wife. But that wasn't something I would share with the detective.

Chapter 26

I couldn't throw my employer's family to the wolves, so I tried to make light of what I knew. "Let's just say it was a sudden announcement. No one had been told he was even dating anyone."

He finally noticed I was sopping wet and had started to shiver again. "Give me the housekeeper's phone number and show me the security camera equipment before you go home and get warm. I'd hate for you to get sick after jumping in the pool."

I clicked through my contact list and sent a text to the detective with Marge's and Janelle's information. Then he followed me as I hobbled back to my office in tattered pantyhose and on bruised feet. I opened the door where the audio/video equipment was housed and brought up the video feed on the computer located in the room. Mr. Skyler's home was high tech, and everything ran through the electronics that lined the walls of the small room.

Mr. Skyler had twelve cameras positioned at various locations on the outside walls and entrances of his home, along with two on his seawall and two on his front security gate. The individual video-feed boxes were black. I tapped on the boxes that should have been recording the pool area, and while the screen showed the date and the time ticking away in the lower right-hand corner of the screen, the feed itself was black.

"This is odd. I can't get it to show the real-time feed." I clicked on other boxes, and the same thing happened. Everything was black.

"How long does it keep recorded video?"

"I think about three weeks for every camera."

"Can you pull up what recorded last night or early this morning?" Detective O'Neill hovered over my shoulder. He smelled of Irish Spring soap.

I didn't want to think about *my* scent after my dunk in the heavily chlorinated pool or what I looked like—a drowned rat, probably. I tucked a strand of sticky hair behind my ear while my other rested on the computer mouse. I opened the menu on the computer and clicked on the request to view recorded video for the pool and punched in the time for six that morning. Once it played, it was obvious nothing had recorded, even though the time stamp was still ticking away. I tried a few of the other cameras with the same results.

"See if it recorded yesterday morning."

I typed in the requested information, and again, the screens were all black with running time stamps. "This is so weird."

"Try last week."

I did as requested and was rewarded with twelve boxes of video showing Mr. Skyler's property. "I wonder what happened to the video from yesterday and today."

"It's apparent our murderer is tech savvy and had access to the house. I'll need the recordings sent to our tech specialists. Hopefully, they'll be able to figure this out." His manner turned curt, almost cold. "Who has access to this room?"

"But that means someone broke in… or are you insinuating it was an inside job?" I couldn't fathom Mr. Skyler strangling his young wife and then calmly catching a flight. "There has to be another explanation."

"I can't rule anything out yet. Is there anyone besides you, the housekeeper, and Mr. Skyler who can access this room?"

"No. Not that I'm aware of."

He put his hand on the doorknob of the equipment room. "I'll inspect the video cameras. Someone might have spray-painted the lens. But they'd still need a way to enter the property without being seen."

After shoving my shoes onto my bruised feet, I followed the detective to the front security gate, where the cameras were easier to see without a ladder. A cluster of crime scene technicians surrounded Detective O'Neill, and I joined the group.

"You can see where the black paint dripped onto the concrete below the camera." He pointed at a couple of minuscule dots below the recorder. "There's no reason anyone would have noticed them."

I strained my neck, trying to see the actual lens of the video camera. Sure enough, instead of shiny glass, an opaque black film covered the lens. There was nothing more I could do here. My body was chilled to the bone, so I headed to my car. Once I cranked on the heater, I sent Tillie a text, telling her I was on my way home and that I needed to talk to her and Brian together.

She sent a picture back of Brian mugging for the camera with a muffin stuffed in his mouth. I laughed then struggled to contain the overwhelming sadness that hit me. It was hard to be sorry that Mrs. Skyler wasn't around anymore to make everyone in Mr. Skyler's life miserable. However, no one deserved to have their life snuffed out, especially at such a young age. I would have rather found something in her past then convinced her to leave Newport Beach and find greener pastures elsewhere.

Once I had taken a hot shower, changed into dry clothes,

and brushed the knots from my tangled hair, I sent Marge a quick text.

Call me!

I didn't expect to hear from her anytime soon, but I felt terrible for not staying there to give her support as she dealt with the police and notified Mr. Skyler. She was going to have a long and difficult day. I walked over to Tillie's house and let myself in. Piper heard me and barreled down the long open hallway. When she reached me, she danced around my legs, begging for love. I scooped her up into my arms and almost staggered under her weight. She wasn't a little puppy anymore, and the thought made tears trickle down my cheeks. Piper licked their salty trails on my skin, and I hugged her close for comfort. After finding two bodies in such a short time, I was on an emotional roller coaster.

Tillie rounded the corner from the kitchen area. "There you are. I thought I heard you come in."

I sniffed and tried to control my voice. It squeaked. I swallowed hard and tried again. "Piper waylaid me."

She moved closer to me and looked at my tear-stained face. "What's wrong? Is it that woman? What did she do to you?"

"No… noth-nothing." I could barely get the words out. "I found her. She was floating in the pool. Dead."

Shock registered on Tillie's face. "What? You poor dear. Come in and let me get you a cup of tea with a drop of brandy."

Knowing Tillie, there would be more brandy than tea in the teacup. I put Piper down and obediently followed her. Brian was sitting at the small table, his laptop propped open in front of him. His green eyes sparkled, and he smiled up at me. When he saw my face, a deep frown replaced his smile. "What's wrong? It's that woman, isn't it?"

Before I could answer, Tillie chimed in. "Emory found her floating in the pool. She's dead."

"Whoa. What happened? How is my father taking the news?" Brian shook his head. "Two wives in just a few months. I hope he learns his lesson."

"Brian." Tillie's voice was harsh. "That's a terrible thing to say."

"He doesn't know yet," I said, my voice quiet and rusty. "He's on a flight for the East Coast."

Brian leaned toward me. "Is Marge at the house? How about that detective who's investigating Mandy's murder? Is he in charge?"

"Yes. At least, he showed up and asked me a lot of questions." No matter how nice Detective O'Neill seemed, I would have to be interrogated by him, in greater detail, about another murder victim. I didn't relish the thought. "Marge was out running errands when I found the body. I gave Detective O'Neill her cell number."

"How was she killed? Did she drown? Or was it murder?" Brian threw questions at me a mile a minute. "I'll bet someone killed that witch. She pissed everyone off."

"Let Emory calm down, kiddo. She doesn't need to rehash her experience right now." Tillie opened a cabinet and retrieved a bottle containing amber-colored liquid. She poured a generous dollop of her favorite brandy into two teacups then added hot tea. She placed the cup and saucer in front of me. "Drink up, and I'll make you another cup."

"Hey, where's mine?" Brian pointed at the bottle.

"You're driving and need to get to work." His grandmother's words scolded, but she had a playful look on her youthful face, thanks to the wonders of the best cosmetic surgeon in Newport Beach. "Would you like some tea?"

"Naw, I'm fine."

Her plastic work reminded me of something. "Brian, did your investigator ever find out Mrs. Skyler's real identity?"

Brian scratched his head. "Nope. I'm going to ask for a

refund. He was worthless. I think you dug up more on her than he did."

I turned to Tillie and laid my hand on hers. "Do you remember talking to Mrs. Dexter, how she said she knew something about Mrs. Skyler?"

"That's right. She did say something like that."

"We need to talk to her again. She or her husband is the connection between Mrs. Skyler and Mandy."

"Wait. What?" Brian was back in question mode. "Why do you think there's a connection between the two women?"

Oops. I wasn't sure the detective would want the method of murder to be public knowledge. Brian wasn't the most discreet person. I would share with Tillie once he left for work. "I can't say, except that it's a question Detective O'Neill asked me."

"Can't say or won't say?" Brian furrowed his brows together. "C'mon, Em. Spill it."

"I'm sure the detective will share what he knows when he contacts you. Basically, I answered a few questions, then he sent me home, since I was soaking wet and freezing."

Tillie's eyes widened. "You went in the pool? You poor dear."

"Why would you do that?" Brian looked puzzled.

I was pretty sure Brian—and especially his brother— would have just left her floating there. I wondered if either of them had an alibi for this morning. They both hated the woman more than anything, and Brian had a past history with Mandy. "I didn't know she was dead. She was facedown, and I was hoping I could pull her out and get her medical attention."

"Again, I have to ask: Why would you do that?"

"Brian, she was a human being and didn't deserve to die." I was shocked he would voice his lack of empathy. I had to consider that he, or his brother, might have it in them to get rid of their new stepmother. On the other hand, how did he know Marge wouldn't be there, or was it luck that she was gone?

"I'm sorry. You're right." His words might have sounded contrite, but his face couldn't hide his relief over the fact that Mrs. Skyler was dead.

"Surely the police will check the security cameras." Tillie stood up, retrieved the bottle of brandy, and brought it to the table. She poured another generous glug into my teacup. "You've got to be in shock, trying to save that woman."

"We checked the security video. Every feed shows nothing but black screens." I gulped and realized that probably made me a suspect now. "Someone spray-painted all the video lenses."

"So the killer premeditated the murder." Tillie poured hot tea into her cup then refilled mine.

"Detective O'Neill thinks it's an inside job." I stared out the large window and watched a seagull perch on the patio table. It was probably hoping to scavenge a missed morsel of food. "It looks like I'm a suspect again."

Chapter 27

"Surely not. You have all sorts of alibis for this morning." Tillie's eyes widened. "Don't you?"

"It all hinges on the time of death. Depending on when Mr. Skyler left for LAX, there's still a large window of time when I could have snuck down there and killed her." I made sure to catch both Brian's and Tillie's gazes. "Which I did not. I am one hundred percent innocent."

"We know you are, dear." Tillie nudged her grandson's arm. "Right, Brian?"

"Uh, yeah. Of course you're innocent. Again."

I glared at him. He didn't need to remind me that I had been arrested for the murder of my ex-best friend the summer before. It was a memory I would rather forget.

He lifted his designer watch and glanced down. "Look at the time. Restaurant duty calls, so I'd better be on my way."

When he stood up and took his leave, Tillie followed him to the front door. Piper raised her head and watched them for a moment then lowered it. She was too lazy to get up from where she was sprawled at my feet, and I was too mad to walk with him to the door. Why was Brian dredging up my past?

Was he trying to divert attention away from him or his brother?

Tillie startled me when she came up from behind and squeezed my shoulder. "Ignore my grandson," she said. "He didn't mean to imply you had anything to do with Barbara. He wants to cook lunch for us at his restaurant to apologize."

"That's nice of him." I gathered the empty teacups to wash and put away. I had a feeling his grandmother had shamed him into the invitation.

"Just leave the cups. Dorie's coming in and can clean up, since Brian needs us to be at the restaurant within the hour." She fluffed her hair. "I need to put on some lipstick, then I'll call Andrew to pick us up in about thirty minutes. You can tell me all about the connection between Mandy and Barbara on the way there."

I looked down at my sloppy sweatpants and T-shirt. "Guess I'd better change. I'd offer to drive us there, but the brandy hit me a little hard."

"That's understandable. You've had a rough morning." Tillie examined my face. "Are you up for going to lunch? I thought we might drop by Mrs. Dexter's house afterward."

"I'll be okay. It'll be a good distraction to help me not think about… you know…"

I collected Piper and headed for my pool house. While I dressed in a floral-print dress with an open-weave crocheted shrug, I considered how we could get Mrs. Dexter to let us into her home instead of slamming the door in our faces. Would a bouquet of flowers make her amiable? By the time I was sitting next to Tillie in the back of the town car, I was downright pessimistic. It was hopeless. I was sure Mrs. Dexter wouldn't give us even one second.

Tillie's voice intruded on my thoughts. "Are you sure you're up for this?"

"I'll be fine." I considered how to word my reservations without making Tillie share my pessimism. "Given how Mrs.

Dexter, uh, felt about us not helping her after our last visit, do you think she'll even open her door to us?"

"It pays to have a cadre of gossiping old ladies at one's beck and call." Tillie laughed, and there was a gleam in her eyes. "My sources tell me that Mr. and Mrs. Dexter have officially separated, and word is she's ready to throw him under the bus. No 'Stand by Your Man' for Shannon, if what I hear is true."

I perked up. "That's great. Oh, I mean it's too bad their marriage isn't working out, but don't you think she's put up with his womanizing far too long?"

"I more than agree. Now tell me why Detective Adonis thinks there's a connection between Mandy and Barbara."

We spent the rest of the drive discussing the coincidence of the white scarves and tossed around possible links between the two victims. I barely noticed the shops, the ocean, or the brush-covered hillside that rushed by as Andrew drove us toward Laguna Beach. It wasn't until the car stopped at the curb that I realized we had arrived at Oceana.

The restaurant was a stone-and-glass building that featured a unique mixture of contemporary and traditional architecture. The restaurant's name was etched in a swooping font on a rubbed-bronze sign, a stark contrast against the patina of the domed copper roof. If I were a tourist visiting Laguna Beach, I would want to eat there. It was elegant yet inviting, and the view of the ocean with Catalina Island in the distance must have rocketed Brian's rent to the stratosphere. He was starting to get good reviews online too. I had checked while getting dressed. The lobster mac and cheese had received rave remarks, and I hoped that was what he had planned for our lunch.

The restaurant only served dinner, so Brian must have been watching for us. As soon as we stepped up to the mahogany-stained French door entrance, he ushered us inside.

I noticed he locked the doors before he followed us to the maître d' station.

"Do mademoiselles have a reservation? This is an exclusive dining establishment and not for riffraff off the street." Brian rested his arm on the mahogany wood counter and lifted his nose in the air to peer down at us. His fake French accent gave me the giggles.

Tillie rattled something off in French then tweaked her grandson's nose. "You always liked putting on airs."

"*Oui*, madame. If you will follow me, I will show you to your table." He extended his elbow so his grandmother could thread her arm through his.

Relieved to see that Brian appeared to be out of his funk, I followed behind the pair. Perhaps I had been too sensitive about his earlier remarks. He led us to a table topped with a crisp white linen tablecloth. A carafe of chilled water waited for us, and a perfectly formed blue hydrangea bloom floated in a shallow bowl. To the side of the table, a stand held a silver bucket with a bottle of chardonnay sitting on ice. The vintage was from a delightful winery in Temecula, a short distance east of us. Our table had a perfect view of the ocean and a boat, its sail unfurled, tacked in the distance.

After pouring us each a generous glass of the chilled chardonnay, Brian went back to the kitchen. Within minutes he brought out three portions of seared scallops with a browned butter sauce. They had been garnished with bits of crispy bacon and fresh chives. Served on scallop half shells, the taupe and pink hues of the shells contrasted nicely with the deeply browned shellfish.

I could have eaten far more than the three rich and succulent scallops served, but the main course would be on the table soon, and I needed to save room.

"Sweetheart, I am so proud of you." Tillie gestured around the room and then to her one remaining scallop. "Not only is your restaurant *fantastique*, but your food is utterly *savoureux*."

"I agree. This is perfection." I smiled at Brian and lifted my wineglass. "Thank you for treating us to the best restaurant in Orange County—no, make that the best restaurant in California and soon to be in the US."

"Thank you." He clinked his glass to mine and to Tillie's. "It means the world to me that you think so. Now, if you'll excuse me, I'll bring out our salads."

I raised my eyebrows and wondered how I would be able to function after such a huge lunch and a couple glasses of wine. Shannon Dexter might have to wait.

Brian placed delicately etched glass plates in front of us and explained that the salad contained vine-ripened tomatoes topped with fresh mozzarclla di Bufala and tender basil leaves from his business partner's herb garden. Barrel-aged balsamic vinegar and virgin olive oil created an artistic pattern around the edges of the plate. He also explained that the goal of Oceana was to source most of their produce and seafood locally, if at all possible, or at least within the state of California.

"You must spend a lot of time researching where to buy the freshest ingredients." I placed a forkful of the tomato and cheese in my mouth. I thought I might have moaned a little, and my eyes rolled back in my head. The combination of sweet, juicy tomatoes mixed with the richness of the creamy cheese was heavenly.

He laughed. "That's part of the fun of the restaurant. Actually, we had most of our vendors set up before we even opened the doors. We needed to have all the ingredients for our set menu. Of course, we look for items we can use for specials, like a new harvest of fava beans or if a boat has a fresh catch of halibut or yellowtail. One of us makes it down to the docks first thing each morning to buy the freshest seafood possible."

By the time I had polished off a large ramekin of his famous lobster mac and cheese and then split an enormous helping of spiced pear crisp with a scoop of homemade vanilla bean ice cream with Tillie, I had practically swooned. We couldn't help but gush over the decadent meal, and the more we gushed, the bigger Brian's smile grew. I was glad we had allowed him to show off his talented chef skills.

When I said as much, he scowled. "I wish Dad and Theodore would accept that this is where I belong. They both point-blank refuse to even consider eating here and instead tell me it'll fail, so I might as well give up now. All they talk about are the statistics of unsuccessful restaurants."

"I'll have a word with them both," Tillie said. "They'll listen to me." I knew that if anyone could change their minds, it would be the matriarch of the family.

"Now that the witch is out of the picture, I'm sure they'll both come around." Brian rubbed his jawline. "She was hounding him to pull the loan he gave me to get started, even though twenty grand is pretty paltry in the grand scheme of things. I'll bet she spent more than that on handbags and shoes in the short time they were married."

Once Tillie and I were back in the car, Andrew headed to Shannon Dexter's house. I remained quiet while I thought about Brian's anger toward Mrs. Skyler and the reasons he had for wanting her out of the picture. He also had access to his father's home and would have known how to get around the video monitoring system. I wondered if he had disappeared for any time during the costume party, but I couldn't remember. I couldn't quite picture him as the murderer, nor did I want him to be. It would break Tillie's heart. I hoped Shannon would have some answers for us.

After stopping to pick up a bouquet, we arrived at the Dexter residence. Tillie reassured me that Shannon had kicked her husband out, so we didn't have to worry about a confrontation with him. I expected for her to slam the door in our faces the second she saw us, but instead, Shannon gushed over the flowers and pulled us into her sitting room, where she popped open a bottle of champagne and filled flutes for all three of us. I would need a nap after my day of drinking and extravagant eating.

Once we all held a filled crystal flute, Shannon toasted us. "Here's to justice being served."

I glanced at Tillie, who shrugged and tilted the glass to her fuchsia lips. After taking a sip, I set the flute down on the glass-topped coffee table. "We're sorry to intrude, Mrs. Dexter—"

She cut me off with a wave of her hand. "Call me Shannon. I'm done with that horrible last name, and I'll change back to my maiden name as soon as the divorce is final. Dexter always made me think of that serial killer show on cable TV."

I shuddered. She was right. Now I, too, would always think of the dark horror-drama every time I heard Senator Dexter's name. Not a good connotation for an elected official.

Tillie lifted her glass of bubbly to Shannon. "We came to offer our condolences, but perhaps it should be our congratulations. You're positively glowing."

She was glowing, and I had to wonder if the soon-to-be ex-Mrs. Dexter had visited a good esthetician or had had a little nonsurgical work done on her face. It wouldn't surprise me if she was back in the dating circuit sooner rather than later.

"Thank you." She clinked her glass to Tillie's. "Guilt can be a wonderful thing, and the senator is seeing our divorce settlement from my point of view."

I sat upright. Guilt? *What is she talking about? Could the senator be a murderer?*

Chapter 28

"Oh, do tell." Tillie practically purred as she refilled Shannon's glass with fresh bubbly. My tipsy head was grateful she didn't add any to ours.

"He's passed himself off as a harmless flirt, but I have actual proof he has had several mistresses and flings since the day before we married." Shannon's lips pursed into a pout, then she drained the glass of champagne. "He started with my maid of honor the night of our rehearsal. The pig."

"You poor dear," Tillie murmured in a soothing tone. She put the champagne bottle back in the bucket of ice after topping off Shannon's glass again.

"That was only the beginning. He made his way through all my bridesmaids within the first year of our marriage." She took a gulp of the chilled beverage. "I don't get what they saw in my husband. Why would they want to sleep with him?"

I choked on the sip of champagne I had just taken. I covered my mouth and tried not to cough.

"Just look at him. He's old and balding. Why would they take him to bed?"

My eyes watered as I tried to keep my coughing at bay. I didn't want to disrupt Shannon's rant. I couldn't help but notice the irony in that she had married the much-older man and must have slept with him, yet she considered him undesirable. Why would she marry him in the first place? I glanced around the room and then at the huge glittering diamonds resting on her earlobes and on her hand. *Ah. Money.* That would explain her motivation but didn't explain the women who had participated in the affairs.

"A powerful man is a huge attraction for some women." Tillie shook her head. "There are too many men willing to take advantage of their position to take what they want. I hope you're well compensated for his betrayals."

"I'll never have to worry about money for the rest of my life." She slumped over on the overstuffed couch and rested her head in her hands.

I wondered if she had been "celebrating" before we arrived. It would explain her demeanor. "Shannon, can you tell us about Barbara Skyler?"

"That witch. She tried to get my husband to dump me." Shannon's words had started to slur.

"You mean she was another one of his conquests?"

"Nope. She's his daughter."

My mouth gaped. I looked at Tillie, whose mouth was wide open too. I snapped my lips together and rubbed my temples. The brandy, wine from lunch, and now the champagne were slowing down my thought process. I was sure I had misunderstood.

"Did you say 'daughter'? How? Did you know about her?"

"Apparently, her mommy had a fling with him—obviously way before my time— and decided a few months ago that it was time for his offspring to collect some of his wealth. He claims he knew nothing about her before she showed up."

"Did she provide any proof?" Tillie put her half-filled flute onto the tabletop.

"She had old photos of her mother and Zach." Shannon scowled and took a gulp of champagne. "He took one look at

Barbara and jumped at the chance to take a DNA test. The idiot."

"And it proved that he was her father?" I tried to direct the conversation so we could get to the important facts faster. The champagne might not have been a good idea.

"Yes. He was happier than I'd ever seen him." Shannon refilled her glass to the brim. "At least, he was happy until she demanded money and threatened to blackmail him over all the women he'd had affairs with. She even had the nerve to demand he divorce me. I guess she wanted his entire fortune and didn't want to share."

"So, Mrs. Skyler knew about Zach's affair with Mandy?" Here was the connection I had been looking for. Mandy and Mrs. Skyler were both blackmailing Senator Dexter. Could he have turned into a serial killer? Maybe. But I wasn't sure he could murder his only child.

"Definitely yes. Those two women were like peas in a pod. Greedy little bloodsuckers, the both of them, and they wanted to take the money I deserved." The bitterness in Shannon's voice made me think she might be capable of murder and would have no qualms about killing her stepdaughter.

"How did Barbara get her hooks into my son?" Tillie didn't sugarcoat it now that her detested daughter-in-law had been exposed.

"You can thank Zach for that. She told her father she wanted a wealthy husband, so he arranged for her to meet David at a fundraiser in London last spring. Zach thought it was better to encourage their romance away from Newport Beach and away from David's wife." Shannon snorted. "He thought if he helped her land someone rich, she'd stop demanding money from him. Instead, her demands increased."

I was reminded of the fake driver's license I had found in Barbara's purse. "Did you know that she was going by the name Benicia Morray in New York?"

Shannon waved her hand in the air as if shooing away a pesky insect. "I don't know about that particular name, but she was a grifter. It wouldn't surprise me if she had a stash of aliases for future marks."

This was getting worse and worse. We would never find the real killer, since too many people wanted those two women dead. It was time to let Detective O'Neill know what we'd found and let him take it from there. With Mrs. Skyler's death and the revelation about the senator and his daughter, there was enough reasonable doubt to prove my brother-in-law's innocence.

We helped a very tipsy Shannon to her bedroom and covered her with her silk duvet. I left a bottle of water on her nightstand along with a bottle of aspirin I found in her bathroom drawer. She would need it when the champagne wore off. She may have said she was celebrating, but beneath it all, I knew she was mourning the betrayal and her failed marriage. It wasn't an easy thing to go through... I had experienced it myself. Although in my case, instead of being left fabulously wealthy by a cheating husband, I had been taken to the brink of bankruptcy.

I grabbed two more bottles of water from Shannon's refrigerator then led a slightly tipsy Tillie to the waiting town car. I had just buckled myself in when I heard a text come through on my phone. It was from Marge.

Just finished answering questions and closed up house. Mr Skyler notified by detective. He's flying home tonite. Can u come to house tomorrow am? Not early.

I thumbed a reply.

I'll come at 10. Narrowing down suspects. Hope 2 have answers soon!

I wasn't sure why I told her that, but I didn't want her to worry that nothing was being done with a killer on the loose. She would also want to reassure Mr. Skyler that the murderer would be found, and I hoped this gave her some confidence. I passed along the news to Tillie that her son would return home later that night.

"I may not have liked Barbara, but this will devastate David. No one should have to bury two wives a few months apart, no matter how awful they were." She looked grim. "I'll come with you tomorrow morning."

I felt like a lightning bolt had seared my brain. "OMG! Do you think there's any connection between the new Mrs. Skyler and his last wife? Do you think she was a murder victim? As far as I know, they never found who ran her down."

"Katrina? Wife number three?"

"Yes. I couldn't remember her first name." I hated to admit that most people had called her Trophy Wife Number Three or, if they had to, Mrs. Skyler.

Tillie pursed her lips together. "Maybe. Although the investigators never said they suspected foul play. They assumed it was a drunk driver who freaked out and left the scene."

From what I remembered from news reports, Katrina had been jogging after dusk, headed for the beach. She had cut through an empty parking lot when a speeding pickup truck struck her down and kept going. Security cameras caught the accident, but the late-model truck had no license plates, and the tinted windows were so dark, the driver wasn't visible. If Katrina's death was a murder, then there was a serial killer on the loose.

As soon as we arrived home, Tillie entered her home to take a nap, and I went to let Piper out into my yard. I sent Randall a quick text about the murder. Within moments he called me. I was warmed by his concern, and although his job had taken him back to San Francisco that morning, he said he would try to get home that evening to be with me. Somehow, knowing he cared reassured me.

After we disconnected, I threw a ball for Piper to chase.

While I waited for her to bring it back to me, I sent Detective O'Neill a text asking him to call me. I didn't receive a response. My arm gave out long before Piper's energy was used up. I collected my iPad and a huge glass of iced water and settled onto a cushy patio chair.

I opened the Notes app and listed the details of what Tillie and I had learned that day. My head spun with the multitude of facts and conjectures I had listed. I hoped the detective could use some of it to get to the bottom of the killings. I chided myself for trying to make it even more complicated by bringing Katrina's death into the equation. However, it seemed like a very suspicious coincidence.

Just as the last rays of the evening sun sank behind the beach fog that started to roll in from the ocean, Tillie sent me a text to let me know she was going out to dinner with a friend and to not worry about her. Within moments, I got a text from Randall telling me he was stuck in meetings and wouldn't return from San Francisco until the following evening. Over dinner with Tillie the previous night, he had explained his partnership in the expanding security firm to us. He was in charge of opening a San Francisco branch and hiring and training new personnel. Once it was up and running, he wouldn't need to spend so much time away from home.

With a quiet evening ahead of me, I mixed up several types of cookie dough to stash in the freezer for last-minute dessert needs. I also experimented with a whole-grain low-fat fruit muffin recipe. The results were okay, but I needed to tweak it before I let my sister critique it. I made notes on my recipe printout to try mini chocolate chips and crunchy pecans the next time I made it. Once the muffins cooled, I wrapped them individually in plastic wrap, placed them in a freezer-safe Ziploc bag, and stashed them in the freezer. I would eat them for breakfast when I was in a rush.

. . .

AT TEN THE NEXT MORNING, I dropped Tillie off at her son's front security gate and drove around the corner to find a parking space. She had been quiet on the drive, and I assumed she was as nervous about facing Mr. Skyler's grief as I was. As I scanned the passing curbs for a space large enough for me to parallel park, I saw Detective O'Neill walking toward the house. The beach fog had burned off early, and it promised to be another warm day. Despite the forecasted heat, he was dressed in pressed black slacks, a baby-blue long-sleeved buttoned-down shirt, and a necktie. He had a suit jacket draped over his bent left arm.

He still hadn't responded to my text from the day before, and I chided myself for not bringing my iPad with the notes I made earlier. Theoretically, I should be able to access the notes via the iCloud, but the reality was I could never quite get a grasp on getting it to work. I had always relied on my ex-husband for stuff like that, and so far, I hadn't caught up with the learning curve of doing it on my own.

He must have noticed me cruising by, because he stopped and pointed at an empty parking space twenty feet behind him. In my opinion, a smart car might have fit in the tiny opening between two Range Rover SUVs, but there was no way I could get my Honda to fit in the space. I shook my head and prepared to keep trolling for a spot.

Detective O'Neill turned and walked after me, raising his voice loud enough for me to hear over my radio. "Stop! We need to talk."

I edged closer to the line of parallel parked cars and came to a stop before I rolled down the passenger-side window. "I'm looking for a parking space, then I'll meet you at the house."

He pointed toward the tiny scrap of curb ahead of me. "What's wrong with this space?"

"That's not enough room for my car to fit." I prepared to put my car back into drive and take up the hunt. "Don't let me keep you. I'll meet with you at the house."

He shook his head. "There's more than enough room for your car. Are you trying to avoid me?"

"Not at all, which is why I asked you to call me yesterday."

"You can't parallel park, can you." It was a statement, not a question.

"Of course I can." My face warmed. "As long as the space is big enough."

He roared with laughter. "Get out and I'll park for you."

"I'm absolutely sure that space is way too small." I would be humiliated if he could park my car and, if he couldn't, I didn't want to be liable for him denting or scratching either of the two expensive vehicles bookending the space.

"Betcha five bucks it's big enough." The twinkle in his amber-colored eyes was irresistible. No wonder Brad was smitten.

"Fine, give it a try. But I'm not a money-betting type of person." My ex's gambling addiction had almost pushed us into bankruptcy, so I tried to avoid any semblance of it. I unbuckled my seat belt and got out of my car. "How about a cup of coffee instead of cash?"

"You're on." He sat behind my steering wheel and moved the seat back to accommodate his long legs. "Stand back and watch how an expert does it."

I moved up onto the sidewalk and watched him crank my steering wheel a couple times then ease into the space. I hated to admit it, but he was right. There had been more than enough space.

"Show-off," I muttered when he tossed my car keys to me.

"I believe the lady owes me a cup of coffee." He flashed a smile. "And I won't even be in interrogation mode when you pay up."

Chapter 29

While we walked to the Skylers' house, I told Detective O'Neill everything Tillie and I had found out since I last talked to Brad. Mrs. Skyler's fake driver's license intrigued him, along with the details of our chat with Shannon Dexter the day before. I mentioned my crazy theory that perhaps Katrina Skyler was a murder victim too. I expected him to scoff at all my speculations, but he listened and asked probing questions. Well, he might have bawled me out first for snooping and then not telling him about the driver's license right away. He was especially miffed I hadn't given the license information to him but had instead passed it on to Brian's private investigator.

After we entered the house, I gave Marge a hug. "How is Mr. Skyler doing?"

She shrugged. "As good as expected, I suppose."

"How about you? Are you okay?"

"I'll be fine." She glanced at the tall man at my side. "Detective O'Neill, I can take you to see Mr. Skyler now. He's expecting you."

"Thank you." Before he followed Marge, he turned back

to me. "I'll need a formal statement from you. Can we meet in a while?"

"Sure. You can find me in my office."

After they headed up the stairs toward Mr. Skyler's personal office, I walked into the kitchen and made myself a barista-style latte using their high-end espresso machine. I had to admit it was a little too easy to drink too much caffeine when I worked at the Skyler residence because the coffee was so good. Plus, Marge indulged my sweet tooth whenever we worked at the same time. She had spoiled me before the new Mrs. Skyler had come along.

When Marge didn't return to the kitchen, I wandered up to my office to go through the mail that had accumulated. I was tempted to tiptoe down the hallway and try to listen to the conversation between the detective and Mr. Skyler, but I couldn't risk getting caught. Instead, I would have to rely on Tillie filling me in. I assumed that was where she was, because I hadn't seen her since I arrived.

With the mail opened and divided into piles according to priority, I wrote checks to pay the bills. Marge poked her head into my office. "Got a minute?"

"Sure." I motioned for her to take a seat on one of the padded chairs. "Is Tillie in with Mr. Skyler and the detective?"

"Yes. I listened at the door for as long as I could but then decided I didn't want to get caught."

"Did you find out anything interesting? Does Mr. Skyler have any ideas why his wife was killed?"

"I think the question is who didn't want to murder that witch?" Marge's face turned red, and her hands clenched.

I didn't think that was helpful, since everyone who'd met Mrs. Skyler seemed to have wanted to kill her—myself included. I was too impatient to wait until Tillie could fill me in. "But did you hear anything that will move the investigation forward?"

"If David hadn't come up with a concrete alibi, he would be suspect number one." Marge narrowed her eyes. "That detective has a lot of nerve coming in here and accusing him. So what if the time of death was around midnight and not yesterday morning like they thought? He's still innocent."

I doubted Detective O'Neill had accused Mr. Skyler of anything, but I also thought the questions he asked were probably leading. "Tell me about his alibi. His flight left early morning yesterday? How would that clear him if she died around midnight?"

She leaned toward me and lowered her voice. "David and Barbara got into a huge argument that last night at dinner. The kind where one of the participants is screaming and throwing dinnerware."

I gasped. I hadn't known the argument had been so intense. "That had to have been Mrs. Skyler."

"David just sat there like a king on his throne, not saying a word. It made her even angrier. I think she broke at least two glasses and three plates."

"I remember you telling me about the argument but not the details." My eyes opened wide as I considered the implications of such a fight. "What did you do?"

"I hid out in the kitchen when I first heard her scream at him, but when the dinnerware starting crashing on the floor, I barricaded myself in the pantry."

"OMG." I shook my head. "How awkward."

"When she clomped away on her high heels and slammed out the front door, I went into the dining room to clean up the mess." Marge sat up straight in her chair but still kept her voice low. "Mr. Skyler was still sitting there, but he looked furious. He was on the phone with his driver, requesting a ride to LAX immediately. I guess he spent the night up in LA before his flight this morning."

"Did he say anything to you?"

"He said thank you for dealing with her and that I'd be

getting a raise for hazardous duty just as soon as he returned."

"Honestly, I don't think there's enough money in the world to make it worthwhile to work for her."

"I'm devoted to David and his family, and it's my job to take care of them. Someone like her, or the last wife, can't scare me away."

I wasn't too sure about that. I had wanted to run after my short time in Mrs. Skyler's presence. "What happened next? Did she come back before you left for the day?"

"No. I left around eight to bring you the wineglass. I never saw her again."

We both heard voices coming from the master-suite wing, so Marge scurried out of my office. I busied myself by writing checks and pretending I hadn't just been gossiping.

Tillie poked her head through the doorway. "What a mess. I'm sure Marge gave you the overview?"

"What? Um, no?" I wasn't about to let the Skyler family know Marge had eavesdropped on them.

Tillie laughed. "Of course she did. That woman knows everything that goes on in this house. If I didn't know better, I'd suspect she bugged the rooms to listen in."

I smiled. "Okay, maybe she gave me a little information of what happened while she was here that last night. But she didn't stick around long enough to find out everything the detective was saying. Anything new come up?"

"Just the time of death was closer to midnight. Thankfully, David was up in LA, so he has an ironclad alibi."

I had thought Mr. Skyler was innocent, yet part of me wondered if he could have hired someone to strangle the mercenary Mrs. Skyler. "This is so frustrating. There are too many people who wanted both Mandy and Mrs. Skyler dead. I guess there could be two different killers, but somehow they're connected, and I haven't worked it out yet."

"These things take time. We'll figure it out."

A deep voice cut through the quiet space of my office. "No, you won't be figuring it out. That's my job."

Tillie turned to look down the hallway. "Hello again, Detective O'Neill. Are you coming to see our Emory?"

He strode into my office, his presence seeming large in the small space. "I want to talk to you both. Can you close the door behind you, Mrs. Skyler, and have a seat?"

She did as asked. In the bright sunlight streaming into the office, Tillie's face looked more lined and fatigued than I had ever seen. Her normally sparkling eyes were rimmed with red, and it looked like she had chewed off her usual layer of lipstick. While there was no love lost between Tillie and her daughter-in-law, she must have been concerned for her son.

Once he had our full attention, the detective cleared his throat. "You've both come up with some good leads. While grateful, I need to ask that you stop asking questions. You've already been warned by the killer once, and I can't risk my conscience, or my job, by allowing you to be in the position of getting hurt… or worse."

"We've only been chatting with people we know," said Tillie, who thrived being in the center of things and puzzling out clues. "We're not putting ourselves in danger."

"Someone you know—and might even trust—is the murderer." The detective allowed his gaze to linger on each of us and waited for the weight of his words to sink in. "If you chat with the wrong person one too many times, you'll pay the consequences."

Tillie broke eye contact with the detective and turned toward me. "I guess he has a point. I'd hate to trigger something that might hurt you, Em."

While I wanted answers, I reminded myself that my brother-in-law was in the clear. Proving his innocence had been my goal all along. "Can you answer one question for me? Is Thomas still a suspect?"

"Let's just say he has moved down to the bottom of the list."

"So he's still a consideration?"

Detective O'Neill nodded. "Everyone is a consideration until the perpetrator is apprehended."

"So you consider me a suspect?"

"Yes, but not a likely one." He leaned in toward the two of us. "Now, ladies, do I have your promise to stop putting yourself at risk by interrogating potential murderers?"

I didn't want to promise, but I didn't want to get into a debate with him either. Tillie reached over to place her hand in mine. I could feel her index and middle fingers crossing each other.

"We'll be on our best behavior, Detective, and won't meddle in your investigation anymore." Tillie's eyes regained some of their sparkle. "But what should we do if someone comes to us with information or has gossip they want to share?"

"Please send them my way." He pulled out his wallet and extracted several business cards. "You can give anyone with information my card. It has my direct phone number on it."

"Some people don't want to talk to the police," Tillie said, pressing her point. "In fact, they'd rather sit on information than have to deal with law enforcement."

"Please use your best judgment. I'm sure most people, aside from criminals, won't have a problem talking to me." Detective O'Neill pointed a finger at me. "Now, if you'll excuse us, Mrs. Skyler, I'd like to have a word with Ms. Martinez alone."

As Tillie stood up, I could hear soft footsteps moving away from the office door and down the hallway. No doubt Marge had been listening in again. "I'll send you a text when I wrap things up here, and I'll drive you home, Tillie."

"No rush. I need to have a long chat with my son."

I wouldn't have wanted to be in Mr. Skyler's shoes right

now. He had twice, in a short period of time, put Tillie's independence in jeopardy because of the women he married.

Once my office door closed, Detective O'Neill loosened his tie, opened a recording app on his cell phone, and settled back into his chair. "Now, Emory, why don't we go over everything you told me this morning so I can record it."

An hour and a half later, my mouth was dry, and my throat was hoarse. The detective took me backward and forward over every interaction and conversation I'd had with anyone and everyone over the preceding week. I was exhausted. As soon as he left to talk to Marge again, I finished paying the bills. Next, I chucked the stacks of catalogs Mrs. Skyler had marked up into the trash then sent Tillie a text saying I was ready whenever she was. She responded she was in the kitchen drinking coffee.

Tillie was placing her coffee cup in the dishwasher as I walked into the kitchen. Marge was nowhere to be seen. "She's in the dining room with Detective Hottie," she said.

"Shh. You don't want him to hear you say that."

"I'm sure he's heard that and more." Tillie showed me her crossed fingers. "Clever, huh? My promise for both of us doesn't mean a thing now."

I was glad to see her acting more like her old self, but I hesitated to put my friend in any danger by snooping further. "I think Detective O'Neill has a good point. We don't need to risk ourselves now that Thomas seems to be in the clear. Besides, he appears to be a very conscientious investigator, unlike the last one we dealt with."

"We can't just stand by and not do something after all we've found out. Where's the fun in that?" Tillie lifted her thumb to her lip and stuck out her pinkie, as if taking a drink. "Besides, can you see someone like Shannon Dexter getting drunk and spilling her secrets to a detective? She wouldn't, so he needs to admit we're invaluable to the investigation."

"Okay, you've convinced me." I dangled my car keys. "Are

you ready to go home, or do you need to speak with Mr. Skyler before we leave?"

"I don't know why you won't call him David. You shouldn't be so formal." Tillie *tsk*ed her tongue against her teeth. "He has an appointment with his attorney and publicist. They're trying to contain this godawful scandal."

Chapter 30

Instead of driving straight home, we stopped off for a late lunch at one of the bayside fresh-fish restaurants. We both ordered salads topped with grilled salmon, and we both stuck to water. I felt like I'd been overcaffeinated and over-liquored the last few days, and it wouldn't surprise me if Tillie felt the same. Instead of rehashing the murder and all the suspects—which, to be honest, was making me feel crazy —we talked about upcoming Thanksgiving plans instead.

Tillie was heading to Hawaii for an interisland cruise with her bridge club, and I would spend the holiday with my family. Carrie planned to host the turkey dinner this year, and I would supply the dessert. Our mother was in charge of the bubbly and wine. I wondered whether Randall would stay in town or fly back east to spend it with his family. Tillie also helped me brainstorm cupcake flavors for the Christmas season so I could develop new recipes before the holidays arrived.

I had planned on going home and working on my new cupcake recipes, but my phone buzzed with a reminder that Piper had a grooming appointment that afternoon. It also buzzed with a text from one of my sister's friends, asking if I was able to provide two dozen lemon cupcakes for her work party the following day. I sent a quick reply that I would drop them off at nine the following morning. All I needed was her address and credit card number.

After seeing Tillie safely to her door, I loaded Piper into the car and headed for the groomer. My dog enjoyed her doggy-spa times, since the groomer pampered the pets, gave them organic client-approved treats, and allowed the dogs to play together in a safe environment. Piper probably got a little lonely being by herself, especially when I had to work away from home. I wondered if I should adopt another rescue dog, since Piper seemed to enjoy socializing. With the holiday season ahead of me, I pushed the thought away and decided to wait to make a decision. I already had a large collection of cupcake orders scheduled for the month of December. I wouldn't have time to train a new puppy.

Once Piper was happily romping around with a beagle at the doggy-spa center, I headed to the grocery store for fresh lemons for the cupcakes. My plan to make fresh lemon curd to pipe into the centers of the cupcakes and top with swirls of lemon buttercream made my mouth water. I also loaded up on fresh veggies and a halibut steak that Tillie and I could share for dinner. The deli's samples of scalloped potatoes tempted me, but my waistband felt tighter than usual, so I steered clear. I blamed it on the stress of the murders instead of all the extra cocktails and cupcakes I'd been consuming lately. I thought I'd better schedule an extra-long walk with Piper after her grooming session.

Tillie left a message on the kitchen countertop saying she was going to the movies with friends and wouldn't be home for dinner. I shook my head as I considered Tillie's active social life compared to my quiet one. I put the halibut on ice and stored it in the coldest part of the refrigerator. If Randall flew back early enough, I would prepare it for the both of us. Otherwise, it would keep for the next night's dinner, and I'd make do with a simple salad, sans croutons or bread.

I had just taken the cupcakes out of the oven when I received a text from Marge.

Can I drop by in approx. 30 min?

I sent a text back saying it was fine and to ring the bell at Tillie's gate. Typically, I'd leave the security gate unlocked if someone planned to come by, but given the recent circumstances, I thought I'd better keep it locked. While I stirred the lemon curd until it thickened on the stovetop, I wondered why Marge had requested to stop by. It was out of character, but I supposed it might be because she didn't want anyone to overhear whatever tidbit she had to tell me. *Couldn't she have called and talked to me when she was away from the Skyler residence instead?*

With both cupcakes and lemon curd cooling, I went to work on the lemon buttercream frosting. While I had put lots of lemon zest into the cupcakes, I preferred a smooth, texture-free buttercream, so I avoided using zest. To ramp up the lemon flavor in the frosting, I added a few drops of lemon oil in addition to the fresh-strained juice. The flavor of the oil was stronger and purer than extract, and a little went a long way. I sampled a few swipes of frosting and adjusted the flavoring until it reached the perfect tart-to-sweet ratio. I loaded half the buttercream into a large pastry bag fitted with an oversize star tip then covered the bowl containing the remaining buttercream with plastic wrap. The cupcakes and curd needed to be completely cool before frosting. Otherwise, I would have puddles of melted buttercream on my hands.

The gate bell chimed, and I used the intercom system to tell Marge to push open the gate once I buzzed her in. I met her at the front door and ushered her into the kitchen, where she plopped into a chair. "Can I offer you a cup of coffee?"

Marge looked frazzled, and she clutched her large patchwork-quilted handbag to her chest. She clasped her hands tightly in front of the handbag then rubbed them together a few times before clasping them together again. "Do you have some herbal tea? I think I've had too much coffee today."

"Sure. I'll fix a mug." I busied myself with the kettle and found the box of assorted herbal teas. "Can I offer you a warm lemon cupcake with a smear of fresh lemon curd? They're still too hot to add the buttercream frosting, but I think they'll taste fine without it."

"Thank you. That sounds lovely." Marge got up from her seat and walked over to the French doors, gazing at the view of the bay. She appeared mesmerized by the sailboats floating by.

I placed two piping-hot mugs of water on the table along with the box of herbal teas and a small jar of honey. She could choose which tea bag to use and sweeten her tea as she pleased. I plated two warm cupcakes—I always made extras and cut them open before placing a dollop of warm lemon curd on each half. I added the cupcake-laden plates to the table with our tea mugs.

Marge seemed to pull herself back to the present and sat at the small bistro table across from me. She was silent as she placed her handbag back into her lap and inspected the assortment of tea selections. She retrieved a lavender-colored packet from the box. Instead of opening the tea bag, she ran her forefinger across the label. Back and forth. Back and forth.

Her demeanor was a little disturbing, and the back of my neck prickled. *Why did Marge show up out of the blue?* I didn't want to disturb her thoughts, so I sat there and tried to unobtrusively observe her. I had thought she was in her early forties, but in the harsh light filling the kitchen, she looked older. Crow's feet framed her faded-blue eyes, and deep lines hovered around her mouth. How had I missed her aging before? Had I been that unobservant? Or had the stress of the last week been too much for her?

She noticed me watching her, and she placed the tea bag into the mug. "Where's Piper? She's a cutie."

"At the groomer's." I glanced at my watch. "I need to pick her up in an hour."

Marge looked around the kitchen, taking in all the details. "How about your sidekick, Mrs. Skyler? I hope I'm as active as she is when I get to her age."

"You and me both. She's at the movies then going out for dinner with some friends." I leaned in, lowered my voice, and winked. "Between you and me, I'd be surprised if she even came home tonight."

Marge frowned and looked away. I guessed she didn't like my insinuations about her employer's mother. "You're probably wondering why I'm here."

"Take your time. It's been a stressful week for you." I pushed the plate holding the cupcake toward her. "Perhaps some sugar will help."

That earned a faint smile. "You do make a tempting cupcake."

I waited until she had taken a bite before I selected my own packet of tea and let the bag brew in the hot water. I slid some warm lemon curd onto my fork and tasted it. The creamy sweetness tempered the tart bite from the lemon, the richness coating my tongue. I could eat lemon curd by the spoonful. Next, I cut off a generous bite of cupcake and dabbed a small amount of curd on top. It was a match made in heaven. The frosting would add an extra layer of flavor and provide a celebratory look to the dessert. I reminded myself to look in the pantry for lemon fruit-slice candies to use for garnish.

I tried to be patient while I waited for Marge to take the lead on why she had dropped by for a visit. She'd been through a nerve-wracking time between Mrs. Skyler's demented reign and her untimely demise. Although, in the back of my mind, the running list of things I needed to get done battered my brain. Time slipped at a fast pace while I watched her take small bites of cupcake with intermittent sips of tea. She finally set her fork down on the empty plate.

I raised my eyebrows and looked at her. Surely she would talk about what was bothering her now.

"Thanks. I needed that." She used the paper napkin to dab at the corners of her mouth. "That Detective O'Neill put me through the wringer after you left."

"I'm sorry to hear that. He's just trying to do his job, so I hope you don't take it personal."

"Oh, I guarantee it's turned personal."

Chapter 31

She shredded the napkin into long strips between her fingers. "Why did you have to bring up the death of Katrina? Why didn't you leave it alone?"

I was puzzled. Why would the hit-and-run death bother Marge so much? She didn't have anything to do with it—did she? She seemed too honorable to have left an accident scene. "It was only a mindless speculation on my part, and the detective just happened to have been around when I voiced the speculation out loud. I'm sure the deaths aren't connected."

"Thanks to you being a busybody, that detective is digging up stuff I'd rather not have exposed." She sighed and stroked her handbag. "I just wanted them to go away and leave the family alone."

A chill struck my spine as I remembered her saying her job was to take care of Mr. Skyler and his family. "Um, what do you mean by 'them'?"

She lifted her head. Her eyes were dark. "You had to keep poking and poking. Why couldn't you let things be?"

"I don't understand why you're so upset. Detective O'Neill is conscientious and won't railroad anyone. He'll find the truth, and everything will go back to normal."

Her laugh—well, it was almost a cackle—split the air. I jumped in my seat. The detective's words rang in my head: *Someone you know—and might even trust—is the murderer.*

I didn't want the killer to be mild-mannered Marge. She was the glue that held Mr. Skyler's family together. She was devoted to him. Was that her motivation—that she couldn't stand by and watch him or his son, Brian, being taken advantage of by the women? The clues started falling in place, and I couldn't ignore the facts any longer.

"I see the wheels turning in your brain, Emory. Figuring it out, are you?" She dipped her hand into the quilted handbag and retrieved a gun. "I'd like to compliment you and say you're smart to have solved the murders. But really, it's just dumb luck."

I glimpsed white silk fabric in her handbag. "If you thought I'd figured it out and the police were closing in, why didn't you head out of town instead of threatening me?"

"I'm doing more than threatening. I'll teach you a permanent lesson for sticking your nose into affairs that don't concern you. Although I'm going to miss your cupcakes." Marge drew the white scarf out of her handbag. "My calling card. I left a scarf by Katrina's body, but some vagrant must have taken it before she was found."

I shivered and wondered how to extricate myself from her wrath. Was I strong enough to overpower her? But if she fired the gun before I reached her, it wouldn't matter. I needed to keep her talking while I considered my options. There had to be a way to save myself. No one knew she was here, and Tillie, thank goodness, wouldn't be home until later that night. "So, you're admitting you killed Katrina, Mandy, and Barbara Skyler?"

She sat rigidly in her chair. "Those witches deserved it."

"But why? I mean, I know they weren't nice women, but no one deserves to die."

"They were taking advantage of David and stealing his

money on top of driving a wedge between him and his sons. I've made it my life's mission to protect him." Her left hand stroked the silk scarf while her right held the gun steady. It was pointed directly at me. I hoped her arm would get tired and she would put the gun down, but I couldn't help but notice the well-developed muscles in her biceps. I remembered her sinewy muscles from the evening she was stirring risotto and the way she had easily hefted the totes of crystal after our party. She wasn't an average sedentary middle-aged woman. I had doubts I was strong enough to overcome her, even if she wasn't holding a gun.

"Wouldn't it have been easier to report them to the police and let the authorities take care of them?"

"I admit Mandy might have been arrested for blackmail, but she would've been back out on the street, back to her schemes with someone else, within a short time. It's all Brian's fault. He should have known better than to date a tramp like her." She brought the scarf up to her cheek for a moment. "It's not illegal for calculating young women like Katrina and Barbara to marry wealthy, older men. It happens all the time. But the way those two mocked David behind his back then filled their own bank accounts with his hard-earned money turned my stomach."

"I agree it's despicable. But surely there had to be another way?"

"Nothing that wouldn't take forever to accomplish. I managed to take care of all the problems in a couple minutes." She pointed the gun at me. "Up you go. It's time to head over to your pool."

I needed to keep her talking. "Why? If you're going to kill me, at least give me some answers."

Marge snorted. "I know those cozy little mystery books you like to read all have the killer spilling their guts before the heroine gets rescued. But you can forget it. No one's going to rescue you, so no more stalling. I've wasted enough time as it is."

My eyes scanned the kitchen while I stood up as slowly as possible. I saw my heavy-duty cupcake tin sitting on the edge of the island. Maybe I could use that to knock the gun out of her hand. I needed to distract her. "Why did you poison Piper? I'm assuming you were the one who gave her the hot dogs with rat poison. You seemed to care about her."

"What kind of monster do you think I am? I'd never hurt an innocent creature, especially Piper. Geez, give me a little credit for being a decent human being." Marge edged closer. The gun barrel felt inches away from my back. "I gave her hot dogs to keep her quiet while I planted the scarf and spray-painted your garage door. I meant to leave the scarf hidden in the garage the night of the party, but I thought I heard someone coming, so I couldn't. Besides, it ended up that I needed to warn you off after you started getting nosy, so I killed two birds with one stone, so to speak. I figured if you were worried about Piper, you'd take the threat more seriously. She couldn't reach the poison unless you were dumb enough to let her get to it."

"What about me? I'm innocent." I decided not to mention the irony of her thinking she wasn't a monster. According to her, it was okay to murder humans, but it was monstrous to kill an animal.

She cackled again. "You were fairly warned. And you still didn't back off. Nope, I wouldn't say you're innocent at all."

I steered us toward the island and pretended to stumble. While Marge was caught off guard, I reached my hand out, grabbed the cupcake tin, spun around on my heels, and threw the tin, Frisbee style. It hit the bridge of her nose, although I had meant to aim for the gun. A huge gash appeared, and blood oozed. It must have been extremely painful, because she howled and fell to her knees. As she clutched her nose with both hands, the gun dropped to the floor.

I kicked the weapon away from her crumpled body. I worried she would try to get it and shoot me right there in Tillie's kitchen. Instead, she screamed in pain and held both hands to her nose to staunch the bleeding. I edged away from her and grabbed the silk scarf from her handbag. Somehow I needed to tie her up so she couldn't escape. I stretched the scarf between my hands and crept up to her.

A deep voice startled me. "Drop it. Put your hands in the air."

Detective Gabe O'Neill stood in the entryway to the kitchen, his gun drawn. I swallowed hard and almost collapsed against the counter. I held the scarf out to the detective.

"Drop it and put your hands in the air." His voice held anger. His eyes were cold.

"But…" When I saw his gun rise and level at me, I did as he commanded.

Marge pointed a bloody finger at me. "She was trying to kill me."

Chapter 32

Several weeks later Brian hosted a Saturday brunch gathering at Oceana for our friends and family. It was a dry run for his restaurant opening for Sunday brunches, but I think he wanted to use the opportunity to say thank you to us for getting his father out of the clutches of so many conniving women. Mr. Skyler came, and I even overheard him compliment his son on the success the restaurant was enjoying. I was happy for Brian, although I wanted to give his brother a piece of my mind for declining the invitation. Hopefully, their father could mend the fractures between them.

Randall hadn't left my side all morning except to refill my champagne flute or load up my plate with more of Brian's delectable food. I took a large bite of eggs Benedict, and a glob of hollandaise sauce dripped down my chin. Detective O'Neill sat down next to me and handed me a crisp white napkin. Brad's eyebrows lifted toward his hairline as he watched us from across the room. I had purposely avoided my friend's crush ever since he arrested me, and I hadn't been happy to find him at the celebratory brunch. The handcuffs slapped on my wrists that day made me want to never forgive the detective who now sat beside me.

"I realize I yelled at you—a lot—when I took charge of the crime scene." Detective O'Neill took a sip of his champagne. He looked across the room toward Brad.

"I understand the yelling. What I don't understand is why you had to point your gun at me and treat me like I was the killer." It had been a long, long night down at the police station. Once again, my stepfather had to call an attorney to straighten out the mess I'd found myself in.

"This is hard for me to say, but I'm really sorry about that." He ran a hand through his hair. The tips stood on end and caught the sunlight that filtered through the window. His hair looked like gold. "But think of how it looked when I walked in. You were holding out a white scarf between your hands while advancing on Marge. And then there was blood all over her face like you'd already battered her. I thought you were trying to finish the job by strangling her."

"You had to know I wasn't the killer." I shook the buzzing in my head. I couldn't tell whether it was from reliving that terrible scene or from drinking too much champagne.

"You didn't have a mark on you while Marge looked like she'd been on a battlefield. What was I supposed to think?" Spots of red appeared on the detective's cheeks. "I'm trying to apologize. My only excuse is that I didn't know you yet, and you'd been involved in three murders in a few months. It made me suspicious."

"I understand, but just so you know, I don't enjoy having guns pointed at me." It had happened far too many times in the last few months.

Randall, who'd been silently looking on during this exchange, brushed a lock of my red hair away from my cheek. "Don't ever scare me like that again, Em."

My face felt warm as I remembered the end of that night. Randall had rushed to the police station and camped out in the waiting room until they released me, then he stayed by my side and chased away my nightmares. Well, that was the story we were spinning, anyway.

"If you hadn't gotten involved, you wouldn't have had a gun pointed at you." Detective O'Neill tried to make his voice sound full of authority, but the corners of his mouth crinkled up. He gave up and laughed. "What am I going to do with you and Tillie?"

Tillie came up and slung her arm around the detective's broad shoulders. "You have to give Emory credit. If she hadn't figured out that Katrina was a murder victim, Marge would've gotten away with all the murders. She was a slippery killer."

I waved away her praise. "It was all guessing. Never in a million years would I have speculated that Marge had it in her to commit murder. If she hadn't panicked, I wouldn't have known."

"I hate to say it, but you did a good job and found out a lot of information I wouldn't have been able to. When we laid out everything we had on her, Marge broke and confessed to all three murders." He lightly punched me in the arm. "But don't ever do it again. I can't take the stress of worrying about you, and if anything bad happens to you, Brad will never talk to me again."

Brian joined our group and hugged his grandmother. "Dad is talking to Addie. I think they're both agreeing it's time to find their daughter."

"Our sister." I reached out and grasped Brian's hand. "I can't wait to welcome her to our crazy family."

Recipes

Bloodshot Deviled-Egg Eyes

Ingredients

6 large eggs
1/3 cup mayonnaise, divided
2 teaspoons mustard (regular or Dijon)
1 teaspoon white vinegar
1/4 teaspoon garlic powder
Salt and pepper to taste
1 teaspoon hot sauce
1/2 teaspoon chili powder
2 teaspoons ketchup
4 pimento-stuffed green olives

Instructions

Insert a steamer basket into a saucepan and add enough water to fill the pan to just below the basket.

Heat water to boiling then carefully add cold eggs to the steamer and cover pan with a lid. Reduce heat to medium and steam the eggs for 13 minutes.

While the eggs cook, prepare the bloodshot sauce by mixing 2 tablespoons mayonnaise with the hot sauce, chili powder, and ketchup. Place in a piping bag fitted with a size 1 or size 2 piping tip. Refrigerate until needed.

Carefully remove eggs from steamer basket and soak in an iced water bath until cooled.

Remove the shells from the eggs and dry the eggs.

Cut the eggs in half lengthwise and separate the yolks from the whites.

Mix the egg yolks with the remaining mayonnaise, mustard, garlic powder, and vinegar until smooth. I like doing this with my handheld immersion blender. Season to taste with salt and pepper.

Place the mixture in a piping bag fitted with a large round tip and pipe into the reserved egg whites.

Dry and then cut the olives into slices and place on top of the egg-yolk mixture for the pupils.

Pipe the bloodshot sauce in squiggly lines on the egg whites.

Refrigerate until ready to serve.

Note:

Recipe can be doubled, but be sure the steamer basket and cooking pot are large enough to cook the eggs in a single layer. Don't stack the eggs, or they won't cook evenly.

Double Dip Jack-O'-Lantern

Ingredients

1 small to medium-sized pumpkin
Guacamole, your own favorite recipe or premade
Tortilla chips

Queso:

1 pound shredded pepper jack cheese
8 ounces cream cheese
1 cup sour cream
1 cup half-and-half
1 10-ounce can tomatoes and green chilies, drained
Chopped tomatoes and cilantro for garnish

Instructions

Cut the top of the pumpkin off and hollow out the inside. Carve a wide mouth near the base of the pumpkin and draw eyes using a nontoxic marker.

Insert a heat-proof bowl into the top of the pumpkin. Place on a large serving tray or baking sheet.

Queso:

In a heavy-duty saucepan set on low heat, cook the cream cheese, sour cream, and half-and-half together until hot. Do not allow to simmer and whisk frequently to make sure no lumps of cream cheese remain. Stir in the shredded pepper jack cheese and continue stirring until completely melted.

Once the cheese is melted, stir in the drained tomatoes and green chilies and continue cooking over low heat just until hot. Do not allow to come to a simmer. Immediately remove from heat and pour into the prepared bowl inserted into the pumpkin. Garnish with chopped tomatoes and cilantro.

Spoon guacamole so that it appears it's coming out of the pumpkin's mouth.

Arrange tortilla chips around serving tray and enjoy!

Graveyard Taco Dip

Ingredients

1 can refried beans

1-1/2 cups shredded cheddar jack cheese

1-1/2 cups sour cream mixed with a half package taco seasoning

1-1/2 cups guacamole, your own favorite recipe or premade

1 to 1-1/2 cups salsa, enough to cover the surface

4 green onions, chopped

7 black olives

1 large flour tortilla

Tortilla chips

Instructions

Preheat oven to 350 degrees (F) for the graveyard scene cutouts.

In a small glass casserole dish (I used 7 x 10-inch), layer the given order: refried beans, shredded cheese, sour cream, guacamole, and salsa.

Refrigerate at least 2 hours.

To make the graveyard scene, cut desired shapes out of the flour tortilla. Place the shapes on a parchment-lined baking sheet. Bake at 350 degrees (F) until browned, 12 – 18 minutes. Keep a close watch so pieces don't burn.

Remove the shapes to a wire rack to cool completely. Once cooled, use edible markers to write text and/or decorate the shapes.

Slice the black olives in half lengthwise. One half of the olive will be the body. Use the remaining half to slice thin crosswise pieces to create "legs" for the spider.

Right before serving, place the tortilla shapes in the dip, carefully pushing down to secure in place.

Arrange the olive spiders and sprinkle with green onions.

Serve with tortilla chips.

Chicken Cordon Boo Casserole

Ingredients

4 ounces wide egg noodles

6 slices white cheese, divided (such as American, white cheddar, or provolone) (don't use thin sliced)

6 small capers (or small bits of black olives for the eyes)

Cheese Sauce:

4 tablespoons unsalted butter

2 cloves minced fresh garlic

1/2 cup finely chopped onion

3 tablespoons all-purpose flour

1-2/3 cups whole milk

1/2 teaspoon ground mustard

1/2 teaspoon paprika

Meat:

1 cup chopped cooked chicken

1/2 cup ham, cubed into small pieces

Topping:

1-1/2 cups panko bread crumbs

1-1/2 tablespoons unsalted butter, melted

Instructions

Preheat oven to 350 degrees (F). Spray an 8 x 8 or 9 x 9-inch casserole dish with nonstick cooking spray and set aside.

Using a 3-inch cookie cutter, cut 3 ghost shapes from 3 cheese slices. Cover the ghosts with plastic wrap and refrigerate.

Coarsely chop the remaining 3 slices of cheese along with the scraps left over from the ghosts and set aside.

Cook noodles according to al dente directions on the package. Reserve 1/2 cup of the pasta cooking water then drain the noodles well. Return noodles to the pot and set aside.

Melt 4 tablespoons butter in a large saucepan over medium heat. Add onion and sauté for 5 minutes. Add garlic and cook for an additional 1 minute. Sprinkle flour over the onion mixture and stir while it cooks for 2 minutes.

Gradually add the milk, whisking constantly to keep sauce from getting lumpy. Cook until mixture begins to bubble, then stir in mustard, paprika, and chopped cheese. Remove from heat. Stir until cheese is melted and sauce is creamy. If the sauce seems too thick, add some of the reserved pasta water to loosen sauce up.

Add the chopped chicken, ham, and cheese sauce to the reserved noodles. Stir until the mixture is well combined, then transfer to the prepared casserole dish.

Stir together the panko bread crumbs and melted butter, then sprinkle over the casserole.

Bake 30 minutes until bubbly.

Remove from oven and arrange the cheese ghosts over the crust and arrange the capers for eyes on the ghosts. Return to the oven for 1 minute to heat ghosts, but don't overheat so that they melt.

<u>Note</u>

Recipe can be doubled. Bake in a 13 x 9-inch casserole dish for the same amount of time.

Yummy Mummy Calzones

<u>Ingredients</u>

2 pounds bread dough (you can use thawed premade frozen bread dough or the recipe below)

1-1/2 cups shredded mozzarella cheese

1/2 cup pizza sauce (your favorite red sauce or white Alfredo sauce)

1 egg, lightly beaten

4 capers or sliced green olives

Pick and choose from filling ingredients or use your own favorites:

(You'll need approximately 2 to 2-1/2 cups of filling for two calzones)

Sliced pepperoni

Chopped green bell pepper

Sliced and sautéed mushrooms

Italian sausage, cooked and well drained

Sliced black olives, well drained

Sliced onions, white or green

Small diced ham

Diced pineapple, well drained

Bread Dough or use frozen, premade dough:

1 cup warm water (105 degrees)
3 tablespoons olive oil
1 egg
2 tablespoons sugar
1-1/2 teaspoons salt
3-1/2 cups (16 ounces) bread flour
2 teaspoons yeast

Instructions

Preheat oven to 350 degrees (F).

Divide dough into 2 1-pound pieces. On a piece of parchment paper, roll each dough portion into a rounded triangle shape about 14 inches high and 11 inches wide at the base. Place each on a baking sheet.

With the tip of a knife, lightly mark a 4-inch-wide rectangle in the center of the dough, reserving 2 inches' space at the top and the bottom. Cut 1-inch strips at an angle up to the score line, leaving the top center of the wide end uncut to create the head.

Spread the pizza sauce, cheese, and desired filling ingredients inside the rectangle marked in the center of the dough. Shape the reserved wide-end dough into a head, then fold alternating strips of dough at an angle across the filling until all but the bottom strips have been folded. Fold the tip of the triangle over the filling, then fold the remaining 2 strips over the top. Press together to seal. Repeat with remaining triangle of dough.

Brush the dough with the egg, then let rise for 15 minutes in a warm, draft-free area.

Press the capers into the dough head for the eyes.

Bake for 25–30 minutes or until golden brown. Allow to rest for 5 minutes before slicing. Serve with additional warmed pizza sauce if desired.

Bread Dough:

Add all the ingredients into the bowl of a bread machine per manufacturer's instructions. Select the dough cycle.

Proceed with the above Mummy Calzones instructions once the cycle has completed.

Note:

Be sure to check dough consistency during the knead cycle. If dough is too sticky, add a tablespoon of flour. If the dough is too dry, add a teaspoon of water. Allow the dough to fully incorporate the extra ingredient before adding additional flour or water. Dough should be tacky to the touch but not overly sticky. Weather and humidity can change the amount of flour you use.

Poison Apple Cupcakes

Makes 12–14

Ingredients

Cupcakes:
1 cup (5 ounces by weight) cake flour
1 cup (5 ounces) all-purpose flour
1-1/2 teaspoon baking powder
1/2 teaspoon baking soda
1/2 teaspoon salt
1 cup (7 ounces) granulated sugar
1/2 cup vegetable oil
2 eggs
1/4 cup sour cream
1/2 cup applesauce
3 tablespoons Crown Royal
2 tablespoons Sour Apple Pucker
1 tablespoon cranberry liqueur (or cranberry juice)

Frosting:
1/2 cup (4 ounces) unsalted butter, room temperature
4-1/2 cups (20.5 ounces) confectioners' sugar
1/4 teaspoon salt

3 tablespoons Sour Apple Pucker

2 tablespoons cranberry liqueur (or cranberry juice)

1 tablespoon Crown Royal

Red food coloring

Garnish:

Tootsie Rolls or fondant tinted brown and formed into apple stems

Leaves formed from fondant tinted green or cut from sour apple fruit leather

Instructions

Cupcakes:

Preheat oven to 350 degrees (F).

Line cupcake tins with paper liners.

Whisk flours, baking powder, baking soda, and salt together in a small bowl and set aside.

Mix Sour Apple Pucker, Crown Royal, and cranberry liqueur together in a measuring cup and set aside.

In the bowl of a standing mixer, mix the vegetable oil and sugar together on medium speed for about 1 minute.

Add the sour cream and applesauce and mix until smooth. Scrape down the sides of the bowl as necessary.

Add the eggs one at a time and beat until incorporated.

Add half the flour mixture to the sour cream mixture and beat on low until mostly incorporated.

Add half the Sour Apple Pucker mixture and stir to combine.

Repeat with remaining flour and Sour Apple Pucker mixture and beat until smooth for about 30 seconds.

Fill cupcake liners 2/3 full and bake 14–16 minutes. The batter will be thin, and I like to use an ice cream scoop for filling liners.

Bake for 16–20 minutes until golden brown and a skewer inserted into the center comes out with just a few moist crumbs clinging to it.

Remove from oven and allow to cool in the cupcake tin for 5 minutes.

Move the cupcakes to a wire rack. Allow to completely cool before frosting.

Frosting:

Mix the Sour Apple Pucker, cranberry liqueur, and Crown Royal together. Set aside.

Place butter and salt into the bowl of a standing mixer and whip until creamy, approximately 2–3 minutes on medium-high speed.

With the mixer running on low speed, add half the confectioners' sugar a little at a time, mixing until sugar is coated with the butter.

Slowly add 3/4 Sour Apple Pucker mixture.

Repeat with remaining confectioners' sugar and 1 tablespoon Sour Apple Pucker mixture.

Add red food coloring until desired shade of red is obtained.

Increase the speed to medium-high and whip for approximately 5 minutes until the frosting is light and fluffy. If needed, add the remaining Sour Apple Pucker mixture if frosting is too thick and additional Sour Apple Pucker 1 teaspoon at a time until desired consistency is reached.

Frost the cooled cupcakes.

Garnish:

Form leaves from green-tinted fondant or cut leaf shapes from Sour Apple fruit leather.

Roll small pieces of the Tootsie Roll or brown-tinted fondant to form stems.

Insert a leaf on top of the frosted cupcake and accent with a stem.

Poison Apple Cake Pops

Ingredients

Cake Pops:

Prepare one batch of Poison Apple Cupcakes or your favorite cake recipe.

Frosting:

4 tablespoons (2 ounces) unsalted butter, room temperature

2-1/4 cups (10.5 ounces) confectioners' sugar

1/8 teaspoon salt

1 tablespoon Sour Apple Pucker

1 tablespoon cranberry liqueur (or cranberry juice)

2 teaspoons Crown Royal

Candy Coating:

16 ounces red candy melts

Additional:

Cake pop lollipop sticks

1/4 cup white chocolate morsels or candy melts

Tootsie Roll or brown-tinted fondant stems

Leaves formed from green-tinted fondant or cut from sour apple fruit leather

Instructions

Cake Pops:

Bake one batch of Poison Apple Cupcakes (12–14 cupcakes) in cupcake tin sprayed with flour-included baking spray. Do not use paper liners.

Allow cupcakes to completely cool, then rub cupcakes between fingers to crumble into fine crumbs.

Frosting:

Mix the Sour Apple Pucker, cranberry liqueur, and Crown Royal together. Set aside.

Place butter and salt into the bowl of a standing mixer and whip until creamy, approximately 2–3 minutes on medium-high speed.

With the mixer running on low speed, add half the confectioners' sugar a little at a time, mixing until sugar is coated with the butter.

Slowly add the Sour Apple Pucker mixture.

Add remaining confectioners' sugar.

Increase the speed to medium-high and whip for approximately 5 minutes until the frosting is light and fluffy. If frosting is too thick, add 1/2 teaspoon Sour Apple Pucker at a time until desired consistency is reached.

Assembly:

Using a spoon, mix 1 cup of frosting into the crumbled cupcakes. Add a little more at a time until crumbs are cohesive when pressed into a ball. You don't want it too dry or overly wet; it should resemble wet sand.

Form the cake mixture into balls, then shape into apples with the bottom narrower than the rounded top. Use the tip of your finger or a lollipop stick to make an indentation on the top of the apple. Place the cake pop on a parchment-lined baking sheet.

Chill the cake pops in the refrigerator for at least 2 hours.

Melt 1/4 cup white chocolate morsels (or white candy melts) according to package instructions.

Remove 10 cake pops from refrigerator at a time. Dip one

end of a lollipop stick into the melted white chocolate and insert into the bottom of the apple cake pop (the narrow end). Repeat with remaining cake pops and return to the baking sheet. Refrigerate for an additional hour.

While the cake pops chill, create stems by pinching off small pieces of Tootsie Roll and rolling into tiny logs. Tint fondant green or use sour apple fruit leather and cut into small leaf shapes. Set aside.

When cake pops are thoroughly chilled, prepare the candy melts.

Candy Melts:

Place half the red candy melts into a deep and narrow container (a 2-cup glass measuring cup will work.)

Melt according to the package instructions. Stir frequently, and make sure you don't overheat.

Final Assembly:

Dip and swirl the chilled cake pops in the melted candy melts, then remove and tap off excess. Immediately position a Tootsie Roll stem and fondant leaf at the top of the apple, then stick the lollipop stick into a sturdy piece of Styrofoam and allow to completely dry. Repeat with the remaining cake pops.

Once the level of melted candy melts is too low to dip the cake pops, add the remaining red candy melts to the container. Melt according to package instructions.

Tips:

If candy melts are too thick to dip cake pops in after melting, stir in 1 teaspoon vegetable oil.

As melts cool while dipping, reheat the candy melts in the microwave for 10 seconds, stirring well after heating.

Keep cake pops refrigerated until ready to serve.

Poison Apple Cocktails

Serves 2

Ingredients

2 ounces Crown Royal Canadian Whiskey

1 ounce Sour Apple Pucker

1 ounce cranberry liqueur

3 ounces Cranberry Apple juice, or more if desired

Instructions

Fill a cocktail shaker with ice and add the Sour Apple Pucker, Crown Royal, cranberry liqueur, and Cranberry Apple juice.

Vigorously shake until thoroughly chilled, then strain into two cocktail glasses.

Poison Apple Cocktails –
Party Size
SERVES 20 GUESTS

Ingredients

- 2-1/2 cups Crown Royal Canadian Whiskey
- 1-1/4 cups Sour Apple Pucker
- 1-1/4 cups cranberry liqueur
- 3-3/4 cups Cranberry Apple juice, or more if desired

Instructions

Mix all the ingredients together in a large pitcher. Thoroughly chill before serving in cocktail glasses.

Cranberry Liqueur

Ingredients

  2 cups sugar

  1 cup water

  1 (12-ounce) package fresh cranberries

  3 cups vodka

Instructions

Cook sugar and water over medium heat until sugar dissolves, stirring constantly. Remove from heat and cool completely.

Place cranberries in food processor and process 2 minutes. Combine sugar mixture, cranberries, and vodka. Pour into clean jars with lids. Let stand 3 weeks in a cool, dark place, shaking every other day.

Strain cranberry mixture though cheesecloth-lined sieve. Discard solids. Store liqueur into clean bottles or jars. Can be kept for one year.

Note:

This recipe makes for a nice holiday hostess gift when bottled in a decorative bottle and gifted with fun cocktail glasses.

Smashed Pumpkin Cupcakes

Makes 15

Ingredients
Cupcakes:
2 cups (10 ounces, by weight) cake flour

1 teaspoon baking powder

1 teaspoon baking soda

1/2 teaspoon salt

1-1/2 teaspoons ground cinnamon

2/3 cup (4.8 ounces) brown sugar, packed

2 tablespoons granulated sugar

2 eggs, room temperature

1 cup (8 ounces) pumpkin puree (not pie filling)

1/2 cup vegetable oil

2 tablespoons Bailey's Irish Cream

2 tablespoons Goldschläger

2 tablespoons Kahlúa

Glaze
2-1/2 tablespoons granulated sugar

1 tablespoons Bailey's Irish Cream

1 tablespoon Goldschläger

1 tablespoon Kahlúa

Frosting

5 cups (22.3 ounces) confectioners' sugar

3/4 cup (6 ounces) unsalted butter, room temperature

1/4 teaspoon salt

2 tablespoons Bailey's Irish Cream

2 tablespoons Goldschläger

2 tablespoons Kahlúa

Orange gel food coloring, optional

Garnish Suggestion

Candy pumpkins

Instructions

Cupcakes

Preheat oven to 350 degrees (F).

Line cupcake tins with paper liners.

Whisk flour, baking powder, baking soda, salt, and cinnamon together in a very large bowl.

In a medium-sized bowl, whisk the brown sugar, granulated sugar, and eggs together until combined.

Whisk in the pumpkin, vegetable oil, Bailey's Irish Cream, Kahlúa, and Goldschläger until combined.

Pour the pumpkin mixture *into* the flour mixture and stir just until combined. Do not overmix the batter.

Fill cupcake liners 2/3 full and bake 15–17 minutes.

The batter will be quite thick, and I like to use my spring-loaded ice cream scoop for filling liners.

Remove from oven and allow to cool in the cupcake tin for 5 minutes.

Move the cupcakes to a wire rack and immediately proceed with glaze.

Glaze

Place the granulated sugar, Bailey's Irish Cream, Kahlúa, and Goldschläger into a microwave-safe bowl.

Heat for 15-second intervals on high heat, stirring in between cycles, until sugar completely dissolves.

Pierce each warm cupcake 4 times with the tines of a fork.

Brush the glaze over the cupcakes, allowing the liquid to soak in before applying more. Be sure to use all the glaze.

Allow the cupcakes to cool completely before proceeding with the frosting.

Frosting

Whisk together the Bailey's Irish Cream, Kahlúa, and Goldschläger. Set aside.

Place butter and salt into the bowl of a standing mixer and whip until the butter is creamy, approximately 2–3 minutes on medium-high speed.

With the mixer running on low speed, add confectioners' sugar a little at a time, mixing until sugar is coated with the butter.

Once the butter-and-sugar mixture is creamy, slowly add the Bailey's Irish Cream mixture.

Add a few drops of orange gel food coloring as desired. If using, it's best to make the frosting the day you are serving, since alcohol can make the food coloring separate from the frosting if made a day or two in advance.

Increase the speed to medium-high and whip for approximately 5 minutes until the frosting is light and fluffy.

Frost the cupcakes and garnish with candy pumpkins, if desired.

Smashed Pumpkin

Serves 1

Ingredients

1/3 ounce Bailey's Irish Cream

1/3 ounce Kahlúa

1/3 ounce Goldschläger

Instructions

Pour Bailey's Irish Cream, Kahlúa, and Goldschläger into an ice-filled cocktail shaker.

Shake until ingredients are chilled, then strain into a shot glass.

Halloween Black Cat Chocolate Cookies

Makes 15 – 20 cookies, depending on size

A yummy and fun Halloween decorating project for kids!

Ingredients

Cookies

1 (15.25 ounce) package devil's food cake mix

1/2 cup vegetable oil

2 eggs

Frosting (Feel free to use your favorite ready-made chocolate frosting)

1/4 cup unsalted butter, room temperature

1/4 cup cocoa powder (either natural or Dutch will work)

2-1/2 cups confectioners' sugar

3–4 tablespoons milk or half-and-half

Decorating Garnishes

Chocolate jimmies for fur (plus rainbow jimmies if your kids like to experiment with designs)

Mini M&M's for eyes

Candy corns for ears

Licorice shoestring laces, cut into 1-1/2 inch pieces for

whiskers (or fondant tinted black and rolled into strands for the whiskers)

Candy-hearts (or red mini M&M's or mini jelly beans) for nose

Instructions

Cookies

Preheat oven to 350 degrees (F).

Add the cake mix, vegetable oil, and eggs to a large bowl and stir until well combined.

Roll the dough into 2-inch balls and place on a parchment-lined baking sheet at least 3 inches apart.

Bake for 7–9 minutes.

Allow cookies to cool on the baking sheet for 5 minutes, then transfer to a wire rack and allow to completely cool before frosting and decorating.

Frosting

Using an electric mixer, whip the butter until smooth (1–2 minutes).

Add the cocoa powder and beat for an additional 2 minutes.

On low speed, add one-third of the confectioners' sugar to the butter mixture and beat until smooth. Beat in 2 tablespoons milk, then add the remaining confectioners' sugar and beat.

Add in additional milk, 1 teaspoon at a time until a spreadable consistency is acquired. You don't want it too thin, but frosting shouldn't be so thick it won't spread on cookie. Once desired consistency is reached, beat the frosting for 1 minute.

Assembling the cookies

Working with 1 cookie at a time, spread chocolate frosting over the top of a cookie. Immediately sprinkle an outline of jimmies along the outside edge of the cookie to represent fur.

Position 2 upside-down candy corns near the top of the cookie for the ears. Position 2 mini M&M's for the eyes and place a dab of chocolate frosting in the center of the M&M's for the pupils.

Place either a red candy heart, a red M&M, or a mini jelly bean in the lower center of the cookie for the nose and add 3 short licorice shoestring laces (or fondant strands) to each side of the nose to represent whiskers.

Allow the frosting to set. Position cookies in a single layer on a serving platter.

Store in an airtight container for up to 3 days. If necessary to stack cookies for storing, place a sheet of waxed paper between each layer.

Chai Cupcakes

Makes 14

Ingredients

Cupcakes:

2 cups (10 ounces, by weight) cake flour

1 teaspoon baking powder

1/4 teaspoon baking soda

1/2 teaspoon salt

1 heaping tablespoon chai mix (premade or use the recipe below)

1/2 cup unsalted butter, room temperature

1 cup (7 ounces) granulated sugar

1/4 cup (1.8 ounces) brown sugar

2 eggs, room temperature

2 teaspoons vanilla extract

3/4 cup buttermilk

Frosting

5 cups (22.3 ounces) confectioners' sugar

1/2 cup (4 ounces) unsalted butter, room temperature

1/2 cup (4 ounces) cream cheese, room temperature

1 tablespoon chai spice mix (premade or use the recipe below)

1 – 3 tablespoons milk or cream

2 teaspoons vanilla extract

Chai Spice Mix

1 tablespoon ground ginger

1 tablespoon ground cinnamon

1 teaspoon ground cardamom

1 teaspoon ground allspice

1 teaspoon ground nutmeg

1 teaspoon ground cloves

1/4 teaspoon freshly ground white pepper

Garnish

Sprinkle tops of frosting with chai spice mix

Halved cinnamon sticks

Instructions

Chai Spice Mix

Mix all of the spices together and set aside.

Cupcakes

Preheat oven to 350 degrees (F). Line cupcake tins with paper liners.

In a medium-sized bowl, whisk flour, baking powder, baking soda, salt, and 1 heaping tablespoon of the chai mix together.

In the bowl of a standing mixer, cream the butter and sugars together for 3 minutes on medium speed.

Add in the eggs, 1 at a time, beating well after each addition. Mix in the vanilla extract.

Alternating 3 times add the flour mixture and buttermilk to the sugar mixture. Beat on low speed to incorporate. After the last addition, beat an additional 30 seconds until smooth.

Fill cupcake liners 2/3 full and bake 15–17 minutes. A wooden skewer inserted into the center should come out mostly clean. A few moist crumbs clinging is fine.

Remove from oven and allow to cool in the cupcake tin for 5 minutes.

Move the cupcakes to a wire rack and cool completely before frosting.

Frosting

Place butter and cream cheese into the bowl of a standing mixer and whip until creamy, approximately 2–3 minutes on medium-high speed.

With the mixer running on low speed, add half the confectioners' sugar a little at a time, mixing until sugar is coated with the butter.

Beat in 1 tablespoon chai spice mix, then add 1 tablespoon milk and the vanilla extract. Beat until incorporated.

Add the remaining confectioners' sugar. If the frosting is too thick, add additional milk, a teaspoon at a time, until desired consistency is reached.

Increase the speed to medium-high and whip for approximately 5 minutes until the frosting is light and fluffy.

Frost the completely cooled cupcakes.

For garnishing, place the remaining chai spice mix into a fine mesh sieve and dust the tops of the frosting and insert a halved cinnamon stick.

*For my husband, Dan, who gives me the support and encouragement
to create and believe in myself.*

*And for my granddaughters, Jaidyn, who bravely fights the Rett Syndrome
monster every day, and her sister, Emory, who is tenderhearted and caring
of her sister. They both inspire me to find joy and laughter in the simple
things in life.*

Acknowledgments

It's true that it takes a village to create a book. I'd like to thank my husband, Dan, for reading and editing my manuscript several times. Not only that, he also toted my pink cupcake carrier to his golf group on numerous occasions to collect a wide variety of comments and critiques on my cupcake recipes from his peers. And to all my taste testers, thank you for your suggestions and encouragement with each tweak I did on the recipes.

I also have to give a shout-out to Lisa Kelley of Lisa Ks Book Reviews for coming up with the title. I am in awe of her quick wit and way with puns! Thank you to my beta readers too, Janet Clause and Kathy Keith.

I greatly appreciate the talents of cover designer Karen Phillips. She captured the spirit of my book and made it come alive.

A special thanks to all of the lovely people who follow my blog, Cinnamon, Sugar, and a Little Bit of Murder, and share in my love for delicious food and mysteries! You inspire me to create stories and recipes to share with family and friends.

About the Author

Kim Davis lives in Southern California with her husband and new puppy, Missy. When she's not spending time with her granddaughters or chasing her energetic pup, she can be found either writing stories or working on her blog, Cinnamon, Sugar, and a Little Bit of Murder or in the kitchen baking up yummy treats. She has published the suspense novel, A GAME OF DECEIT, and the Cupcake Catering cozy mystery series. She also has had several children's articles published in Cricket, Nature Friend, Skipping Stones, and the Seed of Truth magazines. Kim Davis is a member of Mystery Writers of America and Sisters in Crime.

A father's disappearance never solved, a mother's secret taken to the grave, a daughter deceived…

Kathryn Landry thinks her life is just about perfect. She is the owner of a successful interior designer business in Newport Beach, California, and she has an attentive, supportive husband. But her world comes crashing down when her husband, Neil Landry, vanishes without a trace… in a situation almost identical to the disappearance of her father twenty years before.

With her father's disappearance still a mystery, Kathryn is skeptical that the detective assigned to her case will be able to find her husband. Determined to uncover the truth, Kathryn is plunged into a world of politics, high-priced call girls and wealth. As she begins to search for her husband, a decades-old secret her mother took to the grave threatens to destroy all she holds dear. Caught up in a web of betrayals and deceit, and not knowing who to trust, Kathryn must find a way to survive as she discovers the past has a way of repeating itself.

"...Davis deftly keeps readers as up in the air as Kathryn throughout this well-crafted tale. An impressive thriller by an author worth following." – Kirkus Reviews